More praise for
PRIMARY JUSTICE

"A fast-paced mystery that is at times tragic and sad and at other times laugh-out-loud funny. On a scale of one to five, this rates 4¹/₂."
—*Tulsa World*

"A smash. It's funny. It's suspenseful. It's thought-provoking. And most of all, it's entertaining. It's a perfect blend of law-firm politics, romantic tension among co-workers, murder and hidden family secrets, and is a great read from cover to cover....I can't wait for the sequel."
—*The Midwest City, Oklahoma Sunday Sun*

"Impressive, with a likeable main character in Ben Kincaid, the fascinating background of a large corporate law firm, and a nicely worked out plot involving an adoption case and dubious practices by one of the firm's largest clients."
—*Ellery Queen's Mystery Magazine*

"An unexpected treat, one of those non-stop reads that hold something for everybody."
—*Mystery Scene*

PRIMARY JUSTICE

William Bernhardt

BALLANTINE BOOKS • NEW YORK

A Ballantine Book
Published by The Ballantine Publishing Group
Copyright © 1991 by William Bernhardt
Excerpt from *Naked Justice* copyright © 1997 by William Bernhardt

http://www.randomhouse.com

Library of Congress Catalog Card Number: 91-93041

ISBN 978-0-345-47997-6

Manufactured in the United States of America

146442087

for my parents

"Among the virtues, some are primary and some are subordinate to these. The following are primary: wisdom, courage, justice."

Zeno the Stoic
(c. 335–263 B.C.)

"It is the curse, as well as the fascination of the law, that lawyers get to know more than is good for them about their fellow human beings."

John Mortimer, 1979

* Prologue *

"Once again," the man said, pulling the little girl along by the leash tied to his wrist and hers. "Tell me your name."

"I don't remember," the girl said.

"Where do you live?"

"I don't remember."

"Are you from Tulsa?"

"I don't remember." The girl answered emotionlessly, like an automaton.

"Slower. Speak more hesitantly. It must *seem* as though you're trying to remember. Who are your parents?"

"I don't remember."

The two emerged from the bottom of the gray stone stairwell and walked into the sunken parking garage. The rising sun was just visible in the high windows on the east side of the garage. The red corona was just beginning to filter across the skyline and cast an orange halo around the rooftops and skyscrapers of downtown Tulsa. Sunlight barely survived the passage through the dirty glass windows of the garage, though, and since the garage had little lighting of its own, the two figures remained enveloped in gray.

The two moved in concert, past an elevator shaft,

1

across a double aisle of parked cars, toward a black sedan. The little girl, who appeared to be seven, perhaps eight, was dressed in a simple white pinafore over a blue dress, which accentuated the vivid blue of her eyes. Her face seemed unnaturally white, as if she had spent her entire life shielded from the sun. Her long black hair was pulled behind her head and tied in a French braid.

As they came near the sedan, the girl began to drag her heels. The leash connecting the two drew taut. The man turned and looked at her. He frowned but said nothing. He yanked firmly on the leash and pulled her toward him.

At that instant, a woman ran screaming out of the stairwell. She was wearing only a tattered blue bathrobe that flapped open as she ran. Her dark, unwashed hair hung limply from her head. She was barefoot. She was followed closely by another woman, an older, heavy-set woman wearing a white uniform. The large woman was also running, doing her best to catch up to the woman in the bathrobe.

The first woman ran across the garage, whimpering, her arms stretched forward. She looked frantically in all directions, then saw the man and the girl bound to him. She raced toward them. The heavyset woman could not keep pace.

The man stepped forward and pushed the little girl behind him. The woman ran without stopping and collided violently into his body, throwing the man back against the sedan. They wrestled for a moment, arms gyrating wildly, and the woman cut the man's face with her fingernails. Angered, the man grabbed both her wrists and twisted them painfully behind her back.

The little girl began to cry. "Stop it!" she pleaded. "Stop it! You're hurting her!" She kicked the man in the soft part of his right shin.

The man's face was transfigured with rage. Clenching his teeth, he placed both of the woman's wrists into his left hand and, with his right, he clutched the little girl by the neck and slammed her against the side of the sedan. The girl blinked rapidly and fell down in a limp heap on the gray stone floor.

At last the heavy-set woman caught up with them. While the man twisted both of his captive's wrists behind her back, the other woman wrapped a thick, leather belt around her chest and upper arms. She pulled the leather belt tight. Reaching into her skirt pocket, she withdrew a syringe and, almost without looking at it, she pushed the air bubble through the tip and jabbed the needle into the struggling woman's right arm. Almost instantaneously, the woman in the bathrobe relaxed. Her whole body seemed to weaken and become limp.

The man and the uniformed woman exchanged a quick, penetrating look. *This won't happen again,* she told him, without speaking. *Ever.* She took hold of the leather belt and pushed the other woman toward the stairwell.

The man bent down next to the little girl's body. He pulled open one of her eyelids, then placed his two fore-fingers against her neck. *Fine.*

Sunlight was beginning to penetrate the dirty window-panes of the garage, and he realized that he was behind schedule. He had intended to be far away from here long before the sun rose. He opened the car door, bundled the girl into his arms, and spread her across the backseat of the sedan. He untied the leash and tossed it on the floor;

then he closed the back door. Glancing quickly at his watch, he slid into the driver's seat, started the engine, and hurriedly drove out of the parking garage.

PART ONE

*   *

A Bumblebee and Reverie

* 1 *

Benjamin Kincaid glanced at his watch.

It was 9:05. Well, the recruiting coordinator had warned him that orientation might start late. Ben's stomach growled—rather loudly. The other young lawyers looked up. Ben looked away, as if he had heard the rumbling noise somewhere on his far left. Should've gotten up early enough to fix breakfast, he thought. Professionals always eat breakfast. Strong body, strong mind, and all that. But he hadn't risen until the third blast of the snooze alarm; he couldn't risk being late on the first day of work, so he had to do without.

He drummed his fingers on a tabletop. A gnawing sensation, unrelated to hunger, was eating away at the pit of his stomach. He felt uneasy, and he didn't know why.

He surveyed the room. The new class of associates at Raven, Tucker & Tubb were sitting in the office lobby, discreetly appraising one another. Six of them were men; two were women. The men wore suits that came in two colors: blue or gray, with the occasional daring leap to blue-gray or perhaps blue with a gray pinstripe. Every shirt was stiff, button-down, and white. The women were dressed in complex pseudo-suits with scarf ties and high-collar blouses; the kind of suit, Ben supposed, that didn't threaten male colleagues, probably because women don't look very good in them.

There was no conversation. Each young lawyer watched and waited.

Ben glanced at the thin, toothy young man in the gray suit sitting next to him.

"You suppose they've forgotten about us?" the man asked.

Ben smiled faintly. "I doubt it. They're just busy. This is a very busy law firm." What a pompous thing to say, Ben thought, immediately embarrassed by his third-rate small talk. As if he knew anything about the work load at Raven, Tucker & Tubb.

"That's a fact," the young man agreed. He had a drawn, pasty-white face, close-cropped brown hair, and a wispy beard covering a bad complexion. Every whisker was working overtime to create the illusion of a full beard. "Productivity is up by an average of eighteen percent, with variances for different departments. Litigation is up almost twenty-five percent; environmental, of course, is in the sewer. Gross revenues are up half a million dollars over the previous fiscal year. Given the current economic slump in the Southwest, that's an extremely impressive financial performance."

Ben stared at him. "How do you know these things?"

"Oh, I've done my research. I had numerous offers of employment, you know. I was in a position to be selective."

Ben was relieved to find his brief moment of pomposity completely eclipsed. "I see. By the way, my name is Ben Kincaid."

"Nice to meet you. I'm Alvin Hager." Alvin took Ben's

hand and gave it a nerve-dulling handshake. "Maybe we'll get to work together. Are you a Tulsa native?"

"No," Ben replied. "Just moved."

"Got any family here?"

"No. Well, not really. A brother-in-law. Ex-brother-in-law, actually. He's a cop."

"Left Mom and Pop back home?"

"Mom and—" He closed his eyes for a moment, then began again. "How about you? Any family in town?"

"No," Alvin answered. "I'm on my own. Of course, I wanted it that way. I want to pull myself up by my own bootstraps, or not at all."

"Of course."

"Excuse me, but didn't you used to work at the D.A.'s office in Oklahoma City?"

Ben turned and saw a brown-haired woman in her mid-twenties wearing rectangular tortoiseshell eyeglasses.

"Yes, I worked with the district attorney," Ben answered. "How did you know?"

The woman leaned forward. She was dressed in a two-piece gray suit with a paisley scarf wrapped tightly around her neck and a small ivory cameo in the center. Ben wondered if it was difficult for her to talk with a scarf and cameo clutching her throat. "I was clerking at the public defender's office during my third year of law school. I was at the D.A.'s all the time. What made you decide to leave and go into private practice?"

"Oh . . ." Ben searched for words but didn't find any. "A variety of factors."

"Like forty-eight K a year, right?" Alvin said, grinning. "C'mon, Ben, we're co-workers now. You can play straight with us. We understand."

Ben smiled pleasantly but said nothing.

"I am incredibly ill-mannered," the woman said abruptly, slapping herself on the side of her head. "I haven't even introduced myself. My name is"—she hesitated—"Marianne Gunnerson." She shook hands with Ben and Alvin. "Tell me, guys, confidentially. Do you think Marianne is okay? I mean, for a name."

Ben looked at Alvin out the corner of his eye, then back at Marianne. "It's . . . *your* name, isn't it?" he said.

"But don't you think it's too feminine? I mean, for a lawyer." She picked up a magazine from the coffee table and rolled it into a tube shape. "I don't think it's a good lawyer name."

"What would be a good lawyer name?" Ben asked, genuinely curious.

"Oh, I don't know," she said. She began to beat time on the coffee table with the tubed magazine. "Lilian. Claire. Margaret, maybe."

"Forget Margaret," Alvin said. "The firm already has two Margarets. Three, if you count middle names. You'd be lost in the shuffle."

Ben peered at him in amazement.

"Really?" Marianne said. "That's interesting. I didn't know that." She reversed the magazine and tubed it in the other direction. "This probably seems inane to you guys, but they're going to ask us what name we want written on our doorplates today, and I don't know what to say. What are they going to think of a lawyer who can't even tell them her name?"

Ben couldn't imagine a suitable answer.

"Hey, can I join this conversation? I've stared at the rug for about as long as I can stand."

Ben turned and saw another of the new associates, a tall, good-looking man, perhaps a few years younger than himself. His hair was dark, but his face had a bronze cast. He was wearing a blue suit, very similar to Ben's, with a white handkerchief in his breast pocket. He was carrying a white camel's hair overcoat.

His handshake was firm but not crippling. "I'm Greg Hillerman," he said. The other three associates introduced themselves.

"I don't remember coming across your name in my research," Alvin said. "Are you a TU graduate?"

Greg smiled a perfect smile. He had dimples on both cheeks. If the law didn't work out for him, Ben thought, he could get work as a male model, or perhaps a game-show host. "No, I went to law school at UT Austin. Undergrad at the University of New Mexico at Albuquerque."

"Oh, an out-of-state hire," Alvin said. "That explains it."

"I did a year of undergraduate at UNM," Ben said.

"Really?" Greg smiled that marvelous smile again. "Frat man?"

"No. Well, not for long, anyway."

"You hang out with any frat guys?"

"Actually, I tried to have as little to do with that crowd as possible." Ben hoped he didn't sound rude. He didn't want to alienate the one relatively normal person he had met so far.

"Personally, I like *Marianne*," Greg said, shifting his attention to her.

Marianne's eyes brightened. "You think it sounds professional?" she asked.

"No, it reminds me of that good-looking wench on *Gilligan's Island*. Man, I used to love her."

Marianne was not amused.

* * *

By 9:15, Ben had examined every detail of the Raven, Tucker & Tubb reception area with microscopic scrutiny. The lobby was decorated in a style that seemed both ornate and direct, the look of a firm that wanted to tell its clients it was both no-nonsense and expensive. Dark brown hardwood floors with rich burgundy accent rugs. A white wool sofa defining a continuous semicircle around the entire reception area. And in the center of it all, the bronze, human-size statue of Justice, a tall woman dressed in a toga and a blindfold, with her scales balanced in perfect equanimity.

"This really isn't how I envisioned spending my first day at work," Ben said, glancing again at his watch.

Greg arched an eyebrow. "You were expecting maybe tea and crumpets, with a personal address from Arthur Raven?"

"Not likely. Raven is in semiretirement," Alvin informed them. "Of counsel."

"Thank you for setting us straight, Alvin." Greg winked quickly at Ben.

"Do you know who your supervising attorney is, Alvin?" Ben asked.

"Yes. Thomas Seacrest."

"How did you find that out?"

"Well, I conducted an analysis of likely candidates, based upon the firm's historical distribution of assimilation assignments."

Ben took a deep breath. "Yes, but how did you find out?"

Alvin cocked his head slightly. "I asked the recruiting coordinator on thirty-nine."

Ben suppressed a smile. "Have you checked in with your supervisor?"

"Yes," Alvin said, leaning back against the sofa. "I got here early."

"Yeah, well, I didn't. I think I'll run upstairs for a moment and find out who mine is. Don't let them start without me."

"You got it, buddy." Alvin slapped Ben on the back as he rose. Whatta guy, Ben thought.

Ben walked to the elevator bank and pushed the UP button. He was relieved to be out of the reception area. Despite the apparent amiability, the tension in there was thicker than the statue of Justice. Eight overambitious cauldrons waiting to spew forth their juices and prove themselves. What a nightmare.

The elevator did not come. It seemed foolish to wait for an elevator just to go up one floor, especially when orientation might start at any moment. Ben opened a door to the right of the elevators. It was the stairwell. He climbed the flight of stairs leading to the thirty-ninth floor and tried to open the door.

The door wouldn't budge. It was locked from the outside. A sinking feeling crept through Ben's body. He ran up another flight of stairs and tried to open the door to the fortieth floor. The doorknob would not turn.

Ben began to panic. Somehow, he had known this would happen. He didn't know exactly when or exactly how, but deep down he had been certain he would make an utter and irredeemable fool of himself before his first day of work was over. He bolted up another flight of stairs. The door would not open.

His first instinct was to shout and pound on the door, but he checked the urge. What if someone came? Was this really the image he wanted to present on his first day? True, not every floor of the tower was inhabited by Raven, Tucker & Tubb, but about ten floors were, and in the flush of panic and adrenaline Ben found it impossible to remember which were and which were not. He was on the forty-ninth floor before it occurred to him that he was running up a dead end.

Ben remembered Alvin. Alvin was his buddy, right? Alvin would be looking for him. If not Alvin, then Greg. Well, it was possible, anyway.

Ben turned and began to race at breakneck speed down the eleven flights of stairs between himself and the other new associates. He glanced at his watch and saw that it was now 9:24. Great. Orientation had surely begun by now.

He began to feel sweat soaking through his starched shirt and trickling down his collar. His heart was pounding like something out of Edgar Allan Poe. Finally, he jumped the last flight of steps and slammed down on the thirty-eighth floor landing. He pounded his fists against the door and bellowed: *"Alviiiiin!"*

A tall, elderly man with a crown of white hair opened the door and peered down at him. Ben recognized him in a heartbeat. It was Arthur Raven. As in Raven, Tucker & Tubb.

"Yes?" Raven inquired.

"Oh, God." Ben exhaled all the air in his body. He slapped his hand against his forehead and wiped away a layer of sweat.

"Speak up, would you, son? I don't hear as well as I used to." Raven chuckled. "Nothing works like it used to."

"I—I—" Ben swallowed and tried to catch his breath.

"I'm sorry, Mr. Raven. I was trapped in the stairwell. I—"

"Stairwell?" the old man repeated. "You shouldn't be in there. Doors only open on the outside."

"Really? I'll remember that." Ben looked into the lobby. All the other new associates had vanished. "Sir, I need to—"

"Well, that's not true, strictly speaking. You can get out on the first floor and the fiftieth. Fire codes require that. But it's a long way down to the first floor. I remember when we first moved into this building, I thought there ought to be some kind of a back door, so a lawyer could slip out while some client he's trying to avoid cools his heels in the lobby."

"Sharp thinking, sir." Ben tried to edge himself through the door. "Well, I really must be going—"

"But I was overruled. The Executive Committee was afraid the associates would use the door to slip out without being observed by their supervising attorneys." The old man grinned. "You wouldn't do that, would you, eh . . . what did you say your name was?"

It was the crisis point. No matter what Ben did, either the orientation attorney or Mr. Raven was going to be angry. Raven was undoubtedly higher in the firm hierarchy. He also seemed less likely to remember anything about it tomorrow.

Ben gave the old man a gentle push and forced his way through the door. "Sorry, sir. Must dash. Let's talk again." Ben waved cheerily and ran toward the reception desk.

"Which way did they go?"

The receptionist smiled. She spoke in a soft, soothing

British accent. "Orientation is taking place in the north-west conference room."

"Where's that?"

She pointed. "There."

Ben bolted. He had no use for subtlety now. There was just a chance that if he arrived before the meeting was truly underway, he might be able to slip in quietly and wouldn't have to explain where he had been. Ben cruised down the long hallway, zeroed in on the open conference room door, and was just about to scramble through the door . . . when a blond man carrying a coffee cup stepped through the door and began scanning the hallway. He saw Ben a split second before impact.

The two collided with a force that would have left a crater on the moon. The blond man fell backward into the conference room. Both coffee and cup followed a parabolic arc into the man's face. He screamed.

Ben leaped to his feet and gave new meaning to the phrase *apologized profusely*.

"Never mind the apologies," the man grumbled. The coffee had stained his shirt, his tie, and his suit in countless places. His face was dripping. "Give me a towel."

Ben grabbed several paper towels from the box next to the coffee pot warmer, then helped the man up from the floor. As he did so, Ben noticed that the man was wearing a toupee and that it had been so dislodged by the collision that it hung over his forehead like a sun visor.

"What are you staring at?" the man asked angrily.

"Nothing, sir. I mean—" Ben saw the sixteen young lawyer eyes trained on him. "I mean—nothing, sir."

"I take it you're Kincaid?"

"Yes, sir. Well, I can't deny it, can I?" He laughed awkwardly. And alone.

"No," the man replied. "Much as you might care to."
He brushed off the front and back of his suit trousers.
"Where have you been, Kincaid?"

Ben watched the toupee droop even further forward. He
could tell from the jabs and whispers around the conference table that he was not the only one to have noticed.
"It's really a long story, sir. I was trapped."

"Trapped?"

"Yes, sir. In the stairwell. And then there was Mr.
Raven."

"You were trapped in the stairwell with Mr. Raven?"
The hairpiece slipped another inch. It seemed as though
it must be dangling before his eyes.

"No, no, I—"

"Never mind!" he barked. "Let's get on with the business at hand."

"Great," Ben said, taking an empty seat next to Greg.
He smiled enthusiastically. "What's on our agenda toupee? I mean to*day*—"

It was too late. Ben's slip was followed by suspended
silence, as the other associates sucked in air and tried to
control themselves. Ben saw Greg cover his face with his
hand, while Marianne looked absently out the window. It
was no use. All at once, the room exploded with laughter.

The man with the toupee gave them all a stony glare,
and the laughter quickly dissipated. Wordlessly, the man
raised his hand to his hairpiece and pushed it back to approximately its original position. His expression defied
anyone to mention what they were observing.

"To answer what I perceive to be your actual question,
Kincaid, I had just told each associate the name of the
partner who will be acting as their supervising attorney."

"I see," Ben mumbled, not looking up. "And who was I assigned to?"

"Me," the man replied. "My name is Richard Derek. I'd like to see you in my office at ten o'clock. Sharp. And Mr. Kincaid . . ." He paused. "Walk, don't run."

* 2 *

Ben sat in the chair opposite Derek's desk and mourned his existence.

He was trying to shake the feeling that his first day was already a disaster. Try not to think about it, Greg had told him—perhaps the most idiotic advice he had received in his entire life.

Derek chose the cruelest of all ways of referring to the catastrophe in the conference room—namely, not to mention it at all. At least not directly.

"Damn back is killing me," he muttered, a cigarette clenched between his lips. "Acts up whenever my back is subjected to . . . unanticipated stress. A legacy of my Coast Guard days."

Coast Guard days? "Were you hurt in combat, sir?" Ben asked.

"No, I was hurt in boot camp, and that's a damn sight worse." He dipped his cigarette in the near-full ashtray on his desk. "Goddamn sadists."

Derek squirmed in the burgundy chair that perfectly accented the large desk meaningfully placed between Ben and himself. Ben noted that there were two visitors' chairs on the opposite side of the desk, the one in which Ben was sitting and another just beside it. When Derek was talking to a fellow shareholder, or when he wanted to create a feeling of amiability, he could sit on an equal plane with his visitor without the huge desk between them. On the other hand, Ben realized, when Derek wanted to be imposing and autocratic, when he wanted to keep people on edge, he could make them sit alone, on the outside, while he nestled behind his desk and peered out at them. Like now, for instance.

Derek's eyes roved across his desk and came to rest on a brown piece of linen paper Ben knew must be his résumé. "B.A. in music theory, something every lawyer needs to know, minor in English literature, a year in the Peace Corps, a year as a Goodwill Ambassador for Rotary International. Oh, God. Let me guess. You probably went to law school because"—he exhaled a cloud of smoke and curled his lip—"you wanted to help people." He smiled broadly.

"Well," Ben said quietly, "as a matter of fact . . ."

Derek chuckled. "That's so sweet. Well, what's the point of being young if you can't believe in fairy tales?" Derek stretched, grimaced, and rubbed his back in the alleged sore spot. "Of course, if you really wanted to help people, I suppose you would have gone to work at the public defenders' office or a legal aid agency, instead of working at the biggest, richest corporate law firm in the state, right?" Derek grinned, obviously impressed with his own penetrating insight.

"I used to work for the D.A. in Oklahoma City," Ben said.

"Right," Derek said, nodding. "I see that in your ré-sumé. You worked there a year and a half. Just long enough to make yourself marketable."

"It wasn't really like that—"

"Stop." Derek interrupted Ben with a wave of his hand and a demeanor that told Ben he was about to convey some great nugget of wisdom. "Don't bother denying it. I'm not criticizing you. I'm complimenting you." He leaned forward across the desk. "You know what's really impor-tant in the legal world today?"

Ben took a pen from his end of the desk and twirled it between his fingers. "No, sir. What?"

"Marketing. That's what."

"Marketing, sir?"

"Yes, marketing. How are you at marketing, Kincaid?"

"Wha—I . . . I don't know, sir. They don't really cover that in law school."

"Hmmm." Derek pursed his lips and drew on his cig-arette as if he were bringing the smoke in from another county. "I suppose not. They didn't teach it at Harvard, either. Of course, they don't really *need* to teach market-ing at Harvard. One's mere presence at Harvard is gen-erally sufficient."

Derek tapped the Harvard Law School diploma hanging over his desk, just beneath a stuffed and mounted bobcat, poised forever in mid-spring. Funny, Ben thought, Derek doesn't really seem the hunter type. Looks more like a bridge player.

"Of course," Derek continued, "that stuff they teach you in law school is of some value, too. But if you aren't

adept at marketing, you don't have clients, and if you don't
have clients, what good is knowing the law?''

Ben raised the pen to his mouth and began to chew on
the lid, then caught himself. He returned the pen to the
desk and sat on his hands. "I suppose I never thought
about it like that."

"Well, that's the reality, kid, so it's just as well you
come to grips with it now. How old are you, Kincaid?''

"I'm twenty-nine, sir."

"Hmmm. Well, you may be old enough for this. Just
one more tip, Kincaid, and I hope you're not too young
to appreciate it. All that business in law school—you know,
about *stare decisis*, and how the law is the sacrosanct wisdom of the ages, passed down from time immemorial and
applied evenly to different fact situations throughout
time?''

"Yes?''

"It's a crock. A con job by a musty crusty crowd of
academics. You know what the law really is?''

Ben didn't think this was an appropriate time to guess.
"What?''

"It's mirrors and bubble gum. The only thing that's
sacrosanct is your client. Your client needs help, and the
odds are there won't be any law precisely on point to
help him, so *you*, the lawyer, must take what law there
is and perform a little magic. Create the illusion of precedent with mirrors and bubble gum, and make the law
say what it needs to say. That's what being a lawyer is
all about.''

Ben knitted his eyebrows and tried to appear as if he
was absorbing all the erudition.

"That's what Joseph Sanguine liked about me from day
one,'' Derek continued. "I told him the law was a tool,

just like a hammer or a monkey wrench, and I could put the tool in his tool box." Derek leaned back in his chair. "And I've had all his legal business ever since. He's one of the firm's biggest clients. And he's a close personal friend, too."

For some reason, Ben had difficulty imagining that Derek had any close personal friends.

"Am I making any impression on you, Kincaid?"

"Ahh—yes, sir. Yes, you are."

"Not much of a talker, are you, Kincaid?" He smiled faintly. "Perhaps in time." He blew another cloud of smoke into the air. "Well, I hope you'll take what I've said to heart. I have a case I want you to work on, Kincaid. An important case for the aforementioned Joseph Sanguine. President of Sanguine Enterprises. Their principal subsidiary is Eggs 'N' Stuff, Inc., the franchisor for those cute little breakfast joints you see all over the country. Their national headquarters is right here in Tulsa, you know. They've got a problem I think will make an excellent starter case for you."

Ben beamed. "Really, sir?"

Derek grinned. "Now don't get too excited, kid. It's a domestic matter. You took family law in school, didn't you?"

Ben nodded, considerably subdued.

"It's an adoption proceeding. For one of Sanguine's executives. You're meeting him in about an hour."

Ben hesitated. "I didn't think Raven, Tucker & Tubb handled domestic matters, sir."

Derek shifted positions again and groaned, still rubbing his back. "Well, normally we don't, but for Joseph Sanguine, we do. I suppose we'd take the garbage out for Joseph Sanguine, if he wanted us to."

Ben tried not to look disappointed.

"It may not exactly be a blue-chip case," Derek continued, "but it's perfectly adequate for a baby lawyer's first time out." He peered at Ben across the desk. "I suppose you think you're too good to do an adoption case? Too much of a waste of your young upwardly mobile talents?"

"Not at all, sir."

"Well, good. Joseph Sanguine is one of our most important clients. His companies provided Raven, Tucker & Tubb with over three million dollars in gross revenues last year. He likes to think he can depend on us. We don't want to disappoint him."

"I understand, sir."

"Good. If you have any questions about the library or office supplies or anything, just ask Maggie. Maggie is my secretary. We'll share her, at least for a while, until you're settled."

Ben started to rise to his feet.

"Just one last thing, Kincaid."

"Yes, sir?" Ben wasn't sure whether to remain standing or to sit back down. He hovered in between for a few moments, then decided to remain standing, then changed his mind and sat down.

"Did you get a good look at the incoming class of associates?"

"I—I think so, sir."

"Excellent. Let me tell you something about them, Kincaid. For the next three years, they're all going to be working hard, just like you, putting in overtime, trying to be seen by the boss at the office late at night, carrying mounds of work home with them—even if they don't plan to work on it. Basically, they'll be doing the same chores as

you. Some cases will be interesting bits of complex litigation; some will be dogs like this adoption business. Except, when the associates receive their evaluations at the
end of the first three-year period, half of them will be told
that they are on track for partnership, and the other half
will be told that they are not. At the end of six years,
assuming they are all still here, which is unlikely, perhaps
one-fourth of them will be promoted to senior associate
positions, and the rest will not. At the end of eight years,
assuming there have been no lateral hires, which is unlikely, one, perhaps two, of the associates in your class
will be made partners in the richest law firm in the state
of Oklahoma, while the rest will either be offered
nonprofit-sharing permanent associateships or just sent
packing.''

Derek's eyes met Ben's. ''Where will you be, Mr. Kincaid?''

Ben assumed this was a rhetorical question and did not
attempt to answer it.

Derek ground his dead cigarette into the ashtray. ''Now
get to work.''

* 3 *

Ben remembered thinking, after four years of undergraduate school, two years of special studies, and three years of law school, that the days of desperate, last-minute cramming were finally over. He was wrong.

Thanks to his eleventh-hour assignment from Derek, Ben had about forty-five minutes to immerse himself in adoption law prior to counseling a client of indirect but genuine importance. He was confident that Family Law I and the Socratic method didn't come close to providing enough real-life practical experience to enable him to advise other human beings. He polled Greg, Alvin, and Marianne, and learned that none of them knew anything about adoption, or if they did, they weren't telling him. He grabbed a family law hornbook and a copy of the relevant Oklahoma statutes from the library and walked hurriedly toward his new office.

A middle-aged woman with a frosted bouffant hairdo was sitting in the cubicle between Ben's office and Derek's, separated from the hallway by heavy wooden dividers. She was smoking, and her ashtray indicated she went at it as fervently as did Derek. She did not look up as Ben approached.

"You must be Maggie," Ben said amiably.

The woman's gaze shifted from the paperback romance novel she was reading. "Yes." Her voice had a detectable nasal twang. Ben wondered if she had come from back East with Derek.

He smiled. "I'm Ben Kincaid. I guess we're going to be working together."

"I work for Mr. Derek," she said crisply. She returned her attention to her novel.

"Evidently you're working for me, too. I'm the new associate on Mr. Derek's team."

Maggie looked up slowly. "I haven't worked with a new associate in seven years." She removed the clear plastic reading glasses hanging on a chain around her neck and rubbed the bridge of her nose. "New associates are always . . . *writing* things, and always wanting them typed by yesterday. And always changing them once they *are* typed."

"Look, I'm sorry," Ben said, shifting his weight from one leg to the other. "It wasn't my idea. I'll try not to be a bother."

Maggie lifted the receiver to her ear and punched a button on the complex phone console on her desk. "We'll see about this. This isn't supposed to happen to me. We have an arrangement."

Ben decided that his need to hit the books was more pressing than this rewarding conversation. "I'll be in my office," he said.

Maggie didn't even nod.

Ben surveyed his new office. Well, there will be few distractions, he thought.

Raven, Tucker & Tubb provided him with a desk—a table, actually, and a matching chair, both made of a cheap pine Ben wouldn't have used in his college dorm room. The walls were a barren, uninterrupted white. The table held a green banker's lamp and a complicated telephone unit, smaller than but similar to the one at Maggie's station. There was a short, empty bookshelf beside the table and two undeniably hideous orange corduroy visitors' chairs. Apparently, furnishings were passed down from one associate to another—the good stuff going up the totem pole and the wretched stuff going down. Ben hoped his first client didn't have a keenly developed sense of decor.

On the table, he saw a small box. He opened it and found hundreds of preprinted business cards with his name on them, just beneath the firm logo. Ready for business.

He cracked open the hornbook and began to read.

A few minutes before eleven, he was startled by an electronic beeping noise. He pushed the illuminated button on his telephone console. It was Maggie.

"Visitors for you in the main foyer," she said brusquely.

"Thank you, Maggie. Please show them in."

There was a pause, then a slow, inhaling noise. "You understand this is only temporary, Mr. Kincaid."

"Yes, I do, Maggie. But while it lasts, I plan to treasure every precious moment we spend together."

"I'll get your visitors," she said, and rang off.

There was no reason for Ben to be surprised. Derek had not made any representations regarding his visitors' appearances, although he had linked them with one of the most sophisticated and prosperous corporate entities in the state. Nonetheless, when Maggie ushered the visitors into his office, Ben was surprised and vaguely disappointed.

The two adults, a man and a woman, were older than he had expected, perhaps in their early sixties. Both had pure white hair. The man wore blue jeans and a white shirt with a plastic pencil holder in the front pocket and noticeable yellow-gray stains under each arm. The woman wore a simple green print dress, a plain brown coat, and white costume beads.

"My name's Jonathan Adams," the man said, taking Ben's hand, "and this is my wife, Bertha."

The single sentence had been sufficient to tell Ben a great deal about Mr. Adams's origins. He had the thick, slow drawl usually found in rural areas in the western part of the state.

Ben shook his hand, then Bertha's, and introduced himself.

"Honestly!" Bertha said, eyeing him with suspicion. "Are you an attorney?"

Ben tried not to react. People usually thought he looked young for his age. "Yes, I am," he said amiably. "Promise. I've got a diploma and everything. Just haven't coughed up the money to have it framed yet."

"Oh," she said, looking meaningfully at her husband. "I see."

Ben knew exactly what that expression meant. It meant: Jonathan, I thought we were getting a real lawyer.

She turned her attention slowly back to Ben, eyeing him carefully. Ben knew that expression, too. It meant: This case may not mean much to your firm, but it's the whole wide world to us, and we'd like to have a *real* lawyer, not some baby-faced kid who hasn't lost his training wheels yet. Or something like that.

"Princess, don't be standoffish like that," Bertha said.

Ben looked up, startled. For a moment, he thought the

woman was talking to him. Then he saw a small dark-haired girl standing behind the adults. "Mr. Kincaid, this is our Emily."

The girl was beautiful. Her features were simple and smooth; her pale skin was virtually translucent. Her long black hair served to highlight her flawless white complexion. She was a marble sculpture of what a little girl ought to look like, Ben thought, a Botticelli angel. And there was something else about her, he realized, a light, or a *glow*, that seemed to radiate from her.

Ben suddenly felt embarrassed. He was romanticizing a little girl. And he was staring, too.

"Good morning," he said, smiling.

Emily gazed at him with a puzzled expression. Her eyes didn't quite seem to focus on his face. "Good morning, Mr. Kincaid. Have I met you before?"

Ben blinked. "Uh, no, I don't believe so."

"Oh," Emily said. She looked around the office. "Have I been here before?"

Jonathan Adams interrupted. "Good grief, girl. What a lot of questions. Just say hello."

Ben smiled. "It's all right. I like to ask questions myself." He took the pink woolen sweater she was holding and hung it on a hook behind the door. "How old are you, Emily?"

"I'm five," she said, and she held out five fingers.

Five? Ben was no expert on children, but this girl appeared to be at least eight or nine. He saw Mr. and Mrs. Adams exchange another meaningful glance.

Ben squatted down to her level. "And what grade are you in?"

Emily giggled. "Not old enough for school, silly. Mommy dinn't want me to go to kinnergarnen."

Bertha Adams looked out the office window.

Emily abruptly changed the subject. "Do you play pat-a-cake?" She raised her hands with the palms outstretched and chanted. "Pat-a-cake, pat-a-cake, baker's man, bake me a cake as fast as you can—"

Ben winked at Mrs. Adams. "I don't think I know that one."

"I know more," she said. She continued chanting in the same rhythmic pattern. "A bumblebee and reverie. It will do, if bees are few—"

Mr. Adams interrupted. "Bertha, don't you have her crayons or something?"

"Yes." She reached into her purse and pulled out an oversized book. "Emily, honey, I brought your coloring book."

Emily turned and stared at the book. "What is this?"

Bertha pressed the book into her hands. "It's your coloring book, princess. We bought it just before we came here. And here are your colors. You take them and go sit in the lobby."

Emily frowned. "Don't remember no lobby. Don't know this place."

Bertha pointed out the door toward the lobby.

"You won't leave me, will you?"

"Of course not, child," Mr. Adams said. "Now you go sit down and wait for us. We need to talk to Mr. Kincaid here for a spell."

Ben rose to his full height. "Bye-bye, Emily. Maybe we can play again later."

Hesitantly, the girl started to leave.

"Wait, Emily," Ben said. "Don't forget your sweater. It's cool in the lobby. Air conditioning's down too low."

She cocked her head at a slight angle. The puzzled expression again crossed her face.

Ben took the sweater from the hook behind the door. "Remember this?"

The girl looked at the sweater. "It's pretty. Can I have it?"

Ben looked at Mr. and Mrs. Adams, but their eyes were fixed on one another.

"Of course," he said, after a moment. He handed the girl her sweater.

Bertha again pointed toward the lobby. "Now run along, dear."

Emily obeyed.

Ben gestured for the couple to sit down in the orange corduroy chairs. There was an awkward pause as all parties considered the best means of broaching the obvious subject.

Mr. Adams broke the silence. "You probably know this already, Mr. Kincaid—"

"Call me Ben." He felt ridiculous hearing a man thirty years his elder calling him mister.

"Sure. As I was saying, Ben, I work for Joe Sanguine out at Sanguine Enterprises. I'm vice president in charge of new projects and development, have been for fourteen years. I go back even before Sanguine bought the outfit. 'Cept during the time I spent in California, I guess my title changed—"

"Stick to the subject, Jonathan."

He grinned. "Yes, Bertha. Anyway, 'bout a year ago, I was scouting some real estate as a possible location for a new outlet in south Tulsa, out toward Jenks. Place was a vacant lot, out in the middle of nowhere. And who do I find wandering around out there but little Emily? She was filthy and so confused she didn't know up from down. She knew her name was Emily and that she had a mommy she couldn't describe somewhere, but that's about it. Said she woke up nearby but didn't know how she came to be there. Course I figured she was just kinda confused and disoriented from being abandoned.'' He paused, and glanced at his wife. ''Later, we found out just how bad it really was.''

Ben tried to maintain an even, professional composure. ''Is there . . . something wrong with Emily?''

''Yeah, there sure enough is.'' He rubbed his hands against his cheeks, as if rousing himself. ''Korsakov's syndrome.''

''I beg your pardon?''

''That's what the doctors call it. Korsakov's syndrome. With some visual agnosia. Emily has no long-term memory. In fact, she has no short-term memory, really. Anything you say to her or show her, she'll forget as soon as you or it are out of sight. Maybe sooner.'' He paused. ''Emily lives only in the present. And she doesn't live there for long.''

Ben nodded, although he certainly did not understand. ''Why does she think she's five years old?''

''Because that's the last time she remembers,'' Adams answered. ''That's when her memory shuts down. Before that, her memory is more or less intact. Course, there's not really much she can tell you—what do you expect from the memory of a five-year-old kid? Plus there's the visual agnosia. She doesn't seem to see *faces*. Or if she does, she can't describe them. Can't put it into words. Can't draw you a picture.''

He rubbed his hand against his forehead and brushed back his white hair. ''After some point in the year she was five—nothing. She can't even tell you what happened an hour ago. That's why, first thing, she asked you, 'Have I met you before?' She can't remember.''

"She still asks me that sometimes," Bertha added, "and she's been living with us almost a year now." Her stoic expression did not break, but Ben could see her sadness ran deep.

"She's pretty good with voices, though," Jonathan added. "After a month or so, she began to recognize the sound of Bertha and me. Now, once she hears our voices, she seems to remember, at least a little bit, and trust us."

"I never heard of such a thing," Ben said.

"It's a rare brain disorder, according to the docs. An extreme form of amnesia. Usually occurs as a result of alcoholism."

Ben's face wrinkled. "But Emily couldn't have been—"

"No, Ben, she couldn't have been an alcoholic. It can also be caused by a blow to the head, a brain tumor, or anything else that might cause a"—he took a deep breath, as if gearing up for the big words—"neurological dysfunction."

"She's been to see doctors, then?"

"Yes, of course." A tinge of irritation, or frustration, crept into his voice. "She's been checked by damn near every neurologist in the Southwest. EEGs, blood tests, CAT scans, psychotropic drugs, the whole dog-and-pony show. No visible sign of brain damage. But then, they explain, the atrophying of the tiny . . . *mammillary* bodies in the brain that causes this disorder probably wouldn't show up on any of their tests."

"Kind of makes you wonder why they take the gruesome things in the first place," Bertha added quietly. There was no humor in her voice.

"Then no one has any idea what caused this?" Ben asked.

"There is a theory," Adams said hesitantly, "though no real proof, that the syndrome can result from what the docs call . . . hysterical . . . or *fugal* amnesia. Meaning that Emily experienced some traumatic event too awful to remember. Something her mind wants to avoid. So it hasn't remembered anything since."

Ben felt embarrassed about his earlier snap judgment. Jonathan Adams was obviously an intelligent man. "That might explain why her memory stops at age five," Ben said. "But what could happen to a five-year-old girl that would be too horrible to remember?"

Bertha's head was lowered. "I hope she never remembers," she said quietly. "We try not to dwell on it. We love our little Emily and the thought—" She stopped, and her face tightened. She returned her gaze to a fixed spot on the carpet.

"May not have happened when she was five," Adams added, covering the silence. "With Korsakov's syndrome, sometimes the erosion of memory goes both ways. It moves not only forward but backward from the time of the trauma."

The room fell silent. Ben wished to God he had a cactus or calendar or something in the office to which he could divert his attention. After a moment, he realized he had become so engrossed in the discussion of Emily's disorder that he had totally failed to explore the legal matter at hand.

He cleared his throat. "Forgive me for changing the subject, Mr. and Mrs. Adams, but I was told that you were seeking advice on an adoption matter. Do you want to adopt Emily?"

"Yes," Bertha said, not looking up.

"You know, Ben," Jonathan said, "this is probably going to sound ridiculous, but I'm just a feeble old coot so I'm entitled to a little ridiculousness every now and then. I don't think it's any secret how we feel about our little Emily. Took to her from the first moment I saw her in that vacant lot."

"Well, if you're sure, then—"

"We know what you're thinking, Mr. Kincaid," Bertha interrupted. "Don't you think it's crossed our minds? Why adopt such a bundle of trouble? Especially at our age. It's not as if she's ever going to be attached to us." She released a short, unhappy laugh. "She can barely remember who we are."

Jonathan Adams gently laid his hand upon his wife's and squeezed.

"But we love her, Mr. Kincaid, we truly do." For the first time, the strong woman's voice cracked. "We never had any children of our own. Couldn't." She took a deep breath and tried to regain control. "And then, long after I'd given up any hope of children, Jonathan comes home with little Emily. I've spent the last year watching her drift from one moment to the next. And I've been happy, mostly." She sunk back into the folds of her coat. "She's mine now. And I want to keep her."

Ben looked at the woman, then looked away. At last, the impenetrable fortress had been breached. She began to cry.

* 4 *

Ben called Maggie and asked her to bring in soft drinks. After some minor grumbling and a five-minute delay, she appeared with three cans of Coke Classic. As the sodas were served, small talk replaced the previous serious conversation. Ben could feel the tension in the room diminishing.

"She doesn't always seem so . . . unfocused, you know," Jonathan said. "You should see her when she listens to music. We'll play a record, and her entire personality changes. She seems completely absorbed."

"Same thing in church," Bertha added. "When the organ is playing, and they're taking communion."

"She becomes absorbed in the ritual," Jonathan continued. "She likes helping me garden, too. Seems to like repeating the same act over and over. Makes her feel comfortable." He sipped from his Coke. "It's a wonderful thing to see, Mr. Kincaid. All of a sudden, she's not the restless, lost child you saw a moment ago."

"I can't believe you've had Emily for almost a year without getting caught up in bureaucratic red tape," Ben said.

Jonathan and Bertha eyed one another. "Well, when we first found Emily, we reported it to the police, of course,"

Jonathan said. He took another swallow of his Coke. "They claimed they made an investigation and to no one's surprise told us they hadn't the foggiest idea who she was. They told us to take her to the Department of Human Services. We . . . uh . . . forgot." Jonathan winked in his wife's direction.

"But even if you were already attached to Emily," Ben said, "you should have turned her over to the child welfare authorities and then applied to adopt her."

Bertha shook her head. "What would be the point? Let me tell you something, Mr. Kincaid. I'm fifty-nine years old. Jonathan is sixty-one. We've never had children before. They wouldn't let us adopt a puppy, much less a sweet thing like Emily."

"And as time went on," Jonathan added, "we realized just how permanent, how . . . devastating, Emily's condition really was. They probably wouldn't put her up for adoption at all. They'd put her in one of those homes for *special* children. I've heard about what goes on in those homes, Mr. Kincaid. We couldn't let that happen to our Emily. We just couldn't."

Ben frowned. He was hearing damaging information that he knew wouldn't help their case at an adoption hearing.

"So we kept Emily at home," Jonathan continued. "Told the few neighbors we know she was the daughter of a mythical niece of Bertha's in Kansas City. It worked for a while. But you know how neighbors are." His voice took on a shrill tone. " 'Why isn't little Emily in school? When is that niece from Kansas City coming back for her? Maybe the Adamses are one of those old couples that snatch kids in shopping malls.' " He paused. "Eventually, someone called the police."

Bertha smiled wryly. "We got rid of the nosy Parker

with a lot of tea and sincere-sounding balderdash. Or so we thought. I guess our luck couldn't hold out forever." Bertha reached down beside her chair and withdrew a long sheet of paper from her purse. "Some rude young man wearing dark sunglasses served this on us last week."

Ben took the sheet of paper from her. It was a court order commanding Bertha and Jonathan to show cause why Emily shouldn't be taken from them and placed in the custody of the Department of Human Services. The hearing was set for the following Friday.

While Ben reviewed the order, Greg suddenly burst through his office door.

"Hey, Ben, we're taking a poll on Marianne's name—" He saw the Adamses and froze. "Whoops! I didn't know you had visitors." He looked mortified.

"Greg," Ben said, "this is Jonathan and Bertha Adams. Jonathan is a senior vice president at Sanguine Enterprises."

"Really." Greg looked awkwardly at Jonathan, then shook his hand. "Nice to meet you." He turned away hurriedly. "Well, Marianne doesn't have to commit until lunchtime. I'll come by later when you're not busy." He slunk backward out the door. Ben heard him mutter to Maggie in the hallway, "Geez, he's only been here two hours and he's already talking to clients!"

"Is that young man a lawyer here?" Jonathan asked.

"Strange but true," Ben said. He returned his attention to the court order. "Everything seems to be in order. The DHS is apparently taking this very seriously."

"Isn't there anything you can do, Mr. Kincaid?" Bertha asked.

At last, Ben realized, it was time to try to sound like a lawyer. "Of course we'll appear at the hearing on your behalf and try to convince the court it would be in the child's best interests to remain with you. We'll make a formal request for adoption. Other than that, there's not much we can do. I'm afraid the procedures for adoptions are rather rigid. And it won't look good when they tell the court that you kept Emily for a year without reporting to the DHS." He paused. "The best approach would be to go to court with a consensual adoption. But for that, we'd have to know who her mother or father is and obtain their consent."

Jonathan inhaled sharply. "Are you sure that's the only way?"

Ben shrugged. "It's the only approach that is likely to be successful. Absent consent, we can only make our case and hope for the best. Do you have any idea who Emily's parents might have been?"

Adams's face hardened. He seemed to retreat into deep, silent thought. "No," he said, finally. "No, I don't." He took a long time before adding, "But maybe I can work on it."

Bertha's brow creased. She looked pointedly at her husband.

"How soon do you need to know something?" Jonathan asked.

"The sooner the better. I'd like to have an affidavit on file with the court before the Friday hearing."

"All righty. I'll call you as soon as I have any information."

Jonathan and Bertha rose to leave. Ben handed the man one of his freshly printed business cards and asked Maggie to bring Emily back to his office.

The little girl seemed in good spirits. "Hello," she said, looking at Ben. "Have I ever met you before?"

Bertha smiled faintly and took the girl by the hand. The three of them left his office.

Ben plopped back into his chair. The gnawing sensation in his stomach seemed stronger. Why couldn't he have something normal for his first case here? A simple debt collection case maybe, just to get the ball rolling.

He sighed. He tried to analyze the legal ramifications of the case, but found himself daydreaming about Emily, and wondering what life must be like for her. For Emily, he thought with some admiration, everything was now, this instant, present tense. No memory, no guilt, no regrets. An entire life spent in a fixed moment of time.

* 5 *

"So tell me the truth, Alvin," Greg said. "Have you really computed all these demographics about the firm or were you just trying to impress us?"

Ben, Alvin, Greg and Marianne sat in a semicircle on the floor of Ben's apartment. Not for the sake of togetherness but for the sake of necessity—Ben had no furniture, a fact that slipped his mind when he invited them over for a late-night pizza and first-day gossip fest.

"It's the truth," Alvin said proudly. "I take my career very seriously. And why not? Did you see all the new associates today? They were worried sick. Why should I waste my energy worrying when there's a way to find the answers to the questions I'm worried about?''

Alvin turned to Marianne. "How much time have you spent in the last few weeks wondering what names the other female attorneys at Raven were using?'' His gaze shifted to Ben. "And how much time have you spent wondering what associate salaries were at various stages of the eight-year associateship? Well, I didn't just sit around speculating. I found out.''

Greg placed his hand over his heart. "Alvin Hager,'' he said solemnly, "the All-American Boy.''

Alvin ignored him. "I stayed late today, watching everyone leave, trying to see if I could distinguish the associates from the partners.''

"Could you?'' Ben asked.

"Easy. The shareholders all strolled out carrying a nice black leather briefcase, if anything. The associates all left loaded down with books and papers and legal pads. It's their way of crying out, 'Look how hard I work! Shouldn't I be a shareholder, too?' ''

Marianne eyed him suspiciously. "You may be a little *too* smart for my taste, Hager. You're not going to be one of those associates who are always sucking up to partners, are you?''

Alvin waved the suggestion away with his hand. "Of course not. That's not the ticket to success. The up-and-coming associate learns to blend devout servitude with the appearance of independence. You don't want to make the partners uncomfortable, after all.''

Ben shook his head. "Too much for me to handle,'' he said.

The doorbell chimed and, almost simultaneously, the phone began to ring.

Ben headed toward the door. "Greg, would you get the phone?" Greg nodded.

Ben opened the door to find the smiling, sweaty face of the delivery boy from Antonio's. He passed the boy a check and took the pizza box.

"I don't know about this," Marianne said. "We're young urban professionals now. Seems like we should be eating pasta in a classy restaurant with a maître d' named François."

Greg returned and dove into the pizza. "It was your mother, Ben," he said. "She asked you to call her back later."

"Which reminds me," Ben said abruptly to Marianne. "What name did you decide to use on your doorplate?"

Marianne fixed her gaze on the pepperoni slice inches below her nose. "Well, none, actually. I went with initials. M. H. Gunnerson."

Alvin nodded. "Very professional."

Ben suppressed a grin. "M. *H.*, eh? What does the H stand for?"

"I'd rather not say."

"Aha! Now here's a puzzle," Greg said, jabbing Ben in the ribs. "Must be really dreadful."

"Harriet?" Ben asked.

"I'm betting on Hildegaard," Greg said.

"Perhaps Hermione," Alvin suggested.

"Stop," Marianne said, giggling. "I won't tell." She reached for another slice of pizza. "I heard starting associates are expected to bill two hundred and twenty-five hours a month."

"That's *incredible*," Ben said. "That can't be right. Did your supervising attorney tell you that?"

"Nope. My secretary. So it must be true."

"That's over fifty hours a week!"

"What do you think we're here for?" Alvin said with a sort of snort. "We haven't got any expertise or clientele. We're here for one reason and one reason only. To make the shareholders rich." He paused for effect. "And the only way we can do that is work, work, work—and bill dem hours."

"I don't think it's necessary to become a total workaholic just to make the firm profitable," Ben said.

Alvin made a tsking noise. "Uh-oh. Attitude problem. Well, don't worry, Ben, I won't file a report with your supervising attorney. This time."

"At this point, Alvin, there's nothing that could make him think less of me than he already does."

Greg took a bite of pizza and shook his head. "If you're talking about that toupee incident, don't worry about it. It's not that big a deal. I bet he's already forgotten about it."

Ben looked at him, then at Marianne, then at Alvin. They looked back. Simultaneously, all four erupted with laughter.

"Yeah, right," Ben said, wiping his eyes. "What's to remember?"

The phone rang again. Ben frowned. Greg started to rise.

"That's all right," Ben said quickly. "I'll get it." He took three slow steps to the telephone, then lifted the receiver to his ear. "Hello?"

"Hello, Ben. It's Mike. Your brother-in-law."

"*Ex*-brother-in-law. You divorced Julia, remember?"

"Let's not dredge up painful memories, kemo sabe." In the background, Ben could hear the sounds of traffic.

Mike must be calling from somewhere outdoors. "How long have you been in town?"

"Just since Saturday night. I've been meaning to give you a call—"

"Yeah, right. So, you busy right now?"

"Well, I'm snarfing a pizza with some fellow associates."

"Very upwardly mobile," Mike said. "Why don't you come meet me—"

"Mike, I'd really like to see you, but I think it would be rude—"

"This isn't a social invitation," Mike interrupted. "I'm working. I've got a corpse here that looks like he got the bad end of an argument with a Cuisinart."

"My God," Ben muttered. "Who is it?"

"Beats hell out of us. I was hoping you could tell me."

"Me? Look, Mike, I know I helped the police out a few times when I was at the D.A.'s office in OKC, but it's almost eleven and I have to be at work at eight in the morning—"

"You don't understand, Ben. We've got clues."

Ben hesitated. "What clues?"

"Well, just one, really, but it's a zinger. The murderer stripped this poor slob clean—no wallet, no I.D. But he missed something. Something we found in the corpse's shirt pocket behind one of those plastic pencil pouches you see on nerds and accountants. A business card." He paused. "Actually, it was *your* business card, Ben."

Ben said nothing. The air seemed to become very heavy.

"I think you'd better come out here, Ben. On the double."

* 6 *

Ben stood in a dark alley on the north side, the Bad Part of Town in the common parlance, wondering how he got entangled in something so seedy on his very first day on the job. On the street, a red neon sign identifying the Red Parrot Café and a smaller sign providing the key information BEER blinked on and off. A small crowd of disreputable-looking people was beginning to form. Their faces were illuminated by the whirling red and blue lights atop the police cars and ambulances.

Ben watched as the paramedics and coroner's office interns lifted the stiff, blood-caked body onto a stretcher. It had taken them nearly fifteen minutes to lift the body out of the garbage Dumpster where it had been found by a street person.

Ben gazed at the hideous, mutilated corpse, barely recognizable as the remnant of a human being. The body was coated with thick black blood. A violent blow had crushed the left side of the face and left precious little of the right. The jaw was broken and limp, dangling freely from the upper part of the skull.

The body had suffered numerous other blows as well. Something had smashed the knees from the front. Something had split the scalp above the right ear, and again at the base of the skull. And there were numerous puncture wounds, blotted and stained with repulsively large quantities of coagulated blood.

There was no question: these were the remains of Jonathan Adams. True, his face was mutilated beyond all hope of recognition, but he was wearing the same clothes he had worn in Ben's office, with the same distinctive pencil holder. And he had the business card, the only one Ben had ever dispensed, precisely where Ben had seen him place it. But the sense of bearing, of quiet strength, Ben had perceived before was utterly erased; the body had collapsed in on itself like a popped balloon.

The police photographer, a man who must possess a stainless-steel stomach, was photographing the corpse from all heights and angles. Ben winced and looked away.

"Have you found a weapon?" Ben asked.

"No." The man who summoned Ben, Lieutenant Mike Morelli, struggled to light a pipe against a strong headwind. He was wearing a hat and an overcoat—rather heavy gear for summer weather—but Ben knew that for Mike, an important part of being a detective was looking like a detective. "I've got my men combing the area, but I don't have high hopes. Not a cooperative neighborhood. I'm lining up a crew to look for bloodstained clothing. Once morning breaks, they'll be searching refuse collections and dumps throughout the city."

"Think you'll find anything?"

"It's possible. Assuming the killer is from around here and doesn't have the smarts to burn his clothes. Our best shot is to find the knife that made the puncture wounds."

"What kind of knife was it?"

"I can't say for sure. Might know more after the coroner's report. It was a big one. Thick. Sharp. Might be a kitchen knife." He puffed twice on his pipe. "The kind you can find in every home in Tulsa."

"But why would anyone use a knife? It's so . . . *messy.* Any idiot can get a gun from any pawnshop in town. Especially in this part of town."

"You're assuming someone planned this in advance," Mike said. "Remember, Adams's wallet was missing. The five-mile radius now surrounding us houses ninety-five percent of all the lowlifes, drug addicts, drug pushers, and pimps in Tulsa. Probably, Adams was just a stupid rich guy looking for some action who got robbed. The robbery got messy, or maybe Adams was really stupid and tried to fight back. The robber got mad and Adams got offed.

"Also consider, Counselor, that although a knife may be messier than a gun, it's a hell of a lot harder to trace." The exhaled pipe smoke formed a halo around Mike's head. Ben wondered if he practiced that. "No registration numbers. No licenses. No paraffin or ballistics tests. And a knife is quieter, too. Despite the appearance of this neighborhood, it is still inhabited. Some people have been coming here all their lives, and they aren't going to stop now. I understand a lot of older guys come here for a little nonspousal sexual activity."

"Adams wasn't the type to do that."

"Says you. And you've known him for all of what? An hour?" Mike took another puff on the pipe. "This area has also become a favorite haunt for young professionals like yourself who think it'd be fun to go slumming for an evening and score some coke or something."

Resentful? Ben shook his head. How did that happen? Just six years ago, Ben had been a groomsman in Mike's wedding. They had met in college during Ben's junior year, in a poetry-writing class, and discovered they had common interests. Pizza. Music. Saving the world.

They shared an apartment the next semester and started playing together at a local pizza parlor, Ben on keyboards, Mike on guitar and vocals. Mike met Ben's younger sister, Julia, during that time. Two months later, Mike dropped out of school and announced that he and Julia were getting married. Any fool could see that, as they say in soap operas, they came from two different worlds. Ben and Julia's father was an upper-middle-class cardiologist; Mike's divorced and usually absent father was an oil well promoter. But they were in love. The differences didn't matter. At first.

Julia was accustomed to the lifestyle of a successful professional's baby girl. Constant entertainment and all the instant gratification money can buy. Mike got a part-time job as a prison guard and tried to save up enough money for them to pay the bills while he went through police academy training. An impossible dream, as long as Julia had breath in her body and plastic in her purse. Mike, through Julia, had to start asking for loans from his daddy-in-law. Family relations, never good, really started to feel the strain after that.

And, Ben reflected, I started law school and had problems of my own and lost track of my old best buddy and costar. One day Ben got a call from his mother telling him that Julia had left Mike and moved to Montana with an English lit professor. Mom and Dad were mortified. Naturally, they blamed Mike.

With no shopping addiction to feed, Mike had no problem completing the police officer training program. Ben assumed he dealt with the emotional blow in his usual tough-guy manner. Inside of four years, Mike was a detective working in the homicide department. Tulsa PD didn't get near–college graduates that often.

Ben really had meant to call Mike once he got settled. Really.

"So you think it was a robbery that got out of hand?" Ben asked.

Mike took a deep draw on his pipe. "So it appears. The neighborhood, the victim, the missing wallet." He paused for a moment. "But I don't mind telling you, at the risk of sounding trite—something doesn't seem right. One blow would've been enough to rob the old coot. Hell, two blows would've been enough to kill him. Why the hell did the killer feel compelled to turn the guy's body into goulash?"

"Maybe the thief was a psycho. Or high on drugs."

"Yeah, maybe. This is definitely the neighborhood for it. But something about this bothers me, Ben."

A young uniformed officer walked up to Mike. "We had a heck of a time getting the body out of that Dumpster, sir, but it's loaded into the ambulance now. We dusted the corpse, the Dumpster, and the surrounding area for fingerprints. No latents. We also searched for footprints or any other trace evidence. No luck."

Mike exploded, apparently enraged. "Goddamn it, what kind of hack rookie are you?" He muttered a few choice curses under his breath. "I want you to take the whole goddamn squad and fan out for ten blocks in every direction. And *look*, damn it! That means you pick things up, you look around corners. And talk to people. Whether they've bathed recently or not. Don't come back till you can give me something useful."

The young officer swallowed. "Yes, sir."

"And send the hair and fiber boys in with their tweezers."

"Yes, sir."

"And where the hell is the lab biologist? Bolton or Dolton or whatever her name is. Give her another call!"

"Yes, sir."

"And tell McAfferty to get his butt over here. Mr. Kincaid and I are ready to speak to Crazy Jane."

"Yes, sir." The young man turned quickly and disappeared.

"Still doing the hardboiled shamus bit, eh?" Ben said. "Dashiell Hammett would be proud of you."

Mike looked away. "I don't know what you're talking about."

"Right. Forget I spoke. I'm sure it's just a coincidence that you act and dress like a character out of *film noir*."

Mike frowned.

"Don't worry, Mike. I won't tell them you were once an English major."

"I don't have time to put up with you." Mike patted down the ashes in the bowl of his pipe.

Ben decided to leave well enough alone. "What's this about a Crazy Jane?" he asked.

"Street person. She found the body while she was rummaging around in the Dumpster. Looking for supper, probably."

Another young uniformed officer walked toward them, leading by the arm a desiccated woman who had to be Crazy Jane. She was short and hunched, as if from spending her entire life huddling for warmth. Her hair was thin and gray and sticking out in every direction. Ben could see she had a prominent bald spot on the back of her head, the first he had ever seen on a woman. Her skin had a cold, blue, steely texture; she had a large red scab over her left eye. A black plastic garbage bag was wrapped around her upper body. A poor woman's over-coat.

"Did you sober her up, McAfferty?" Mike asked curtly.

The young officer seemed hesitant. "I poured a lot of coffee down her throat, sir, but as for sobriety, well . . ."

Mike understood. He squared himself in front of her. "How long have you been in this alley, Jane?" he asked.

Her mouth was a straight, horizontal line. "All my life, handsome."

This was going to be more difficult than he had imagined. "Have you seen anyone in this alley tonight? I mean, other than the deceased?"

She looked at him oddly. "The snowbird done it."

Mike's eyebrows raised.

"The snowbird, the white bird of peace. It cum down and took 'em away to the clouds." She gazed up toward the sky.

Mike and Ben glanced at one another. "I see . . ."

"It's heaven!" Suddenly she was shouting. "Great God Almighty open them doors at last!" The woman shook free of McAfferty's hands. "The time has cum. It's the cummin' of the Lord! Praise God halley-luah!"

Mike let out a deep sigh. "Well, that's all we need from you now, Jane. Thanks, though."

Crazy Jane brought her gaze and her voice back down to earth. "Cert'ly, handsome." Officer McAfferty led her away.

After they were gone, Ben made a long whistling noise. "Wow," he said. "What a case. Total crackpotdom. Must be the Oral Roberts influence. Infects the whole city."

"Yeah, well, you try living on the streets for a while and we'll see how sane you come out. Those people have a hell of a hard life. Cuddling sewer vents for warmth and scraping garbage bins for food." He frowned. "If you don't have any additional insights on this matter, Ben, you may leave."

"Darn. And just when I was learning to love the north side. So how long till you catch the guy that killed my client?"

"Forever, probably."

"What?"

"You heard me."

"It's a little early in the investigation to abandon all hope, isn't it?"

"I'm just trying to be realistic," Mike said, "and the fact is we don't have anything to go on. Maybe the lab or the coroner will turn up something, but it's not promising. The killer was probably some transient loony who took the cash and is now sitting in a motel room in St. Louis." He glanced at Ben. "What with the business card, you're my number-one suspect. But I can't see hauling you downtown. Since you're family and all."

"I can't believe you're giving up on this before you've even begun."

"Who's giving up? Tomorrow we'll go to this breakfast food factory where you say he works, and we'll quiz everybody who's spoken to him in the last ten years. We'll get a subpoena for the Message Unit Detail sheets from the phone company, and we'll trace every call he's made from his home or office for the last six months. The physical evidence boys will continue to scour the city. For as long as they can. Until Chief Blackwell decides it's hopeless, or until the next gruesome homicide comes along."

Mike was becoming agitated. "Tulsa isn't New York City, but we haven't got so little to do that we can piddle away our time on hopeless cases. This murder was a one-man show, possibly a one-lunatic show, and that one lu-natic hasn't left many traces and isn't likely to confess. Unlike those TV cop shows you grew up on, some real-life cases just can't be solved." He paused significantly. "At least not by traditional police methods."

Ben's eyes narrowed. "What do you mean?"

"C'mon, Ben. You're the shyster; you don't need me to tell you the law. There's plenty you can do that I can't."

"Like what?"

"Like what happens if I break into a house without a search warrant and take some crucial evidence?"

"It probably can't be used at trial."

"And what happens if you do the same thing?"

Ben shrugged. "Nothing. No state action."

"Well, not exactly. I'd have to arrest *you* for breaking and entering, but the evidence you found could still be used at trial. Geez, what kind of grades did you make? Maybe *I* ought to be a lawyer."

Ben didn't honor the remark with a reply. "What are you getting at, Mike?"

"Well, my quick-witted friend, I'm saying if you really want to find the guy who deep-sixed your client, hire a private investigator. Do some investigating yourself. And check back with me from time to time. Unofficially, of course."

A black-and-white police car slowly cruised to a stop on the other side of the street. Ben could see Bertha Adams sitting in the backseat on the passenger side.

"Does she know yet?" Ben asked.

Mike nodded. "Told her on the phone. But it's not the same. It never really sinks in till they see the body."

Ben began zipping his jacket. "I don't want to be around for this, Mike."

"Don't blame you. Consider what I said, though, okay? And stay in touch. Oh. Last thing . . ." Mike reached into the pocket of his overcoat and withdrew a crumpled bit of white paper. "You can take this with you."

Ben took the paper from Mike. It was his business card. "Don't you need this for evidence?"

"Oh, I think I can remember the name." Mike winked, then thrust his fists into his overcoat. "You know, Ben, I really loved your sister."

Ben shoved the card into his pocket. "Yeah." He turned and walked back to his car.

* 7 *

"Absolutely not. Under no circumstances. Good God, Kincaid, this was supposed to be a starter case. Simple and cheap. A favor."

Derek slammed the flat of his hand against his desk. "I can't believe this happened. I mean, Jesus, I've lost clients before, but not like this!"

Ben sat on his hands as Derek paraded around the office.

"How could I justify the expense? This is an adoption

case, for God's sake! Why do we need a private investigator?''

"Lieutenant Morelli told me—''

"Sure!'' Derek threw his arms into the air. "Morelli
would love for us to do his work for him. But we've got
work of our own, Kincaid. Lesson one about relatives,
kid. If they don't want money, they want you to perform
some legal hocus-pocus for them gratis.''

"Excuse me, sir, but it seems to me this is part of *our*
job—''

"No. Our job was to go through the motions and gen-
erate some paperwork so a sweet old couple could try to
adopt a brain-damaged wretch they found in a vacant lot.
We were not asked to find a murderer, and we were not
asked to cast a private dragnet for the girl's parents, whoever they may be.'' He fished around in his shirt pocket
for a cigarette but didn't find any. "Hell, for all we know,
the woman may not want to adopt the kid now that . . .
that . . .'' He sputtered for a moment, then waved it all
away with a dramatic skyward gesture.

"She does, sir. More than ever.''

"Fine. Just fine.'' Derek kicked the wall next to his
desk. He grimaced, then grabbed his right foot. He hob-
bled behind his desk and plopped down into his chair.
"Sprained my ankle playing squash last night. Meant to
stay off the damn thing.''

He took a deep breath and regained his train of thought.
"So do the adoption. That's your assignment. But no private investigators, no bells and whistles, no tickets to the
prince's ball, understand? I'm not even authorizing you to
make long-distance phone calls.'' He rubbed his ankle
tenderly. "Do you have any idea what a private investigator would cost?''

"Not really, sir," he admitted.

"Well, it's a bundle. Let me remind you, Kincaid, that this job does not actually benefit our client or his business. It's a charitable gesture on his part. Lots of mega-rich business types like Sanguine want to provide a little employee-oriented charity every now and then. Good for the image. Makes them feel virtuous. But they don't like the charity to put a dent in the bottom line. You know what I mean?"

"You see, sir," Ben started, hesitantly, "Mrs. Adams is unlikely to be permitted to adopt Emily by the Department of Public Welfare or the Department of Human Services. She's elderly, she has no child-rearing experience, and now"—he swallowed hard—"now she's a widow. Adoption agencies have lists of hundreds of couples who satisfy every condition but who nonetheless have to wait years for a child. The only scenario I see that gives Mrs. Adams a prayer of adopting Emily is if we can tell a judge, acting as *parens patriae* for Emily, that Emily's natural parents have consented to the adoption. And for that, we need to find a parent."

Derek drummed his fingers on the table. "What makes you think you can find the parents? Do you know who they are?"

"Sir, I haven't the slightest idea who Emily's parents are. But Mr. Adams seemed convinced he could find out. And a few hours after he sets out to do just that, he's murdered. Sure, maybe it's just a hideous coincidence, but I find that hard to swallow. Lieutenant Morelli says we can help—"

"If Lieutenant Morelli wants to hire us as lawyers," Derek interrupted, "and pay us at our usual rates, we'll accommodate him. Tell him to give me a call—I get a hundred and eighty-five dollars an hour. Otherwise, forget it.''

Derek gently lowered his right foot to the floor. ''Look, kid, I know how you feel. On his first day out of school, every new lawyer wants to be Perry Mason. You watch enough television, you start to think the job of lawyers is to solve mysteries. Well, it isn't. The job of lawyers is to please their clients.''

Ben started to speak, but Derek stopped him with a raised finger. ''If you need to do some investigating, fine. Be a lawyer. Use the traditional discovery methods set forth in the Oklahoma Rules of Civil Procedure. But don't forget about the number of hours this firm expects you to bill. I think Joseph Sanguine will accept five, maybe eight hours being billed to him for this matter. More than that, he'll balk. So will I.''

Ben opened his mouth to respond. Again, the upraised finger stopped him.

''That's it, Kincaid. I've had two new files placed on your desk, and I want you to be up-to-snuff on them tomorrow morning. One of them involves a motion for preliminary injunction with a very short fuse. It's another Sanguine matter. We've asked for an expedited schedule because of the so-called looming threat of economic disaster by trade dress infringement. Our reply brief is due Monday. That means I want to see it Friday. Early.''

He waved his hand at Ben in a dismissing gesture. ''You've got a lot to do, Kincaid. So get to work.'' Derek pointed at the door.

Clenching his teeth tightly, Ben walked out of Derek's office.

* 8 *

Perry Mason indeed! What a jerk!

Ben shuffled a few papers around on his desk and muttered angrily to himself.

"Well, at least you've turned your light on. That's an improvement."

Ben looked up and saw a woman of medium height not much older than himself standing outside the doorway.

"The last guy who had this office," she continued, "never turned his light on. Lance Caldwell. Liked to work in the dark. And that's not the half of it." She shook her head from side to side with disapproval. "Weird, weird, weird. He finally left. I don't know if he got fired or disbarred or taken away by extraterrestrials or what." She leaned further through the doorway. "Aren't you going to ask me in? I'm Christina McCall. I'm your designated legal assistant."

Ben smiled. "I'm sorry, please come in and sit down. I'm Ben Kincaid. Pick a chair. Either chair."

She stepped inside and shut the door behind her. Although Ben could see several barrettes and rubber bands, her long strawberry-blond hair was not arranged according to any coherent plan that he could detect. Her face was soft and thin and pleasant in a natural way, rather than a *Vogue* magazine way. Her attire was the real eye-catcher, though. She was wearing a brown leather dress that came perilously close to being a miniskirt. And yellow leotards.

She scrutinized the two orange corduroy options. "I hope come bonus time they compensate you for these chairs."

"Good idea," Ben replied. "Why don't you prepare a memo for upper management?"

"Right." She settled into the chair on the left and crossed her yellow legs. "So, did you and Dickie have a nice chat? It's not that often we can hear him through a closed door. You two must have a special relationship." She grinned. "What was he, kicking the wall or something?"

Great. The word was out. "We were discussing a troublesome problem."

"Right. The adoption-murder case. I heard."

Ben stared at her. No secrets in this firm, evidently.

"That must be spooky," she said. "You meet a nice guy, you talk to him awhile, and the next thing you know, he's in rigor mortis. Brrrrrr."

Ben didn't say anything.

Christina changed the subject abruptly. "Are you going to the Raven, Tucker & Tubb dinner and dance gala Friday night?"

"Do I have any choice?" They laughed. "How about you?" he asked.

"*Faux pas, faux pas.* Legal assistants are not invited. Only lawyers and their chosen companions."

Ben's face reddened. "Oh. Sorry . . ."

"It's all right. It gave me a chance to speak French. Are you impressed that I know French phrases? I love the way they sound. Especially *faux pas*. It's my favorite. I can spell it, too. Can you?''

Ben blinked. "I was never very good at spelling."

"Don't sweat it. You'll enjoy the party. I mean, not that I'd know, 'cause I've never been. Don't let that spoil it for you, though. I'm sure I'll find something else to do. Of course, nothing could compare with the thrill of going to the Excelsior ballroom and mixing with the Tulsa *crème de la crème*." She paused. "More French. *Crème de la crème*."

"I noticed."

"Do you know what it means?"

"I think so."

"Can you spell it?"

"Ahhh . . . no."

"Oh, well. *C'est la vie*." She uncrossed, then recrossed her legs. "Now, if I had a boyfriend, I might consider gate-crashing. The party, I mean. On Friday night. But on my own? No, it would never do."

Information received and catalogued, Ben thought.

Christina reached into her satchel and withdrew a thick pad of printed paper, then passed the pad across the desk to Ben. "These are your time sheets. There are spaces here for the name of the client, the computer code number of the billing matter, the number of hours worked, and a brief, not-very-informative description of the work performed. This is how we bill clients."

Ben scanned the billing sheets. "Thanks," he said. "I was wondering about the mechanics."

Christina brushed her hair away from her face. "Ben, do you mind if I give you some advice?"

"Thanks, I've already had plenty from Derek."

"Yeah, but this advice will do you some good. I don't

want to be presumptuous, but you seem like a nice guy, not like the usual young lawyer zombies we get around here. You've got a certain *je ne sais quoi*."

"More French," he noted.

"Yeah." Her broad smile flashed again. "Didn't you formerly work for a legal aid society or something?"

"The D.A.'s office."

"Well, you're at a private law firm now, a big one, and the rules of the game are entirely different. Let me tell you what I, based on my five years at Raven, Tucker & Tubb, perceive to be the three principal guidelines for new associates. If you don't mind."

Ben shook his head. "Please. I need all the help I can get."

"First, fill out your time sheets every day. Don't put it off till the end of the week or when you think you'll have more time. If you do, you'll forget things you did, and you won't understand your notes, and every minute lost is a minute Raven doesn't get paid for. The shareholders may tell you they're concerned with . . . oh, associate training or family or inner growth or whatever; but when they're making the decisions about issues that really matter, like raises and bonuses and making partner, shareholders care about two things. Billing big hours and bringing in new clients. You've just moved to Tulsa, so barring a miracle, you ain't gonna be bringing in any big new corporate clients. So fill out your time sheets. Generously. Every day."

Ben pretended to be making notes. "Time sheets, every day. Got it. What's rule number two?"

"Lunch at the Oil Capital Club every Thursday. That's where the shareholders hold their weekly meetings. You can't go to the meeting, of course, but they can see you on their way in or out. It seems ridiculous, and it costs bucks, but it makes a lasting impression. So remember, rule number two: future shareholders lunch at the Oil Capital Club.''

"I'm pretty fond of Carl's Coney Island myself.''

"Future permanent associates lunch at Carl's Coney Island. That's rule number three.''

"I see.''

"So make a sacrifice for your career.''

"Is this Oil Capital Club a decent eatery?''

"Beats me. No women allowed.''

Ben's eyes widened. "You're kidding.''

"Scout's honor.''

"How could female shareholders attend the meetings?''

Christina offered a thin smile. "Fortunately, that contingency hasn't arisen yet.''

Ben rubbed his eyes. "Okay. Any other words of wisdom?''

Christina batted her lips with her index finger. "I'm going to offer you a specially tailored rule, because I think you're subject to special circumstances. You've got Richard Derek for a supervising attorney.'' She looked over her shoulder and verified that the door was shut. "Derek comes from an oil-rich Tulsa family; he's the baby boy in a family of five; he's Harvard-educated; he did a short stint with a Philadelphia law firm, then returned home to Tulsa. He's well connected and knows a lot of important people. He's incredibly intelligent and evidently is an effective, if undiplomatic, lawyer. He's egotistical, imperious, thoughtless, and generally difficult to get along with. He's made a career out of good looks and a fondness for bullying.'' She caught Ben's eye. "And you haven't exactly gotten off to a great start.''

Ben groaned. "Don't tell me you've heard.''

"About the toupee tragicomedy? Everyone has." She grinned. "It's made you very popular in certain circles. We always suspected the egomaniac wore a rug. Thanks for the confirmation."

Christina laid her hand on the edge of Ben's desk. "The fact is, Ben, you *have* to get along with him. Maybe later, a year or so down the road, you can ask for a transfer, or ask to work for a variety of masters. The shareholders will understand, believe me. But not yet."

"First I've got to pay my dues, eh?"

"Something like that. You don't want to develop a reputation for being a troublemaker. Nothing is more expendable to a big firm than a young, salaried troublemaker. So tread softly. Humor the jerk."

Christina glanced at her wristwatch. "Good grief, I didn't mean to prattle on." She rose to her feet. "I must be moseying. I just wanted to introduce myself. Don't hesitate to ask me for help. I'm working for four other attorneys in addition to you, but I can always do a little more." She glanced at the files on Ben's desk. "Looks as if you're already behind."

Ben followed her gaze. He'd forgotten all about the new files, and he was supposed to familiarize himself with both cases by tomorrow morning. Could she help? He realized he didn't even know what legal assistants did.

"I can help with proofreading, cite checking, document control, cataloguing, deposition summaries. You name it— I can do it."

And read minds, too, apparently. "Could you . . . summarize a case file?"

"No problem." She reached toward the two files on the desk. "Which one?"

"Take your pick."

She took the thicker of the two. "When do you need it?"

Ben averted his eyes. "Tomorrow morning."

"Ahhh," she said, "a Richard Derek test. He'll want to know about the most obscure details imaginable, everything you're tempted to skim over because it doesn't seem important. I'll come in early tomorrow, and we can discuss the file. Good thing you called me in. You'd never have made it alone."

She made a clicking noise with her tongue and walked through the door. "Of course, after I do this favor for you, you'll owe me. Kind of a *quid pro quo*." She smiled. "Another French phrase. Classy, huh?"

Ben hesitated. "Actually," he said slowly, "I think that's Latin."

Christina raised her chin defiantly. "Well, I still like it." She grinned and left the office.

Ben leaned back in his chair. She was right about one thing. Life at the big law firm was not what he expected.

He opened the remaining file on his desk and began to read, but he couldn't concentrate. He kept flashing back to his brief glimpse of Jonathan Adams's bloodied remains—and of Bertha Adams riding to the scene of the crime to identify the body.

Whether Derek liked it or not, he had to do something. But he couldn't figure out what.

* 9 *

Raven, Tucker & Tubb threw only two formal bashes a
year, the summer cotillion and the obligatory Christmas
party, so when those occasions rolled around, Raven could
afford to go all out. In fact, according to Ben's sources,
the parties could actually turn a profit, not merely by
boosting the self-image of the shareholders, but also by
reaping benefits from selected clients who enjoyed a night
of high-class revelry. Raven's bashes had become so elaborate and costly (and well covered in the newspapers),
particularly for a big-small city such as Tulsa, that an invitation had become a prestige item. And the only way for
a non-Raven attorney—who wasn't married to or sleeping
with a Raven attorney—to get an invitation was to be a
client. It was a surprisingly effective incentive.

The ballroom at the Excelsior was enormous. Yet, by
congregating all the dining tables in one quarter of the
room and reserving a spacious area for dancing, the room
was made to feel both festive and intimate. There were
also separate smaller rooms adjacent to the ballroom con-
taining pool tables, card tables, and similar amusements
for small groups.

The band was an exercise in acoustical compromise,
intermixing big-band melodies with Muzaked versions of

popular rock songs. The dance floor was almost empty this early in the evening, with never more than ten couples, mostly elder shareholders who had nothing to lose by embarrassing themselves. Shareholders, Ben observed, tended to take the floor with someone else's wife, or some female associate normally only seen in a gray suit with a scarf bow tie.

After dinner, the plates were cleared, and approximately five hundred people began milling about, trying to shake the right hands, flirt with the right wives, and flatter the right egos.

Ben was sitting at a large round table with the other new associates, including Alvin, Greg, and Marianne, all in formal dress. He had hoped the new associates would be distributed throughout the room so he could meet some new people, but instead they were all seated at the same table. As Alvin pointed out, there was no margin for the shareholders in taking the time to learn all the new names, at least not until they had a better idea of who would be staying and who would not.

The only non-new associate at the table was Tom Melton, a gregarious fifth-year associate assigned to supervise and assimilate the incoming class. Tom, Ben thought, was the sort of person who made partying and flattery seem like professional skills. His ability to tell boisterous, bawdy, often self-deprecating jokes was matched only by his ability to butter up shareholders and shamelessly bolster their sense of self-importance. Probably on the partnership track, too.

The male associates at the table were talking sports—predictions of success and failure, with reenacted instant replays. Ben was reminded of the crucial importance of a superficial knowledge of sports for male bonding and ca-

maraderie. When Ben was interviewing, he always made
a point of memorizing the day's sports headlines so that
he could drop names into the conversation at strategic
points, usually in sentences that began "How 'bout
them . . ." Tonight, he was unprepared.

And there were other problems as well.

"You and I seem to be the only ones here without
dates," Ben said to Alvin. "Of course, I just moved to
Tulsa last Saturday. What's your excuse?"

"I find it easier to function at these formal exercises in
social foreplay when I don't have to worry about whether
my date has her head in the punchbowl."

"I see. Want to shoot some pool?"

"No. I find that the bullets tend to deflect off the surface
of the water."

Oh, it's going to be one of those conversations, is it?
"Excuse me," Ben said. "I mean, would you like to
play a game of billiards?" He turned toward Marianne.
"Boy, a minor imprecision, and this guy jumps all over
you."

"Actually, I never jump all over anyone," Alvin replied.

"Really," Ben said. "Must be hell on your sex
life."

"Actually, I don't have a sex life. I'm celibate."

There was a hush at the table. "Sorry to hear that,"
Ben offered.

"No, no, no," Alvin said. "It's by choice. I swore an
oath of celibacy some time ago. I prefer it this way."

"I see. That must be . . . trying."

"Not at all. I prefer it. Never had it, don't miss it."

"Ah." Ben nodded his head.

Greg decided to join the fun. "Well, better stay away

from Raven's new wife, then,'' he advised Alvin. ''You may not have any choice.'' Several of the men at the table laughed in a knowing fashion.

''Raven has a new wife?'' Ben asked Alvin quietly.

''Boy, you don't keep up at *all*, do you, Kincaid? How are you ever going to make it in the murky world of firm politics?'' He shook his head with disgust. ''Yes, Raven has a new wife. His sixth.''

''Have you met her?''

''Not personally. But I've heard about her. They say she's considerably younger than he is.''

''She could hardly be much older.''

''Good point. They also say she's on the prowl.''

''On the *prowl*?''

''You heard me. On the prowl. And she likes young associates.''

''Get real.''

''That's the word on the street. I suppose a woman in her position would come to appreciate anything young, don't you?'' The men all laughed boisterously.

''Kincaid,'' Greg said, ''you're single, decent-looking, as far as I know, heterosexual—and not celibate. This could be a tremendous opportunity for you.'' He smiled his perfect smile, but it was more like a leer this time.

''Thanks, but no thanks.''

Greg frowned. ''C'mon, Ben, it's a career move.'' He jabbed his elbow into Ben's ribs. ''Close your eyes and think of England.''

Ben half smiled. ''I'll give it some consideration.'' He craned his neck around, looking for an avenue of escape from this conversation. Immediately behind him, he saw his old pal, Richard Derek.

"Good evening, Mr. Derek," Ben said, rising to his feet. "Enjoying yourself?"

"Oh . . ." Derek sniffed. "Trying to. I've got this damn cough and"—he inhaled deeply—"sinus congestion. Flu, probably. I wouldn't be surprised if I had pneumonia."

Somehow, neither would I, Ben thought.

Derek turned toward a diminutive blonde in a floor-length sky-blue gown. "Have you got those cough drops, Louise? Oh, Kincaid, this is my wife."

Like soldiers at inspection, every male associate sitting at the table rose to his feet. "A pleasure to meet you, Mrs. Derek," Ben said.

"Oh, call me Louise." She smiled weakly and nodded her head. She was a slight woman, and somehow, standing next to Derek, she seemed even slighter. "Dick, I don't know where the cough drops are."

"Figures." He cleared his throat, loudly enough to attract attention at the next table. Ben noticed that Derek didn't even look at his wife when he was ostensibly speaking to her. "Well, glad you could make it tonight, Kincaid. By the way, you did a decent job summarizing your two new cases. Didn't miss too much. I look forward to reading your brief on the trade dress injunction." He sniffed again, then turned away, departing with his wife for cough drops unknown.

Cozy little marriage, Ben thought. He sat back in his chair, only to find every associate's eye fixed upon him. Receiving public accolades from shareholders, however minor, was probably not the way to endear oneself to one's fellow associates. He stood again and pushed his chair away from the banquet table.

Greg sidled up next to him and whispered in his ear.

"Psst, Kincaid." He gave Ben a conspiratorial look. "Let's break into the good stuff."

Ben looked back at him blankly. "The good stuff?"

"You know. Booze."

"Greg, there are open bars all over this place."

"Yeah, but not the good stuff. Courvoisier. Dom Pérignon."

"I understood that was strictly for the senior shareholders to dispense to megafees-paying clients."

Greg smiled his trademark smile. "I found the cabinet where it's kept. In the adjoining room."

"I'm sure it's locked."

Greg wiggled his fingers in the air. "There was never a liquor cabinet I couldn't break into. These fingers can open any lock, crack any security system." He jabbed Ben in the ribs. "And they say you don't learn anything in a fraternity."

Ben shook his head. "I don't think so, Greg. I'd like to wait until my second week at least before I get caught confiscating firm assets."

"C'mon, Kincaid, don't be a wimp."

"No." He turned away from Greg and found himself standing face-to-face with Mr. Raven. Raven was peering into a short piece of paper held close to his nose.

"Let's see," the elderly man said. "Are you Amberson?"

Ben swallowed. Didn't Raven recognize him from the incident in the stairwell?

"Er . . . no, sir."

"Hager?"

"No, sir."

Raven continued his microscopic scrutiny of the paper. "Well, I give up then. Who are you?"

"Kincaid, sir. Benjamin Kincaid."

"Ahh, Kincaid!" he exclaimed. He took a pencil from his jacket and drew a line through one name on his list. "Good. Nice to meet you." They shook hands.

Ben stared at the old man. Was this some sort of bizarre test, or did he really not remember? Ben decided to play along.

"It's a true honor to meet you, sir."

Raven nodded and returned his gaze to his list. "All right," he said, "who's Amberson?" He moved around the new associates' table in search of the other names on his list.

"Well, if he won't introduce me, I'll have to do it myself."

Ben looked away from the table and saw a thin, black-haired woman in an exquisite décolleté black gown. It was trashy, but an expensive, tasteful sort of trashy. Black mesh at top and bottom, covering her figure just enough in strategically chosen places.

"I'm Raven's new wife, Mona. And you're . . . ?"

"Ben Kincaid," he said, suddenly flustered. He realized he'd been caught staring. He offered her his hand.

Standing closer to her, Ben saw that Alvin was right. She was nowhere near Raven's age—late thirties, maybe. He wondered how much of the rest of Alvin's information about this woman was accurate.

"Ben. Very nice to meet you." She took his hand and held it tightly between both of hers. Her fingernails were painted black. She made eye contact and smiled. The smile seemed to answer most of Ben's questions.

The band returned from their break and began plugging in their instruments for the next dance. Mr. Raven bowed gallantly beside Marianne.

"May I have the pleasure of this dance?" he asked. Marianne laughed, adjusted her glasses, and let him lead her to the dance floor.

"That husband of mine," Mona said dryly. "Always on the make. Well, I guess that leaves you and me, Benjy." She linked her arm through Ben's and before he knew what was happening, he was being hauled toward the dance floor. Ben realized any protest was probably futile.

"So what are you working on, Ben?"

"Oh, several projects for Richard Derek—"

"Derek? Oh, poor boy." She looked nostalgically at Derek, who was standing at the opposite side of the room. "Nice enough in the looks department, but he couldn't sustain, if you know what I mean."

Ben hoped he didn't.

"Just do what he says and try not to laugh when he tells you about his old polo injury. You'll do okay. Got any oil-and-gas work?"

"Ahh, not yet. I'm working on a domestic matter for Joseph Sanguine—"

"Really? Have you met him?"

Ben shook his head no.

"He's here, you know. I'll introduce you." She waved her free hand in the air. "Joey! Yoo-hoo, Joey! Over here!"

Ben's face reddened. He wanted to meet Sanguine, but he had hoped for a more respectable introduction.

After a moment, a tall, distinguished-looking man with a full head of gray and black hair and a thick mustache walked toward the yoo-hooing Mona. He had a dark, rugged face that bespoke many hours exposed to the sun. Native American descent, Ben guessed, at least in part.

Sanguine's lips turned up slightly when he saw Mona. "Mona! Good to see you again. Where's Arthur?"

She poked Sanguine in the side. "Oh, you know how he is. He's got some nymphet on the dance floor. You look awfully good tonight, Joey."

"Thank you," he said quietly.

"Joey, I want you to meet a new Raven associate. He's working for you."

Ben stepped forward and extended his hand. "Benjamin Kincaid, sir."

They shook hands. Ben felt an inexplicable shiver run up his arm. This was a man with presence. A presence that he wore like an overcoat and that seemed just as tangible.

"Pleased to meet you," Sanguine said. "I always like to know who Raven's got working for me. They've got so damn many lawyers doing so damn many things, I can't possibly keep track of them all. What are you working on, son?"

Ben hesitated. "Well . . . I'm working on the adoption matter for Bertha Adams, the woman whose husband . . ." He trailed off.

"Yes," Sanguine said. "Very much a tragedy. Jonathan had been with the company for a long time, even before I bought it. He seemed like . . . part of the furniture to me." He paused. "You never know just how much you depend on someone until you lose him. I hope there won't be any problem helping that sweet lady adopt that child. I want us to do anything we can to help her."

"In that regard, Mr. Sanguine," Ben said slowly, "I'd like to speak to you at your convenience. You and perhaps some of the other Sanguine employees who knew Mr. Adams."

Sanguine's brow wrinkled. "Really? I can't imagine what help I could be." He scrutinized Ben's face. "Still, if you think it will assist you, fine. Come up to my office Monday morning."

"Thank you, sir. I will."

Mona decided to reassert her dominance of the conversation. "Enough, enough. You two are starting to talk about business. Ben has promised me a dance. At the very least."

Sanguine looked at Ben with an arched eyebrow. Ben tried his best to communicate his denial nonverbally. Mona's arm again clamped down on his.

The band was in full swing now. They were playing a Bruce Springsteen tune, but making it sound like a Lawrence Welk standard. Ben and Mona reached the dance floor and began to sway roughly in time to the music. Ben was not much of a dancer, and given that he had worked at Raven for less than a week and had no idea what shareholder might be watching him, he decided to play it low-key.

Mona, he discovered to his dismay, was from the full-body, free-spirit school that perceived dancing as a tribal rite of foreplay. She wriggled, she squirmed, she heaved. When they were close, Ben heard strange guttural noises emanating from between her teeth. And stealing occasional furtive glances over her shoulder, Ben saw that many eyes in the ballroom were understandably fixed upon Mona. And, by association, Ben.

And then, just when Ben thought he had reached the apex of embarrassment, matters got worse. The band finished the Springsteen and began another song. A slow dance.

"Well, thanks," Ben said, edging away. "I enjoyed the dance."

Mona seized his hand. "You're not slipping away yet, my sweet young thing. Come cuddle with Mona."

Ben felt his face burning. He was finished. He knew it. Might as well get the résumés back in the mail. He extended his arms to hold her in the traditional waltz posture, but she insisted upon the full-body press more popular in junior high schools. Blissfully, the lights dimmed.

Ben tried to keep in step with the music, but he found Mona was more interested in groping than dancing. He felt her hot breath in his ear.

"Let's do something crazy," she whispered, breathing hard.

"Like what?" he responded, wishing he hadn't.

"Don't play games with me, Kincaid. You've been teasing me all night long. You don't give a girl a chance, do you?" She leaned forward and nibbled on his ear.

"Stop that!" Ben said. He looked around quickly to see if anybody was watching. "You could get me fired."

"You could get me fired up." She blew into his ear.

"Please!" Ben pleaded. "You're the senior partner's wife. If anyone found out—"

"So don't tell anyone. I think boys who kiss and tell are naughty." She licked her lips suggestively. "I'm ready to go."

"I can't afford to lose my job the first week—"

"Well, that's just what will happen, Benjy, if you don't meet me in the hallway outside the ballroom in two minutes." Her voice had a new edge to it. "Don't forget, I talk with the boss on a regular basis. I can have you out of this firm in a heartbeat." She stroked him under his chin and smiled. "And I'd hate to see that happen. Such a waste. So meet me in two minutes."

Ben sputtered, "But what will I tell everyone?"

"Tell them you're going out for fresh air."

"Where will we go?"

Mona released him and stepped back. "Come on, Benjy, this *is* a hotel, after all. And bring me a glass of champagne." She lifted the hem of her gown and ran quickly off the dance floor. Ben walked slowly in another direction, doing his best to look as if he had come with someone else.

Ben paced back and forth in the hallway with a glass of champagne in each hand. It had been five minutes. If she didn't show up soon, he'd just leave and claim he thought he'd been stood up. But what if she told some lie about him to Raven? No, he needed to talk with her, to make her see the error of her ways. He was certain he could reason with her as one logical human being to another. He didn't have anything personal against her; it was just an impossible proposition.

He heard a commotion at the other end of the hallway, by the escalators that led to the hotel lobby one floor up. Louise Derek was standing at the base of the up escalator, facing her husband, who was riding up. They were arguing with one another, in loud, strident voices.

"I've never even *seen* your goddamn cough drops!" Louise shrieked. For a petite woman, she could muster an extremely powerful voice.

"Sure," Derek said, not even deigning to look at her. "Right. Then where are they?"

"How the hell should I know? Maybe you left them at your *girlfriend's* place."

Derek stepped off the up escalator and stepped onto the down. "Don't start that again. Every time you get upset about something you fall back on—"

"Don't tell me what to start up! I'll start it up if I want to. You're a walking viral infection! God knows what you've brought home to my bed!"

"Louise, that's all in the past."

"Sure, that's your story. How the hell would I know?" Her face was becoming red and blotchy. "It's not as if you're ever home!"

Derek sighed, stepped off the down escalator, brushed past her, and rode back up again. "I work very hard—"

"At certain things, yes."

Derek began to get angry. "Look, I do it for *you*. You and the kids."

Louise laughed bitterly. "The hell you do. Look, *Dick*, if you're doing it for me—*don't*. I'd rather have a husband than a super-stud lawyer." She laughed again. "The only person in your whole life you've ever done anything for is yourself. You're the most goddamn selfish man *ever*!" Tears were beginning to stream from her eyes.

Derek started back down again on the other escalator. "You're not being fair."

"Who says I have to be fair? God knows you've never been fair, you egotistical son-of-a-*bitch*!" Derek stepped off the escalator and moved toward her. "And you keep your fucking hands *off*!" She wrapped her arms around herself and walked away.

Derek sighed, got back on the escalator, and rode all the way up. He strode into the lobby and disappeared.

Louise began walking toward Ben. Her face looked as if it had aged five years in five minutes.

Ben decided this would be an opportune moment to make himself scarce.

He turned left down a narrow hallway opposite the north side of the ballroom. Almost immediately, a door on the left opened and a familiar hand with long black fingernails reached out to him.

"Pssst. In here." The hand gripped Ben's wrist and gave him a tug. Champagne spilled on Ben's tuxedo. The hand pulled him into a tiny dark room.

"What is *this*?" Ben asked.

"Janitorial closet," she whispered. She took the champagne glasses away and yanked off his jacket.

"But I thought—"

"This is better," she said. "More intimate. More dangerous." She started untying his bow tie.

"Right," Ben muttered. "Just what I was hoping for. More danger. Ow!" He banged his head on an overhead shelf. Shifting positions, he managed to rest himself against a dusty shelf loaded with cleaning fluids. "Not much room in here."

"That's right, Benjy, nowhere to go but into Mona. Come to Mama."

Ben reached out into the darkness to stop whatever overture she was making, but his hand alighted on soft warm flesh that could be nothing other than a woman's breast. With a sudden *frisson* of horror, Ben realized that she was not wearing any clothing.

Ben began to feel queasy. "Look, Mrs. Raven, let's examine this rationally—"

"Examine *this*, you tease." She bit down on his earlobe and pressed her hot naked body against his. "First you lure a girl into the janitor's closet, then you play hard to get. You sexual sadist! Stop talking and get on with it."

Ben felt a skilled hand systematically eliminating the pearl-studded buttons on his shirt. She was out of control, an unstoppable, elemental force of nature. He prayed that no one in the hotel got a sudden urge to do some dusting.

* 10 *

Ben was awakened the next morning by the harsh sound of a ringing telephone. He gave it six chances to relent, but the fiend demanded to be answered. Groaning, Ben crawled out of the sleeping bag he was using for a bed and snatched the phone receiver from its cradle.

It was Mike.

"What gives? Don't tell me you were still in bed?"

Ben sighed. "Yes, Mike, I was still in bed. Sound asleep. Dreaming sweet dreams. Until you called."

"Well, you should thank me. It's almost ten o'clock."

"And I do thank you, Mike. Truly." He rubbed his tongue across his dry, fuzzy teeth. "I was up late attending a Raven festivity."

"Oh, well, that explains it. Get lucky?"

"*No,*" Ben said immediately and with great force. "No, I most certainly did *not* get lucky."

"All right, all right, ease off. I'm not your mother."

"Is this why you called, Mike?"

"Actually, no." Ben heard him shuffling papers. "Dr.

Koregai is starting his autopsy of Adams. I thought you ought to be there.''

Ben felt an unpleasant sensation in his stomach. "Why in God's name should I be there for the autopsy?''

"Come on, Ben. Don't wimp out on me now. You knew the man.''

"What's that got to do with the autopsy?''

"I want you to be present when the evidence comes in. Besides, I have some new information to share with you.''

Ben massaged his temples. "None of this convinces me that I need to be present for an autopsy.''

"I think it's important, Ben. Do it for me.'' He paused. "If you won't do it for me, do it for Bertha Adams.''

Ben took a deep breath, then exhaled slowly. "I'll meet you in twenty minutes,'' he said. He slammed the receiver back into its cradle and started searching for his toothbrush.

Ben arrived in twenty-five minutes, after stopping for his traditional early morning fix of chocolate milk. This was definitely a two-carton morning.

He met Mike outside the coroner's office and accompanied him into the examining room of Dr. Koregai, a middle-aged Japanese man who seemed to approach autopsies with the same matter-of-fact manner one might bring to disassembling a model airplane. Mike said he was the best. He was a little strange, true, but what do you expect from a man who cuts up corpses for a living? At least he wasn't the type to tell jokes or eat lunch while he was cutting. He was very observant, if very temperamental. To get Koregai to answer your questions, Mike explained, you have to give him the impression that you're here for the sole purpose of serving *him* in his quest for truth, justice, and autopsic excellence.

Ben covered his mouth and nose with a paper towel as he entered the room. Be brave, he told himself. This is only the preliminary examination, not the actual postmortem. He considered the relative merits of watching a series of violations of bodily orifices as opposed to watching the slivering and dismembering of body tissues. He was barely in the room and he already felt ill.

The first thing Ben noticed was the odor. The odor of formaldehyde and God knows what other chemicals were thick in the air. The second thing he noticed was a string quartet, Vivaldi, he thought, playing over the built-in intercom system. Maybe Koregai needed his nerves steadied, too.

Three bright white ceiling lamps shone down on the mutilated corpse of Jonathan Adams. Ben stifled the instinct to gag. If anything, the body looked better now than when they had found it in the Dumpster. Most of the caked and coagulated black blood had been scraped away; the jaw and other loosened and detached body parts had been rearranged and returned to their proper places. The skin was an eerie, translucent color, sort of green and sort of not.

Dr. Koregai took a thin rotor saw from his worktable and held it in his latex-gloved hands. His mouth and nose were covered by a blue mask.

"If you could give us an idea about the cause of death," Mike said, with extreme deference, "we might be able to obtain information in the field to assist you in detailing your report."

Evidently, the doctor's talents included the ability to chat while he worked. "I already know how he was killed," Dr. Koregai replied. "With a knife."

"What a breakthrough," Ben mumbled under his paper towel.

"The blade of the knife was three-quarters of an inch wide," Koregai continued. "And it was serrated."

"Like a saw?" Ben asked.

"Or a carving knife," Mike suggested. "Unfortunately, even with that extra information, the weapon is still something you could find in nearly every home in Tulsa."

"But it's not something a person would just happen to carry," Ben thought aloud. "Unless he was planning to kill someone."

"What else could we possibly find that would help you, Doctor?" Mike asked obsequiously. "Point us poor working slobs in the right direction."

"Marks left on the neck by fingers," Koregai noted, as if dictating a report. "Coupled with the bruises on the back and shoulders, it suggests the victim was pinned against a wall or floor. Probably a wall. He struggled to free himself—that explains the bruises on both elbows and his hands. Also, bruising of the throat and voice box indicates that the grip on his neck was quite strong."

"The killer overpowered Adams?"

"Perhaps."

Ben took slow, deep breaths and tried to pretend he was in Rio. "You haven't even mentioned that horrible blow to his face. And why so many gashes all over his body?"

Dr. Koregai did not look up from his work. "Very low correlation of bruising to blows."

"No bruises?" Ben said. "What does that mean?"

Mike turned to look at Ben. "It means Adams was already dead when the killer ventilated him,'' Mike said. ''Right, Doctor?''

''Right.'' Koregai set down the saw and took a thin stilettolike knife from his worktable. ''Corpse was killed by two knife wounds, one through his head and neck and one to his torso. Mutilated afterward.''

Ben heard himself literally gasp. The paper towel clung to his face.

''One entry slit penetrated the floor of the skull, cut through the jugular vein, through the neck muscles between the arches of the first and second cervical vertebrae and just reached the center of the brain stem. He would've been unconscious immediately.''

''Thank God for that,'' Ben murmured.

''But that left him defenseless,'' Mike said. ''It left his body at the mercy of the sick bastard who took him apart.'' Mike took a step closer to Koregai. ''Is there anything we could provide to help you reach a conclusion regarding the time of death, Doctor?''

The doctor was holding the stiletto in one hand and using his free hand to peel away thin layers of skin and body fat from the corpse's midsection. ''I already know the time of death. Corpse's body was still relatively warm when found. Over eighty-five degrees. Given that the murder was followed by a series of mutilations that took at least five to ten minutes, and given that the corpse, which would be quite heavy at that point, was dragged into a garbage Dumpster, I'd place the time of death at 10:15 or 10:30. Preliminary analysis of stomach contents also supports this estimate.''

''Relatively early for a robbery-murder,'' Mike mused. ''Still a lot of people wandering around.''

Ben nodded in agreement.

"Anything else I can do for you, Dr. Koregai?" Mike asked.

The doctor looked up briefly. "Not at this time. The lab work from Forensics should be done in a day or two. Anything new I discover during the p.m. will appear in my final report. If I require anything further, I'll let you know."

"Aye, commandant," Mike whispered. He turned to Ben. "Anything I can do for *you*, pal?"

"Yeah," Ben said. He looked toward the door and saw two orderlies wheeling in another cadaver. "Get me the hell out of here."

* 11 *

Ben cooled his heels in the outer lobby of Sanguine Enterprises.

He noted that the entire area had been decorated in the orange and white colors of the Eggs 'N' Stuff trade logo. He made a mental note, in case he ever decorated a house or office, that orange was the least agreeable color for carpeting. Staring at it made him wish he had not eaten breakfast.

Eventually, there was a buzz on the receptionist's desk, then: "Mr. Sanguine can see you now."

Ben followed the woman—who, Ben noted with disgust,

was wearing an orange and white dress—past a desk used
by a security officer, through a winding corridor, and into
the elevator lobby. After a short ride, they emerged on the
second floor, which, she explained, was used exclusively
for the offices of Sanguine and his vice presidents. Ben
emerged from the elevator and walked down a long black
marble-tiled hallway to Sanguine's office.

Which was magnificent. Deep oak library paneling on
all walls. Furniture that retained the rich hues of the
woodwork. Snuffboxes, porcelain figurines, and other European objets d'art were scattered throughout the office.
Tasteful framed paintings, mostly Old Master–style oils,
lined the wall above Sanguine's desk. The adjoining wall
was lined with books from floor to ceiling. All hardback,
mostly leather-bound volumes. The man who worked in
this office was either a cultural connoisseur of the highest
order, or wanted others to believe he was.

In one corner, on the bottom shelf of a cabinet to the
left of Sanguine's desk, Ben spotted a display of Native
American artifacts. Kachina dolls, tom-toms, turquoise
jewelry. A tribute to his ancestry? Ben wondered. A tribute tucked away in a quiet corner in a room otherwise
devoted to a celebration of European excellence. A curious man.

Sanguine was poring over a stack of papers on his desk.
Ben made a quiet, coughing noise. Sanguine looked up.

"Ah, Ben, you're here." He stood and extended his
hand. "I didn't hear you come in. I get absorbed in the
work sometimes." Discounting the noisy hubbub of the
Raven party, Ben was hearing Sanguine's voice for the first
time. It was a voice like still water, steady, even, strong,
and without predictable inflection.

Sanguine gestured toward the chair opposite his desk. "I was examining a new franchise contract."

Fascinating, Ben thought. "I see," he said.

Sanguine sat in his chair and leaned back comfortably. "So what can I do for you? Let me tell you up front, Ben, anything I can do to help out . . . Jonathan's widow, I'm going to do. Jonathan was a loyal, hard-working executive who helped build this operation from the ground up and, to be frank, I admired him. What's more, I *respected* him, and I believe he respected me. I wish I had more like Jonathan."

Ben watched the man as he talked. There was something slightly askew, something about the man, and his office, and the whole situation. Something didn't seem right, even more than Sanguine's not remembering Bertha's name.

"Well, Mr. Sanguine," Ben said, clearing his throat, "as you know, I was asked to help Adams with his attempted adoption of the foundling girl, Emily. In fact, I interviewed him on the day he was killed."

"Yes. It's a tragedy. An honest-to-God tragedy."

Ben continued his story. He told Sanguine about the interview and explained why he thought it was important to find Emily's parents, if possible.

"I'm convinced that this adoption matter and the murder are connected in some bizarre way," Ben concluded. "Adams intimated that he might be able to find Emily's parents. It was very important to him. I don't think he would have done anything else until he accomplished whatever it was he planned to do. And I don't think he would have finished that without talking to me."

Sanguine remained silent throughout Ben's narrative. Silent face, steady eyes, still water. "The only thing I don't understand, Ben," he said, his fingers pressed against one another, "is what I can do."

"Do you have any idea what Mr. Adams was going to do?"

"I'm afraid I don't. Let me call someone in." He pushed a button on his desk telephone. "Darryl, could you step in for a moment?"

A moment later, a middle-sized man, balding, with thinning black hair on either side of his head, stepped obediently into the office. "You wanted to see me, Joe?"

"Yes, I did. Benjamin Kincaid, this is Darryl Tidwell, my personal secretary. Vice versa." They shook hands. Tidwell wore an apricot shirt with a muted floral tie. Ben judged him to be in his late forties or early fifties.

"Darryl is also my vice president in charge of management and all-around right-hand man. I hate to admit it, but I just don't have time to pay attention to all the minor details anymore. I have to focus on the big picture, and I'm lucky if I have time to do that. That's where Darryl comes in. He's the detail man."

Sanguine briefed Tidwell on their conversation in short, clipped sentences. "Do you have any idea what Jonathan might have been referring to, Darryl?"

"I can't imagine," he answered. He tapped his clipboard against his free hand. "We talked quite often. I knew about his finding that little girl. In fact, when he told me he was worried about the DHS hearing, I came to Joe and asked if we couldn't get someone in legal working on this."

"We like to help out our employees whenever we can," Sanguine interjected. "After all, if you can't help some people along the way, what's the point of it all?" He waved his hand across his office, as if offering a definition of *it all*.

Tidwell continued. "But I never heard anything that indicated that John knew who the kid's parents were. Quite the opposite, in fact. If he knew something, I think he would have told me."

Sanguine checked his watch. "I'm sorry to rush this along, Ben, but I have to take *White Lightning*—that's my Lear—to Dallas right away. Big powwow at the Southwestern division office."

"Well, I don't have much else to ask," Ben said. "I'm sorry I've taken up so much of your time."

"Not at all."

Ben rose to his feet. "One other thing, Mr. Sanguine. Do you suppose I could look through Mr. Adams's office? I know it seems unlikely, but who knows, I might find something that would give us a clue to what happened."

Sanguine took a moment to collect his thoughts. "Well, I don't think we can allow that, Ben, as I'm sure you'll understand. For one thing, the police have already sent a man to search the office, and afterward, he sealed it up. You know, locked the door and stretched that yellow tape across it. I don't think they want anyone disturbing things in there. Furthermore, his poor widow hasn't had a chance to go through his effects yet, and I think she ought to have the first go at it, don't you? Could be belongings of a personal nature there, who knows?"

He walked around the desk and patted Ben on the shoulder. "If we do hear anything or find anything that could be of use to you, though, we'll let you know, won't we, Darryl?"

"You bet."

"Of course we will. Now, I've got a jet to catch. Darryl, would you see this conscientious young man out?"

Ben and Tidwell walked down the hallway toward the elevator. "He'll be back from Dallas tomorrow morning," Tidwell said. "It's a much more important meeting than he let on, so if he seems preoccupied . . ." He let the sentence trail off, then changed the subject. "So, you're really a lawyer?"

"Yup. Really. Got a diploma and everything."

"Oh, I didn't mean to suggest . . . It's just that you look so young. Hey, here's a joke for you. What do you need when you've got a lawyer up to his neck in sand?"

"I don't know," Ben said, suppressing a sigh. "What?"

"More sand!" Tidwell laughed heartily at his own joke. "Pretty good, huh?"

"Yeah."

"Oh, I've got more. Why don't sharks attack lawyers?"

"I give up. Why?"

"Professional courtesy." He erupted into laughter again.

Ben realized that he didn't even know what his hourly billing rate was, but whatever it was, he was going to double it for time spent listening to lawyer jokes.

Tidwell wiped his eyes. "Oh, wow. Those are great. Hey, I hope you don't take it personally."

"Of course not."

They reached the elevator. Ben punched the button and, after a moment, stepped inside.

"Let me assure, you, Ben, if I find out anything that might assist you in this adoption matter, I won't hesitate a second before calling you."

"I appreciate that, Darryl."

They shook hands again, and Ben rode the elevator down

to the lobby. During the walk through the parking lot, Ben replayed the entire meeting with Sanguine in his mind. Sanguine had by all appearances been forthright, honest, helpful, concerned. He seemed to be a model employer. And yet Ben couldn't shake the feeling of distrust. There was no good reason for it, but nonetheless, it was there. Something bothered him.

* 12 *

Ben invited Christina to join him for a working lunch at Tulsa's downtown outdoor mall.

The protocol policy at Raven, she had explained to him, was that fraternization between attorneys and staff members, such as secretaries and legal assistants, was seriously frowned upon. Too much potential for impropriety or the appearance thereof. But if the attorney tucked a manila file under his arm before he left, it became a *working lunch* and, of course, he or she would be expected to have a secretary or legal assistant along. So Ben grabbed a manila file, and they embarked on a working lunch. Ben's manila file, however, was empty.

It was a green day for Christina. She was wearing a short green dress and complementary green hose, with a black leather belt wrapped around her waist. Ben thought she looked like Robin Hood.

Ben pointed toward a tall man in a blue floral Hawaiian shirt and white pants. He was probably only a few years older than Ben, but his face was aged and wrinkled from too much exposure to the sun. He was standing with his face upturned toward the sky, a Bible clenched in one hand, the other hand outstretched toward the sun. He seemed to be humming, or perhaps chanting. Then, abruptly, he started bellowing. "What's your rush?" he shouted in a deep, penetrating baritone. "Why spend your life scurrying from one appointment to the next? Don't be slaves to time! Don't be worshipers of the passing of the sun! Tick, tock, tick, tock, tick, tock . . ."

"Who's the wacko?" Ben asked.

"Are you serious?" Christina said. "You don't know?"

Ben shook his head. "I'm familiar with Tulsa's standard repertory of revival preachers who shout about how AIDS is a plague of the pharaohs and so forth, but I've never encountered this particular Looney Tune before."

Christina smiled enigmatically. "That's Lance Caldwell."

"Who's Lance Caldwell?"

"Don't you remember? He's the guy who had your office. The last associate Raven, Tucker & Tubb assigned to Richard Derek."

"You're kidding! This guy is a lawyer?"

"Well, I don't know if he paid his bar dues this year. But he used to be."

Ben knocked himself on the side of the head. "I don't understand."

"You will, kiddo. Being an associate in a pressure cooker like Raven, Tucker & Tubb is bad enough. Trying to work with Richard Derek is lunacy. He's broken better men than you."

"Great. Dandy."

Ben and Christina ordered burritos from a Mexican food cart, then sat down on a bench next to the fountain farthest from Lance Caldwell. While consuming their burritos, Ben told Christina about his meeting with Sanguine.

"So Sanguine gave you the brush-off?"

"That's how it seemed to me. His private secretary was practically apologizing for his rudeness. Suggested that I try again when Sanguine wasn't so busy."

"Do you think Sanguine is involved in this somehow?" Christina asked. "Seems unlikely."

"I don't know if he's involved or not. But I suspect he knows something he's not telling. And I'd like another chance to talk to Tidwell. He seemed willing—almost eager—to talk."

Ben wiped a bit of sauce from his mouth. "And why all the subterfuge about Adams's office? I called Mike. He told me the police finished searching the office last week, and that they found nothing particularly helpful. So why wouldn't Sanguine let me look at it? I'm not buying this business about letting the widow have first dibs."

"The police were looking for clues to a murder. Maybe there's something that doesn't relate to murder, but that Sanguine still doesn't want you to find."

"Yeah. Maybe." He pointed across the mall. "How about an ice cream?" he asked. "My treat."

Christina's eyelashes fluttered. "Ice cream is my *raison d'être*."

They walked across the mall and stood in the short line. "So what's your game plan, boss?"

"I don't know. I want to help Mrs. Adams, but I don't know what I can do. I'm stymied." He purchased two ice-cream cones, and they returned to their seats by the fountain.

"Sounds to me like you need to take a look inside that office," Christina mumbled. She was focusing on her rapidly melting dessert, trying to get more of it in her mouth and less of it on her hand.

"You know, it's possible that Sanguine hasn't had a chance to look through the place himself. The cops were already there before he found out about the murder. But when he gets back from Dallas tomorrow morning, I bet he remedies that."

"Then you need to work fast," Christina said.

Ben's eyebrows raised. "Oh? And do what?"

"Break in, I suppose."

"Are you kidding? What if I got caught? I could go to jail! Even if I got off, I'd almost certainly lose my bar license. My career would be over before it started."

"Well, you know what I always say, Ben. *Qué será será.*"

Ben glared at her. "It's out of the question."

"Okay. Do you have any better ideas?"

Ben was silent for a moment. "No."

"So the options are, basically, you either try to get into that office, or you just give up, right?"

"We should wait. We might get another lead."

"Look, Ben," Christina said. "If you're right about Sanguine, and you wait until tomorrow, everything worth looking at in that office will be gone."

Another long pause. "How would we get in?"

Christina shrugged. "Don't look at me. They didn't cover breaking and entering in my legal-assistant courses."

Ben returned his attention to his ice cream. "This has

got to violate the Rules of Professional Conduct,'' he said, shaking his head.

"The rules say you have an obligation to zealously represent your client to the best of your ability,'' Christina countered. "That's all you're doing.''

He swallowed the last of his ice cream silently.

"Don't worry, *mon ami*,'' she said, giving him a mock punch on the arm. "I'll be with you.''

Ben smiled thinly. *"Merci beaucoup.''*

Ben had been pacing outside Greg's office for about five minutes, but it seemed longer. Where the hell was he, anyway? Probably off putting the make on a secretary. Didn't he have work to do like everybody else? Ben shoved his hands into his pockets and waited.

After a few more moments, Greg emerged from the men's room down the hallway. He greeted Ben in the hall and they walked into his office together. Ben shut the door behind them.

"A closed door meeting. Must be important.'' Greg situated himself behind his desk and smiled. "What can I do for you, Kincaid?''

"I've come to consult.''

"Really? I'm flattered.''

"I have need of your expertise.''

"No kidding?'' Greg's eyebrows raised. "Oh, I see. You want to get laid.''

"No. Well, not at the moment. I'm talking about what you said the other night at the party.''

A puzzled expression crossed Greg's face. "What I said at the party? You mean about your sweetheart Mona?''

"No.'' Ben wiggled his fingers in the air. " 'These fin-

gers can open any lock, crack any security system.' Was
that true, or were you just bullshitting?''

"Ben, I'm offended. I never bullshit. I was simply tes-
tifying as to wisdom gained from years spent as a social
reprobate.''

"Good.'' Ben pulled his chair closer to the desk. "We
need to talk.''

* 13 *

Ben was surprised when Emily opened the door. He had
assumed Bertha handled matters of hospitality, since Emily could hardly be expected to greet a visitor.

He and Christina stood on the porch staring at Emily.
She didn't seem scared of Ben, but she clearly did not
recognize him.

"Hello, Emily,'' he said. "I'm Ben Kincaid. Remember? We met at my office the other day. Nice to see you
again. Is Mrs. Adams at home?''

Emily smiled, as if relieved that she needn't confess she
couldn't identify him. She didn't answer his question. She
couldn't.

Bertha Adams appeared in the doorway. She looked ex-
hausted. "Hello,'' she said quietly. "I'm sorry. I usually
answer the door myself, but I was in the back bedroom
napping. I've been so tired lately.''

"I understand," Ben hurried to say. "Mrs. Adams, this is Christina McCall. She works with me."

Bertha eyed the new woman uncertainly, a response Christina had told Ben to anticipate during the drive over. Bertha was of a generation of women that still had not come to expect, or trust, other women in professional positions.

They walked into the living room, furnished with a tasteful but inexpensive collection of unmatched items. The room was tidy but simple. Ben and Christina sat on a thin-cloth sofa upholstered with a familiar green floral pattern; Bertha sat in a fake leather recliner facing opposite. Emily sat at her feet.

"This is a surprise, Mr. Kincaid," she said in an even tone. "I didn't expect to see you before the hearing. If I'd known you wanted to speak to me, I'd have come to your office. There was no need for you to come here. I know you must be very busy."

Poor woman, Ben thought. She's embarrassed about the shabby state of her home. Maybe I should have telephoned first.

"Call me Ben, please," he said. It seemed stupid, but he felt they should be on a first-name basis.

"Ben, then," she murmured.

"I'll be very brief, ma'am," Ben continued. "I have a couple of additional questions, and then, well, kind of a strange request."

He paused, trying to choose the right words. "First, in light of, well, what's happened . . ." He immediately regretted starting the sentence he hadn't the courage to complete. Imbecile. He could see the tears welling in her eyes. "I'm sure the police asked you already, but do you know of anything that would make someone want—'' He stopped.

The woman said nothing. Ben wiped his brow. "Was anything . . . out of the ordinary happening between your husband and Joseph Sanguine?"

Bertha raised her head a bit but remained silent.

"Mrs. Adams," Christina said, "we should remind you that Ben is your attorney. Everything you tell us is confidential. Every court in the country will honor that privilege. We only ask for information because we think we can help you."

Bertha seemed to be searching for an assurance she could not find. Finally, she said, almost in a whisper, "There was something going on, I believe, but I honestly don't know what. Jonathan never talked about his work. But during his last month or so, he was very excited about something. He started getting phone calls at odd hours and spending lots of late nights at the office. I think it had something to do with Sanguine. We . . ." She searched for the right words. "We weren't always pleased with Joseph Sanguine. He made several promises to Jonathan that he didn't keep." Her eyes darted down to her lap.

Ben could see there was no point in pushing her for details. She was good for one, maybe two more questions, so he had to choose judiciously. Maybe later, after she'd had more time to heal, he could try again.

"Do you know any reason why Sanguine might not want me to look through your husband's office?"

Bertha looked up, then quickly away. "No," she said. "I don't know what the reason would be."

But you don't deny that it's possible, either, Ben noted. He decided to cut to the quick. "Bertha, Lieutenant Morelli of the homicide department tells me they returned the few personal belongings found on your husband's body."

"Yes."

His eyes connected with hers. "Could I borrow your husband's keychain?"

Don't ask, Ben thought. Just don't ask.

She didn't. "I'll get it."

She walked into one of the inner rooms, then returned holding a chain filled to capacity with keys of various shapes and sizes.

"Thank you, ma'am. I'll return these as soon as I can."

The woman nodded. Christina and Ben rose.

"Leaving so soon?" Emily asked. "We could play pat-a-cake."

"Not today," Ben said, smiling at her. "But later. I promise."

He rubbed the top of her head affectionately. He felt compelled to be nice to her. Foolish, he thought. I'm trying to make a favorable impression, but the minute the door closes behind me, she won't even remember that she's met me before.

Ben stopped at the door. "I'm going to do everything I can for you, Mrs. Adams. You and Emily. Really."

Bertha nodded slightly, then turned away.

Ben and Christina let themselves out.

* 14 *

"How much longer?" Christina whispered. "It's as dark as it's ever going to get."

Ben glanced at his watch. It was still a few minutes before midnight. He stared out the window of his car at the tall glassy office building across the street. As long as they stayed in the car, they couldn't be arrested for anything. But as soon as they stepped out . . .

"Talk me out of this, Christina."

"No way, boss. It's for a good cause. Remember the Alamo."

Ben nodded nervously. They had been sitting in Ben's Honda Accord for over an hour. As far as they could tell, there was but a single security officer watching the place, and he alternated between prowling through the building and prowling around the grounds. The man moved in cycles of about twenty-five minutes inside, twenty-five minutes outside, and so forth. About half the outside cycle was spent in the wooded area behind the building.

As near as Ben could tell through his binoculars, the security guard plodded through his routine like a sleepwalking zombie. That was fortunate. He also appeared to be an older man. That, too, was fortunate. Alas, he was making his rounds with a Doberman. That was unfortunate.

They had their routine planned in detail. Obviously, they needed to pass quietly through the front door while the security officer and his dog were in the back. Then they could search Adams's office freely for about twelve minutes or so until the man came back inside. They'd hide while he made his cursory indoor sweep and leave when he returned to the wooded area in the back. They could be in and out in under an hour. It should work. Really, it should, Ben kept telling himself.

"We'll enter as soon as the guard comes outside and goes to the back. Be ready. We won't have a lot of time to mess around."

"Aye, aye, Cap'n," Christina answered.

Ben examined and reexamined the twenty-odd keys on Adams's keychain. Based on their varying sizes, shapes, and logos, he had selected five that appeared to be keys that might open the front office doors. Assuming Adams had a key to the front door.

That left the question of an alarm. There were three small keys on the ring of the sort that Greg said usually controlled alarm systems. Or opened suitcases. Or briefcases. Or diaries. Ben wiped his brow. He felt extremely warm.

"Have you ever done anything like this?" Ben asked, eyes glued to the building.

"Nope. You?"

"Not really. I mean, when I was with the D.A., I went on a few police stakeouts, but that was different. Then I *knew* where the police were. They were right in front of me. On my side."

"Yeah," Christina said. "Well, try to relax. You look tense."

"Imagine that."

"Concentrate on something else."

Ben continued to stare at the office building.

"How did a nice guy like you ever get into law?" Christina asked.

"Well, what I really wanted to do was pitch for the Cardinals, but I kept breaking training."

"Ahh," Christina replied, "an athlete."

Ben laughed. "Hardly. I was the most miserable athlete that ever was. Voted Least Valuable Player year after year." He glanced away from the building. "Some of my most miserable childhood memories revolve around my pathetic efforts to curry favor by going out for sports. Only thing I could play at all was baseball, and that only barely."

"Mom wanted her son to be a jock, huh?"

"Mom didn't care. It was—" He stopped short. "But that's another story."

He shifted in his seat. "I remember playing Little League when I was in grade school. They played me at second base—you don't need a great arm, and the ball doesn't come your way that often. We had this one coach, a short, skinny psychopath named Shedd. God forbid, he must've been some poor kid's father. He used to throw baseballs at us if he didn't think we were hustling enough."

Christina giggled softly.

"Shedd was bad news in the locker room, too. 'Hey, look everybody, Kincaid's gonna do a strip show for us.' Cripes, what a jerk. Used to give holy hell to this inept little Jewish kid—only guy on the team worse than me. He couldn't control his bladder—always used to wet his pants during practice. 'Get a load of Litvack,' Shedd would say. 'The widdle baby wet his pants again. Awww!' '' Ben shook his head. ''Man, I hated that bastard.''

''Sounds like the kind of trauma that eventually causes people to shoot total strangers at the A & P.''

''No, that would be the tap-dancing lessons,'' Ben said. He was becoming more animated. ''One afternoon I'm at home peaceably munching potato chips and trying to watch *Daniel Boone*, when my parents come in and announce that I'm going to take tap-dancing lessons. 'But why?' I kept asking. I was sure it was a sinister plot to complete the total humiliation of Benjy Kincaid before his peer group. If my parents had given me a choice, I'd have opted for castration.''

He turned toward Christina. ''Enough about me,'' he said. ''Now you tell me a story of childhood mortification.''

She placed a finger against her lips. ''That's hard. I was always sort of an outsider in my neighborhood.''

Ben wondered if she had dressed then like she did now.

''I always had the feeling everybody else knew something vitally important I didn't know about. Heard some kids mention *fucking* one day in the third grade. Hadn't the foggiest notion what they were talking about. Some kind of sport maybe, I thought. So I asked my mother.'' She pressed her hand against her chest. ''I thought she was going to have a stroke right then and there. I suppose I should've waited till after the Bridge Club meeting.''

They both laughed. Christina wiped a tear from the corner of her eye.

''My mother would have died,'' Ben said. ''On the spot. Mother was very big on appearances. Was, hell, *is*. She especially worried about me because I'm partially color-blind. Can't distinguish subtle gradations of some colors. No big deal. When I went away to college, though, she pinned little notes on all my clothes to tell me how to match them up: *I would look delightful with your blue sports coat or, for more casual occasions, your green corduroy slacks.*"

"You're kidding!"

"Nope." Ben crossed his heart. "Strange but true tales of suburbia."

"As long as we're playing *This Is Your Life, Benjamin Kincaid*, let me take a wild guess, based on the few days I've known you and on my profound understanding of human nature. You got into law because"—she took a deep breath and affected a stiff British accent—"you wanted to help people."

"That's what Derek said! Is this engraved on my forehead or something?"

"Let's say I can see it in your eyes."

"I can't deny it. I was out to save the world. Raised on *Owen Marshall, Counselor at Law*. First, I gravitated toward environmental law. Save the trees, the rain forests. Then I thought, maybe the public defender's office. After I got out of school, I worked for over a year at the D.A.'s office."

"So what happened?"

"What do you mean?"

"I mean what are you doing at Raven? Public defender is a far cry from corporate defender."

Ben returned his gaze to the office building. "I don't know. Things . . . happen. I seem to have a hard time standing still.

"I thought I'd be happy at the D.A.'s office. But I wasn't.

I felt like I was taking the easy way, not challenging my-self. I got very little satisfaction out of the work. Putting pathetic wretches behind bars. Plea bargaining. No pres-tige. No money.''

"So you came to Raven," Christina said, filling in the blanks.

"And I've been here a little over a week, and already I wonder if I've made a mistake. I miss the idealism of the D.A.'s office. Pompous or not, at the D.A.'s, everyone saw the law as the strong lance of the crusaders. At Raven, everyone pokes fun at that. At Raven, the law is bubble gum and mirrors.''

Ben looked back at the office building. He could tell from the movement of the flashlight beam in the windows that the guard was heading downstairs. Soon it would be time to go in.

"So enough of this poor-me routine. Tell me about yourself, Christina McCall.''

"Oh, not much to tell.'' She waved her hand with a flip-pant air. "I'm thirty-one—an older woman—devastatingly attractive, dressed in solid black clothes, and getting ready to break into a corporate office building.''

"I wanted facts, not self-parody. Married?''

"Not anymore.''

"No kids?''

She hesitated a moment. "No.'' Her face bore an odd expression, but it passed quickly. "No, I'm over thirty, single, and working as a legal assistant with a slew of filthy rich lawyers. Obviously, I am stalking a husband.'' She laughed, a bit too heartily, Ben thought.

"But why be a paralegal? Not that there's anything wrong with it, but there must be more rewarding ca-reers.''

Christina pushed herself back in the seat. "Well, I'm not what you'd call well educated. I was a whiz in high school—really, all A's and B's—but then I married Ray and ended up not going to college. I bet that surprises you, doesn't it?"

Ben shrugged noncommittally.

"Most people think I've been to college. I've taken night-school short courses at TJC. Trying to improve myself."

"You should have skipped the class on French phrases."

Christina looked astonished. "What do you have against French? I consider it sort of my trademark. My way of making people sit up and notice."

"It does do that."

"I had to find an occupation where I could make some decent money without a college education. For a while, I tried modeling. That was a disaster. Too much boob, not enough leg. I tried being a secretary, but I never managed to work a week for a boss I didn't end up wanting to kill. I decided paralegaling would be better."

"You never considered being a housewife?"

"With my ex-husband? Ray? Cheez—fat chance."

"Where is he now?"

"Oh, somewhere in OKC. He's remarried, some blonde bimbette, just out of high school—just like me twelve years ago. Last I heard, he was trying to get into night dental school." She laughed again. "It figures. He's married to me, he drives a delivery truck. He marries her, he's a friggin' dentist." She took a deep breath, then mumbled something under her breath.

"What was that?" Ben asked.

Christina looked up suddenly, as if she wasn't aware she was speaking aloud. "Oh! I was chanting."

Ben stared blankly at her.

She added: "That's how I relax myself. I induce a self-hypnotic state."

Ben's eyebrows raised. "Really? You can do it that quickly?"

"After a while. Not the first time."

"Really. Self-hypnosis. Do you do astrology, too?"

Christina gave Ben a look that could chill a supernova. "No. I've lived several past lives, though, if that makes you happy."

"Past lives? You're not serious."

"After you've heard yourself on tape talking for two hours about your former life in ancient Mesopotamia, it's kind of hard not to take it seriously."

"Who have you been?" Ben asked. "I see you as sort of the Madame Curie type."

Christina looked past him through the car window. "He's out," she said simply.

Ben turned and saw the guard and his dog emerge from the building. After a few minutes of wandering around out front, they walked to the left side of the building and out of sight.

"This is it," Ben said. His voice trembled embarrassingly. "Time to go."

Christina got out of the car first and started across the street. Ben followed, bringing the keys and a flashlight. They both moved quickly, running bent at the waist, as if they were afraid of enemy strafing. To avoid attracting attention, they had both dressed head to toe in black, like cliché cat burglars in a situation comedy. They had, however, resisted the temptation to wear black stocking caps.

A large fluorescent light illuminated the front of the

building but did not penetrate the shadow cast by the orange and white awning over the front doors. Ben and
Christina skittered through the lighted area and took shel-
ter in the shadows surrounding the two smoked-glass pan-
eled front doors.

Without pausing, Ben shoved the first key in the door.
The key went in, but he couldn't turn the lock. Was it the
wrong key, or was it one of those stubborn keys that never
work easily? Ben tried to force the turn.

"Give it up," Christina whispered. "If the key breaks
off in the lock, we'll never get inside. Try the next one."

Ben tried the next one. Same song, second verse.

"Damn," he said, clenching the key in his fist.

"Don't get frustrated," Christina whispered. "Try the
next one."

The sound of crunching gravel told them that a car was
driving along the road in front of the building. They froze.
What if someone noticed their car parked on the shoulder?
What if someone was coming? *Oh, hi, we just dropped by
for a casual visit in our burglar clothes.*

The crunching sound faded. Apparently, the car had
driven on. Ben exhaled audibly.

He tried the next key. The lock clicked open.

"Success," Ben whispered. He pushed the door forward several inches—and stopped. They had not noticed
before because of the smoked glass, but the door was
chained and padlocked from the inside. There was enough
room between the doors to reach through and open the
padlock. If you had a key.

Ben groaned. "That's it. I don't have any keys that
would open a lock like that. Let's split."

"Don't give up so easily," Christina said. She pushed
the doors forward. They gave enough to create a gap of

about six or seven inches. "Not chained very efficiently. I suppose the guard gets tired of going through the routine, especially since he knows he'll be back in twenty minutes. We can get through this." She turned sideways and poked her head through the gap in the doors.

"Are you kidding?" Ben exclaimed. "I'm a lot thicker than that."

"Only in the fatty places," she said, edging her body into place. "Fat can be squeezed through."

Christina took a deep breath, crouched under the chain and eased herself between the doors. Most of her generally slim body passed easily, though she had to wriggle and twist to get her hips through. But she made it. In fact, Ben thought, she made it look easy.

"Here, give me your hand."

Ben did as he was instructed. Her hand was warm. He could feel her pulse thumping.

Following her lead—head first, wriggling midsection, legs last—he slid in beneath the chain and pulled himself through the narrow space.

They walked into the main lobby. Ben's sneakers squeaked on the tile floor. Almost immediately, he heard a soft but insistent electronic beep, sounding about every three seconds.

"Is it an alarm?" Christina asked. She was still holding Ben's hand.

"I don't think so," he replied. "If Greg is to be believed, the beeping means the timer on the noise alarm has been activated. We probably have one minute to find the control box and shut it off before it turns into a piercing alarm and automatically dials the police. It's designed to allow people who are supposed to be here a chance to deactivate the alarm.''

''Then don't waste time talking. Find that box!''

They scanned the spacious lobby. There were a million possible places. Elevators, hallways, receptionist stations.

''Over here,'' Ben said hurriedly. He ran toward a booth in the front left corner of the lobby. ''This is where the security guard was sitting when I came to see Sanguine earlier today. It's the logical place for the alarm control box.''

They examined the security booth. The beeping noise seemed louder here, but Ben could see no control box. He dropped to his knees. On the underside of the desk, he saw a small box with a red light flashing in time to the beeps. A digital display showed eleven seconds, then ten, then nine. Next to the display, there was a keyhole.

Ben tried the first small-size key on Adams's keychain. It would not go in.

Suddenly, the beeping noise stopped. ''It's about to blow,'' Ben muttered.

He inserted the second small key and turned. The red light shut off.

Christina put her arm on Ben's shoulder. ''Hey,'' she whispered, ''once you get into the spirit, you're a natural at this breaking and entering.''

Ben declined to respond.

Quickly, they sprinted up the emergency stair to the second floor. From the outer hallway, they entered the office bearing Adams's nameplate. The door was not taped or locked. Rather than turning on the lights, something the guard was bound to see, they used the flashlight Ben brought.

"All right," Ben whispered, "we've got maybe ten minutes."

They began searching, Ben at the desk, Christina at the bookshelves and credenza. Ben noticed that the office, although considerably larger than Ben's at Raven, was not one of the larger offices he had seen in this building. In fact, it seemed amazingly small for the vice president of new developments.

The desk was light brown oak—at least in color. Probably a nouveau antique, Ben mused. A framed photograph of Bertha that must have been taken forty years ago rested on top. Ben examined the desk drawers. The desk was not locked, mercifully sparing Ben another agonizing key search. He systematically, if hurriedly, combed through everything, but found nothing helpful.

"Bertha said that the night he was killed, Jonathan never came back from the office," Ben whispered to Christina. "So if he set up a meeting, he probably did it here. I hoped we'd at least find some kind of note or a scrawled address or phone number." He picked up a thick memo pad from the desk. The top sheet was barren. "A total blank." Disgusted, he dropped the pad back onto the desk.

"Wait a minute," Christina said. She took the memo pad, and held it up to the moonlight. She tilted the pad at different angles, catching the light. Then she took a pencil from the desk and lightly sketched over the top sheet of paper. A white impression resembling words or numbers began to appear.

"It's the imprint of whatever Adams wrote on the sheet of paper above this one," Christina murmured. She finished sketching and scrutinized the result. "Hmm. It worked a lot better for Sherlock Holmes."

Ben looked at the pad. Only a few letters were clear. A
p and an *a*, and after that, something indecipherable. Below that, an *a*, followed by either an *f* or an *r*, followed
by a *c*.

"Archer," Christina said. "It's an address on Archer
Avenue."

"His body was found in an alley off Archer," Ben said.
"You might be right. What's the *p-a*? Parent maybe?"

"Maybe he was saying he found Emily's parent on
Archer Avenue," Christina suggested.

Ben snapped his fingers. "Or *p-a* could be part of the
Red Parrot Café. That's the bar across the street from
where Adams was found. Maybe he planned to meet
someone there."

"Could be," Christina murmured. "Or perhaps *p-a* is
part of Sapulpa or St. Paul—or the Panama Canal, for that
matter—"

She stopped short. Footsteps. In the outer hallway by
the elevators.

Ben shut off his flashlight. They dropped to the floor
and hid behind the desk.

The footsteps grew louder at a steady but unhurried
pace. Ben and Christina could see a light come on in the
hallway in the airspace beneath the door. The footsteps
slowed. A door opened, then closed.

"Is it the security guard?" Christina whispered.

Ben shook his head. "It's too soon for him."

The footsteps began again. They were heavy and drawing closer.

Christina held her breath. The door to the office opened.
A light flickered on.

Ben and Christina did not move, or breathe, or think.

They were completely hidden by the oak desk, or so Ben
thought. *If only whoever-it-is doesn't look behind the
desk.*

An eternity passed in what was probably a few seconds.
Ben's entire life (past, present, and future) unreeled before
his eyes—including his expulsion from the bar and a long
prison sentence.

Then the light went off, and the squeaky office door
closed. Christina looked at Ben, and together they quietly
exhaled. The footsteps moved away at an intolerably slow
pace. Finally, the stairwell door opened, and they heard
the visitor walk away.

Christina started to stand up, then noticed Ben staring
at the underside of the desk. "What is it?" she whispered.

Ben pointed to the bottom of the middle desk drawer,
the one he had last opened before they dropped to the
floor. A medium-sized manila envelope was taped to the
bottom of the drawer.

"I can't believe the police missed this," Ben muttered.

"They probably weren't crawling on their hands and
knees when they searched the place," Christina replied.

Ben reached up and removed the envelope.

"We've got to get out of here," Christina whispered.
She stood up and tried the window behind the desk.
"Locked," she said. "But not hermetically sealed." She
flipped the latches on both sides of the window and
pushed. The window opened.

"You can't be serious," Ben said.

"We don't have any choice. With this mystery man
creeping around, our previous plan is unworkable. Besides, we're only on the second floor."

Ben gazed out the window. There were few lights on

the back side of the building, although there was a half moon. Where is the security guard? he wondered. He realized that he simply had no idea. He had lost all sense of the time scheme.

He looked down. The window was twelve, perhaps fifteen feet above the ground. She was right, though. They had no choice.

He pushed Christina aside. "Time for some macho posturing," he said. "I'll go first." He put his feet through the window first, hung with his hands on the sill for a few moments, then dropped.

He landed off-balance on his left leg. The impact of the fall drove his knees into his chin. He fell onto his back. He blinked, then took a personal inventory. His teeth felt like mashed potatoes, but he was all right.

Christina followed close behind. She landed more gracefully, rolled on her heels, and softened the impact on her knees by rolling down onto the backs of her arms and shoulders.

"Nice job," Ben whispered, standing over her.

"It's the modeling training," she murmured, taking her bearings. "Teaches bodily coordination and grace under fire."

"You're okay then?"

She nodded.

"Then let's get the hell out of here." He clasped her hand and helped her up. They started to run back around the side of the building toward the car.

Behind them, a dog barked.

"My God," Ben said without breaking his stride. "We forgot about the dog!" They bolted toward the front of the building without looking back.

If they had looked back, they might have noticed a dark silhouette in the open window from which they had jumped. Someone was watching them.

PART TWO

*   *

The True Embodiment

* 15 *

There was a loud, deliberate knock on the door.

The heavyset woman in the white uniform recognized his knock. She rose quickly and, after peering through the peephole, opened the door.

The man walked into the apartment and took off his jacket. "How is she today?"

The woman hesitated. "She's . . . fine. Stable. Very good, under the circumstances." She paused. "I know what I'm doing."

The man smiled. "That's why you get paid the big money." He glanced down the hallway. "Get her."

Nodding obediently, the woman walked halfway down the hall and called out.

After a few moments, there was a shuffling noise, and another woman, much thinner and younger, poked her head through the bedroom door. She had a vacant, distracted expression.

"Someone here to see you," the nurse said quietly.

The younger woman looked down the hallway and saw the man standing in the main room of the apartment. A panicked expression spread across her face. She slammed the door shut.

The man frowned. "I'll handle this," he muttered. He

pushed the woman in white out of the way and walked down the hallway.

"Open the door," he said, quietly but firmly.

There was no response.

"I said, open the door," he repeated, a little more loudly than before.

Still no response.

A sudden rage came over him. Gritting his teeth, he threw his full body, shoulder first, against the door. The door shuddered but did not open.

Even more enraged, the man began to kick the door. His pounding dented the outer wood surface.

He stopped, breathing heavily. His entire body was trembling. "All right, then," he said, "see what you think about this." He leaned close to the door and whispered a few brief words.

After a moment, the woman slowly opened the door. She was crying. Red blotches appeared on her face and neck just above her blue bathrobe.

"Please don't hurt her," she said. Her face was wet with tears.

"We'll see," the man said. With both hands he shoved the woman back against the bed.

He smiled. The rage had passed. He turned and looked back at the heavyset woman. "You're dismissed."

"But I haven't prepared her for the evening yet."

"I said you're dismissed!" the man growled. He slammed the bedroom door shut.

* 16 *

"What is it with you, anyway, Kincaid?"

Derek closed the door to his office and began his ritu-
alistic pacing. Glad to see the ankle's healed up, Ben
thought.

"I asked you to try to get a kid adopted. A simple
matter. The hearing is already set; you either win or lose.
Except, for some reason, the next day you tell me you
need a private detective to investigate the kid's"—he
hunched his shoulders together like a ghoul and rolled his
eyes to the tops of their sockets—"myster-r-r-rious past."
He resumed his normal posture. "And now you want to
hire an *accountant*, for God knows what reason. What is
going *on*?"

"Mr. Derek, I think these papers I discovered are very
important." Ben neglected to mention where he discovered them.

"Why? What can they tell us that's relevant to an adoption hearing?"

"I don't know, Mr. Derek. That's just it. I'm *not* an
accountant. I got C's in algebra—"

"Stop." Derek thrust the palm of his hand forward as
if he was doing a bad imitation of the Supremes. "No
more."

119

He sat down behind the desk. "I will tell you this one more time, Kincaid, and *only once more*, if you catch my drift." He leaned forward and stared meaningfully into Ben's eyes. "This is *not* a *pro bono* case, but it's damn close. This is not a money-maker, for us *or* our client. Our client does *not* want to spend a bundle of bucks on this. All he wants is to sleep nights with his guilt assuaged because he *tried* to do something nice for an old employee's widow. And, frankly, if we're unsuccessful"—Derek shrugged—"well, he did what he could."

Ben stared back at the man. It was useless. Like arguing ethics with the Great Wall of China.

"Speaking of Sanguine," Derek continued, "have you finished the brief for our preliminary injunction motion in the trade dress case?"

"Yes," Ben answered. "I placed it on your desk this morning—"

"I've already read that draft," Derek interrupted. "And I've made changes. It's in your in box."

"I'll see that Word Processing makes the changes, sir."

"What about my opening statement? Have you written that?"

"N-no. I didn't realize you wanted—"

"What did you think I was going to do tomorrow morning? Stand at the podium and twiddle my lower lip?" He struck a match against the side of the box and lit a cigarette. "You see, Kincaid? This is exactly what I've been talking about. You're behind in your work, you're really only making an effort on one case, and you're not accomplishing anything on *it*!"

He took a deep, calming draw on his cigarette, then used the cigarette as a pointer. "A good associate doesn't have to be told to do something. A good associate *sees* that it needs to be done and does it. Period. I know you've just started, but frankly, your work to date has not been up to the usual Raven standards. And if your work isn't up to snuff, Kincaid, nothing can save your butt from the shredder. Not your mother, your minister, a shareholder—or his wife." Derek's eyes flashed.

Ben didn't know how to respond. No secrets at R T & T.

"So get humping, Kincaid. The trade dress hearing tomorrow is before Old Stone Face, Judge Schmidt. He's a would-be author of a few unimportant legal articles and fancies himself a celebrated literary figure. So pepper the opening statement with obscure quotations and polysyllabic prose. You should be good at that." He took a final drag from his cigarette. "And forget about this asinine accountant crap!"

Ben left the office without saying a word. As he walked down the corridor, every secretarial eye was fixed upon him. Ben realized just how loud Derek's shouting had really been. Was it just Ben or was Derek still on the skids with his wife? That would explain volumes. It seemed as if Derek opposed his investigation of this case at every step.

Ben ducked into the elevator lobby and pushed the DOWN button. Tom Melton and Alvin Hager joined him just as the doors opened. The three of them stepped into the elevator.

"So, Mr. Harvard gave you a bad time, eh?" Alvin asked in a boisterous voice. The elevator descended.

"Do you lurk outside of keyholes or what?"

"Not necessary when Derek's doing the shouting," Tom said. "What a prima donna. I did think that jab about shareholders' wives was unfair, though. I mean, it's not as though it was your idea, after all." Tom and Alvin looked at each other solemnly, then broke into broad grins.

Tom regained his solemn expression. "Seriously, Ben, try not to worry about him too much. Everyone knows what a prick he is."

"That's an understatement," Alvin added. "Do you realize no associate assigned to Derek has lasted over three years with the firm? Ever. In the twelve years since Derek came here from Philadelphia."

"That's pathetic," Ben mumbled. "Someone needs to do something about him."

The bell rang, and the doors opened on the ground floor. Alvin and Tom headed toward the fast-food restaurants and ice-skating rink in the mall adjoining the office tower.

"Before we run off, Ben," Tom said, "are you coming to the recruiting function tonight?"

"Recruiting function? I've already been recruited."

"For next year's class, Ben. Now that you're an associate, you have an obligation to pull your weight in recruiting. I'm in charge of the recruiting program, and I'm organizing a little soiree tonight. The firm likes to have new associates in attendance—to tell the new recruits how wonderful life is at R T & T. They're more likely to listen to someone closer to their own age."

Ben shook his head. "I don't think I'd be the ideal pitchman for R T & T."

"I wouldn't say no if I were you, Ben," Alvin remarked. "Just speaking as a friend. The firm higher-ups want tonight's guest in a bad way. He's 3L Yale, decent grades, law review. If we can be part of the team that reels him in, it'll be a feather in our caps. Given your current standing in the firm, you can't afford to pass up a chance to impress shareholders.''

Ben sighed. ''I'll think about it and get back to you guys. Okay?''

They nodded.

''Is Marianne coming?''

Tom and Alvin exchanged a naughty look. ''I don't think so, Ben,'' Tom said. ''That wouldn't be quite appropriate.'' They looked at each other again and burst into laughter. Tom swatted Alvin on the shoulder, and the two of them walked off toward the fast-food zone.

Ben watched Heckle and Jeckle recede into the distance. Great, he thought. What next?

After they were gone, he walked until he reached the shopping mall area. He stood at the banister on the third level, looking down on the ice-skating rink below. There was only one person on the ice, a girl, probably in her early teens. She had dark hair and was wearing a skimpy, sequined outfit. She was skating to a classical piece—one of Chopin's preludes, Ben thought. She raised her arms and executed a nice aerial double spin. She was trying to maintain balance, to remain smooth and graceful, and yet there was something imperfect, something slightly awkward about her execution. Perhaps she was new at this, Ben thought, or was performing a new routine, and was still working out the bugs, still perfecting her art.

Ben stared down at her until the itching in his eyes grew too strong. He turned and, holding his head down so that he could not be seen, raced to the nearest men's room. He entered one of the stalls, closed the door behind him, sat down on the toilet, and began to cry.

* 17 *

When Ben finally returned to his office, Christina was waiting for him.

"What ho!" she said, saluting. "It's Benjamin Kincaid, Man of Adventure!"

Ben slammed the door shut. "Don't say that!" he whispered harshly. "Someone might figure it out. Sanguine's bound to report a break-in. After all, we left the window wide open."

Christina plopped into one of the orange corduroy chairs. "Sorry, boss. Didn't mean to get you riled up. Any luck on the accountant?"

"Are you kidding?" He threw himself into the other chair. "Derek is determined to do this case for next to nothing and doesn't care if we lose it in the process."

"Really?" Christina said. "That seems odd." She meditated for a moment.

Ben dialed the combination on his briefcase and withdrew the manila envelope he had found beneath Adams's desk drawer. He pulled out ten pages of paper, stapled in the upper left corner. Each page contained five vertical columns; the first contained letters, apparently in code, while the other four all contained numbers. At the top left of the first page someone had scribbled in pencil *Comp*

Sang Summ. Some of the figures had been underlined in red.

"Have you figured out what it is?" Christina asked.

"No," Ben replied. "I got into law so I wouldn't have to deal with addition and subtraction and other forms of higher mathematics." He threw the document back into his briefcase. "How about you? Weren't you an accountant in a previous life?"

She smiled thinly. "Well, I was going to offer my invaluable assistance, but now I'm not so sure."

Ben laughed. "C'mon," he said. "Give me a second chance."

"Well . . ." She brushed back her long strawberry hair. "I do have a friend in Bookkeeping here at Raven. Sally might consider taking a look at this on the QT, but you'll have to make it worth her while."

"That's awfully suggestive. Remember, I'm just a naive waif from the suburbs."

"Don't worry, Ben. I'll play chaperone and protect your virtue. I'll call you when it's arranged. Will you be home tonight?"

"No. I'm going on a recruiting function with Tom Melton."

Christina gave him a long, questioning look. "Well, I'll expect a full report in the morning. Don't spare me the details."

She departed, leaving Ben to wonder what that was supposed to mean.

The neon sign pulsed with irritating regularity in garish red: THE BARE FAX. The lights in the second A and X had almost entirely burned out, however, and from a distance the sign read THE BARE F. The windowless building was a small, flat rectangle, made of sloppy stucco and painted a dirty brown color. It looked as if it hadn't been repainted in ten years, but then, Ben mused, there was no reason why it should be. It was not the aesthetics or architecture that drew in the customers.

The Bare Fax was conveniently located just outside the Tulsa city limits, about a twenty-minute drive from the plush downtown seafood restaurant where the group had eaten dinner. What a deal for a new recruit. A three-hundred-dollar dinner and a strip-joint chaser. How could the guy say no?

The guy—one Dewey Stockton—was at the front of the R T & T assemblage with Tom Melton. Stockton was tall, blond, reasonably attractive, well spoken, and intelligent. Ben had to admit that he seemed like a promising attorney. He had the courage to decline wine with dinner even after Tom selected a bottle and ordered glasses all around. Ben admired Stockton for that. Besides, it was a lousy vintage.

Close behind Donald and Tom were Greg, the grizzled party veteran, and Alvin, the celibate sensation. Ben had witnessed enough winking and jabbing between those two to fill a lifetime. Unlike Dewey Stockton, Alvin had opted to drink wine with dinner. Too much, near as Ben could tell. He suspected Alvin was not accustomed to heavy drinking. Or even light drinking, probably.

Tom did a little negotiation regarding cover charges with the beefy humanoid guarding the front door. A Ben Franklin passed hands, and the man waved the whole group inside. "Treat these fellas extra special, ladies," he shouted behind them.

The room was smoky, smelly, congested, very noisy, and none of it mattered. When there are eight waitresses running through the room wearing nothing above their waists, Ben realized, one tends not to focus on the ambience. Along the east wall, an old-fashioned wooden bar was situated, with a large single-plate mirror behind it. A young, bearded bartender was working furiously, filling pitchers of beer and sliding them down to the barebosomed babes.

In the opposite corner, along the same wall as the entrance, was a small wooden dance floor with a guardrail separating the dance floor from the peanut gallery. A long iron bar in the middle of the dance area ran from ceiling to floor. And coiled around the iron bar, Ben spotted a leggy blonde twisting and gyrating in a pair of leopardskin panties. And nothing else.

Tom motioned everyone around a vacant table directly in front of the dance floor. The woman currently onstage was not exactly pretty, Ben noted, although *pretty* generally refers to a woman's face, a feature barely noticeable with regard to the body in question. She seemed as if she were dancing through a dream, as if she had forgotten, or was trying to forget, that the hooting and howling audience existed. Occasionally, a patron would catch her eye and she would bare her teeth and release an animalistic growl, thereby completing the leopard theme of her presentation.

"So what can I get you, darlin'?"

Ben turned his head. The waitress's breasts were dangling about an inch from his nose.

"So answer the woman, Kincaid," Greg said. He gave Ben a shove on the shoulder, which propelled his face even further forward.

She was a redhead, with freckles that seemed to cover her entire body, or at least as much of it as Ben could see, which was quite a bit. She was older than most of the Bare

Fax babes—mid-thirties, probably. Her skin drooped a bit in places, as if worn down by constant scrutiny. Thick, caked makeup couldn't hide the wide half moons under her eyes.

"Uh . . . what do you have?"

"Beer," she answered.

"Oh." Ben leaned back for air. "What kind?"

"Beer," she repeated.

"Oh. Well, I'll have some of that."

"Two pitchers," Tom shouted over Ben's shoulder. He slapped Alvin on the shoulder. "We need to get you loosened up, pal."

The waitress vibrated a bit, pivoted on her gold lamé high heels, and walked back to the bar.

"Third round," the redhead said cheerily. As before, she insisted on thrusting herself in Ben's face as she unloaded her refreshments. Ben trained his eyes on the pitchers of beer.

The floor show continued as the waitresses donned costumes and took turns dancing. The leopard woman had been replaced by the fairy princess, the Egyptian catwoman (played by their waitress, stage-named Delilah), and the schoolmarm. The schoolmarm (Jezebel) had removed her thick eyeglasses and the bobby pins constraining her hair and was currently demonstrating the creative use of a chalkboard pointer.

Suddenly, Alvin, urged on by Tom and many, too many, beers, stood in front of his chair and shouted, "Baby, baby, you're *killin'* me! I'm ready for ya, babe! Come and get me!" A chorus of grunts and cheers echoed Alvin's sentiment.

Ben stared at him, horrified. "Alvin! Sit down!" he
hissed. He yanked Alvin down by his arm.

Tom leaned close to Alvin's ear. "Loosen up, pal." He
thrust a glass in Alvin's hand. "Here, drink another beer."

Ben snatched the glass away, splashing beer on his arm
and lap. "*No*. Definitely no more beer. I think he's loose
enough."

Greg slapped Alvin on the shoulder. "Don't get yourself arrested, Al. You still have to take the bar exam come
October. The bar examiners tend to frown on lawyers with
a criminal record."

Delilah bent over, cupped her hand around Ben's ear,
and whispered, "Isn't this silly? I think so. I'm just trying
to get enough money so I can go to college and dedicate
my life to Christ." Her freckles bounced before his nose
for a moment, and then she disappeared.

What was that all about? Ben wondered. Had she sin-
gled out the only guys in the place that were better dressed
than the usual jeans and cowboy boot crowd? Dangerous
place for suckers.

Ben turned to face his companions. Tom and Dewey
were deep in what appeared to be a very serious conversation, although they had to take turns shouting into one
another's ears to be heard over the din. Ben marveled.
How can you talk about insurance benefits and profit-
sharing plans while you're staring at a schoolmarm's
G-string?

Alvin was on his feet again. "Baby, *baby*," he shouted,
stretching his arms out to Jezebel. "Teach me a lesson.
Give me some homework." He grinned a goofy, toothy
grin and let loose a high-pitched drunken squeal.

The dancing woman studiously ignored Alvin. She had
progressed to working with her clinging, diaphanous

shawl. Evidently what she was preparing to unveil was not enormous, so she was making a great show of the unveiling itself.

"Sit down, Alvin." Ben yanked again at his arm, but Alvin would not obey.

"I said *homework*, woman! C'mon . . . do your pedagogical duty." His tone was becoming abusive. Again, Ben told him to sit down and again, Alvin ignored him.

And then Alvin stepped up onto the guardrail, balancing himself by placing one arm against the wall. He wobbled uncertainly. Instantly, the schoolmarm stopped her undulations and cowered back into the corner of the dance floor. Two muscle-bound toughs emerged from nowhere and barreled toward the dance floor, along with the bouncer from the front door.

"All I wanted to do was say hello," Alvin mumbled, with a hiccup.

Two thick, hamlike hands slapped down on Alvin's shoulders. He lost his balance and began falling backward. He waved his arms in large circles, hopelessly trying to regain his balance. He tumbled back onto the table the Ravenites were sitting around. Glasses, pitchers, and beer went flying in every direction. Everyone tried to move out of the way, and no one was quick enough. The table rocked several times before falling over and dumping Alvin onto the floor.

The three bouncers began to close in on him, but before they could, Delilah ran in and knelt beside him.

"Stay back!" she said, motioning them away. "He needs air."

She brushed his hair out of his eyes and wiped the sudsy,

splattered beer from his face. She dabbed her spill cloth against the gash on his forehead.

Alvin blinked several times and groaned. Apparently he was still alive.

"Are you all right?" she asked.

"I guess so," Alvin said uncertainly. "I can't feel a thing."

"Can you stand up? I have some Band-Aids in my locker in the dressing room. Can you make it?"

"Sure," Alvin said. He pushed himself upward by the palms of his hands and groaned. "Oh, my God!"

"You can do it," she said. She put her arm around him and wrapped his arm around her bare midsection. "That's it. Easy does it."

Eventually Alvin was on his feet, more or less. "Come on back to the dressing room, and I'll get you all fixed up." She walked him toward the back of the bar. "I'm so sorry this happened. You know, I'm just trying to get enough money to go to college and . . ." Slowly they disappeared into the background of the bar.

"Oh, well," Tom said. "Looks like he's in good hands. Party animals, *resume!*" He winked at Dewey, and they resumed their serious conversation.

Ben watched as Alvin and the waitress disappeared behind a bead curtain. He hoped Alvin wasn't hurt badly. He hoped Alvin wasn't too drunk to know what he was doing.

He hoped Alvin remembered his oath.

* 18 *

Ben arrived at the office early, carrying the script for Derek's opening argument before Old Stone Face. Maggie told him Derek hadn't come in and hadn't called, so Ben went to his own office.

He found Mike Morelli sitting in one of the corduroy chairs, puffing his pipe.

"Morning, shamus," Ben said. "What's the good word?"

"Shamus?" Mike winced. "You've got to stop watching so much television."

Ben hung his suit coat on the hook behind the door and sat down at his desk. "Give me a break. It's too early in the morning to take any grief from you. At least I didn't call you a dick."

"I've got some preliminary reports," Mike said, ignoring him. "I thought you might be interested."

"You were right. Shoot."

"Dr. Koregai thinks he's determined the cause of death. Adams died from cardiac shock and blood loss induced by rapid-succession knife wounds—"

"No kidding," Ben interrupted. "How much do you pay this guy?"

"—received by the victim after imbibing a considerable quantity of alcohol."

"Really?" Ben said. At the Red Parrot? he wondered.

"You're missing the main point here, Kincaid," Mike said, fumbling in his coat pocket for a pipe-bowl stamper. "Death was induced by the first two or three knife wounds. This confirms the hypothesis Dr. Koregai made at the autopsy based on the low incidence of bruising. The body was mutilated *after* death."

Ben let the words sink in. He suddenly felt weighted, immobile. What were they tracking?

"I haven't even told you the best part. This is where Dr. Koregai really earns his salary. He found a fingerprint."

"The *coroner* found a fingerprint?"

"Yep. Noticed Adams's wristwatch was smudged. Called Pulaski, my best duster. Sure enough, a beautiful, unsmeared right thumbprint on the watch crystal." He pulled a police print sheet from his coat pocket. "Based on the unusual position and freshness of the print, our guys think it's almost certainly the killer. Probably happened during the struggle."

"That's great. Have you run the print through the AFIS computer?"

"Of course," Mike growled. He placed his pipe between his lips and stared at the print sheet for a moment. "We don't have the killer's thumb on file. Which tells us that he's never committed a felony, served in the military, or worked for the government. The *other* quarter of a million people in Tulsa are still suspects."

"Rotten luck," Ben murmured.

"Not really. At least now when we do catch the killer, we'll have a positive means of ID."

Ben pulled a legal pad from his desk drawer and made a few notes. "What about hair and fiber analysis?" he asked. "Your guys ever find anything?"

"Not much," Mike said, relighting his pipe.

"How can you inhale that disgusting crap at seven-thirty in the morning?"

"Breakfast," Mike mumbled. He puffed several times, then released the smoke. "The hair and fiber guys analyzed everything they could find on Adams. Most of it matches Adams or his clothes or his house or the kid or his wife, but not everything. Two straight black hairs didn't match up. Definitely human. Definitely male."

"Might be the assailant."

"Might not."

"Right," Ben said, nodding. He made another note. "Very helpful. What about fibers?"

"A few, all very common. Everything we can positively identify can be traced to Adams's house or his car or his office."

"Anything else?"

"Yes. We got served a subpoena on the phone company for the MUDs for Adams's home and office phones. They tell us it will take them a few days to put it all together. I'll call you as soon as I have something."

Mike took another hearty drag on the pipe. "Oh. I almost forgot. We think we've got a blood sample. Found some blood on Adams's left hand that didn't come from him. Maybe Adams managed to cut his assailant before he got shish-kebabed. It would be nice to think so." He removed a crumpled lab report from his coat pocket and handed it to Ben.

Ben took the sheet of paper and scanned it, trying to

remember what little he had learned at the D.A.'s office
about blood analysis.

Adams	*Unknown*
Rhesus Pos	Rhesus Pos
ABO A	O
AK 2–1 (7.6%)	I (92.3%)
PGM 1 + (40%)	2+, 1−(4.8%)

Ben made a few notes on his legal pad. "Is the unknown a secretor?"

Mike raised his eyebrows. "I'm impressed. Maybe
you did learn a thing or two in OKC. Yeah, he's a
secretor, not that that gets us far in this kind of case.
We're not likely to stumble across any sperm samples."

"Still," Ben said, "a blood match gives you a second
means of positively IDing the killer."

Mike nodded. "Once we find him. But enough about
me. What have you been up to, Ben?"

"Nothing very productive. Why?"

"Funny thing. A burglary occurred two nights ago at
the Sanguine offices. Someone got in—we don't know
how. There's no sign of forced entry. Burglar escaped
through a second-story window. Damn near got caught."

Ben stared intently at his legal pad. "Did they take
anything?"

"Why do you say *they*? I just mentioned a burglar."
Mike smiled. "Nothing taken that we know of. That
makes it even stranger. You don't know anything about
this, do you?"

Ben spoke nonchalantly. "Of course not. How could I?"

"I had to ask. Matter of procedure." He removed the pipe from his lips and stared at it. "Frankly, if it had been you, I wouldn't want to know, because then I'd have to ask if you found anything, and if you did I'd have to ask what. I'd be exposed to illegally obtained evidence, and some jerk lawyer would make a fruit-of-the-poisonous-tree argument and I'd *never* get a conviction in this case. True, the police didn't break into the office building, but some shyster might suggest that I urged my brother-in-law to do this dastardly deed."

Message received and understood, Ben thought. "Ex-brother-in-law," he said.

"Right."

"Anything else?" Ben asked.

"Nope. Just keep me posted, and I'll do likewise. I'm going to send some more men with Adams's picture around the neighborhood where we found the body. See if anyone recognizes him."

"You mean anyone in that neighborhood who will talk to the boys in blue. Lotsa luck."

"Yeah, exactly. Well, I'll see you around." He started out the door. Ben followed him.

"You have a message," Maggie said as Ben stepped out of his office. "Mr. Derek called in twenty minutes ago. He says he'll meet you at the courthouse."

"*Twenty minutes ago?* Why didn't you tell me?"

Maggie fluttered her eyelids. "You were in conference."

Ben rolled his eyes. "Great. See you around, Mike." He dashed back into his office, grabbed his suit coat and script, and ran for the elevator.

* 19 *

Ben dashed into Judge Schmidt's courtroom, briefcase in hand, coat slung over his arm. Christina was waiting for him at the plaintiff's table.

"Where's Derek?" she asked.

"You mean he's not here yet?" Ben threw his briefcase and coat in a chair by the table.

"Don't worry. He works well on his feet. Just get the script out."

A tiny blonde in a plain red dress walked up to the table. Her hair was disarranged, and she looked as if she hadn't slept in several nights. Mascara had been applied to her eyes with an unsteady hand.

"Where is he?" the woman asked.

Ben looked up. "Mrs. Derek!" He corrected himself. *"Louise."*

"Where is he?" she repeated.

"You mean Mr. Derek?" Ben exchanged a glance with Christina. "He's not here yet. He's still . . . not here yet."

Louise released a short, bitter laugh. "He's not at home. He hasn't been home all night."

"I see," Ben said, nodding his head. He drummed his fingers on the table. What to say, what to say? "Can I . . . give Mr. Derek a message when he arrives?"

Louise was staring at Christina. "You're the one, aren't you?"

Christina pressed her hand against her chest. "Me? No, I'm not . . . I mean, I don't know what you mean, but whatever you mean, it isn't me."

Louise repeated the bitter laugh. "I don't suppose you'd admit it if you were. I couldn't even expect him to commit adultery in an honorable fashion."

She returned her gaze to Ben. "Yes, you can take a message. On one of those little pink sheets of paper. Check the box labeled *no return call required*. This is my message: don't come home—we don't want you." She took a deep breath. *"Ever."*

With that, she pivoted on her heels and marched out of the courtroom.

Ben pursed his lips and blew. "Whew. You get the feeling Derek has crossed the line once too often?"

Christina nodded. "Evidently. I don't care much, though, for being linked with Derek. Particularly not as the homewrecking floozy. Next thing I know, I'll be hauled into divorce court."

Behind Ben, someone cleared his throat. "I have the exhibits Mr. Derek asked for."

Ben looked up and saw Darryl Tidwell, Sanguine's personal secretary. He was wearing a blue sports jacket and, beneath it, a pink cardigan sweater and darker pink tie.

"These are the photographs we took of the interior and exterior of this Eggs 'N' Such place." Ben looked at each of the photographs as Tidwell handed them to him. "As you can see, their street sign is extremely similar to our Eggs 'N' Stuff logo—same colors, same font. Similar on the inside, too. Same decor, practically identical menu— the whole ball of wax." He handed the entire packet to

Ben. "I'd have gotten these to you sooner, but I was delayed."

"I'll see that Derek gets these."

"Where is he, anyway?" Tidwell asked.

"He's—" Ben began.

"—out for the moment," Christina interceded. "He'll be here any minute."

"Oh," Tidwell said. He ran his fingers through the thinning hair on either side of his bald head. "Say, Ben, do you know why they're replacing laboratory rats with lawyers?"

Ben sighed. Remember: courtesy to the client. "No. Why?"

"Lawyers are more plentiful, and you don't get so attached to them." He laughed heartily. "Also there are *some* things a rat just won't do." He laughed even louder.

Ben tried to smile.

"Well, I guess I'll find a seat. Sanguine wants me to give him a full report on the hearing."

"Good plan."

Tidwell turned and shuffled back to the courtroom gallery.

Christina glanced toward the door leading to the judge's chambers. "There's the bailiff. If Derek doesn't show up in about two minutes, Ben, I'd say you're about to give your first oral argument."

Ben's eyes widened.

"All rise."

The court bailiff stepped through the door and behind him, in a long black robe, was Judge Schmidt.

"You may be seated," he intoned solemnly. Schmidt appeared to be in his early fifties. He had an orange-brown mustache the same color that his hair probably was back when he had hair.

"Stone Face is right," Ben whispered to Christina as the bailiff began calling the docket. "What a humorless character."

At that instant, Ben saw Derek sliding into the chair next to his at the plaintiff's table. The hair on the right side of his head was sticking straight out and he wore a day's growth of stubble. His clothes reeked of smoke. "So where's the script?" he growled quietly.

"Right here." Ben patted the papers on the table.

Derek glanced down. "Lots of highbrow literary allusions?"

"You bet."

Derek quietly grunted his approval. He set his briefcase atop the table and raised the lid so as to cut off the judge's view of his face.

Ben watched as Derek removed a plastic disposable razor from his briefcase and scraped it across his chin. That must sting, Ben thought, but Derek didn't seem to notice. Derek licked his fingers, ran them through his hair twice and, after checking that no one was watching, discreetly positioned his toupee. As if by magic, everything seemed to settle more or less into place. He removed two tablets from a smoked plastic pill bottle and popped them into his mouth. "Hangover remedy," he murmured.

The bailiff finished calling the docket and formally announcing the appearances of the attorneys. He returned to the first case on the docket.

"Sanguine Enterprises vs. Martin Food Corp., doing business as Eggs 'N' Such, case number CJ-92-49235-S, is now called before this court. Are the parties present and ready?"

Attorneys on both sides announced that they were.

"Very well," Judge Schmidt said in a heavy voice, as if he'd rather be anywhere else. "Opening statements, please. And be brief," he added wearily.

"Thank you, Your Honor." Derek rose, buttoned the top button of his jacket, and strode to the podium. He seemed calm and self-assured, not remotely as if he had been up all night, had a hangover, and was about to deliver a speech he'd never seen before.

"Your Honor, the motion for injunctive relief before the court today presents only a single issue, but it is an issue of great importance both to Sanguine Enterprises and to the business world in general. The question presented to this court, simply stated, is this: has Martin Foods, through the Tulsa restaurant known as Eggs 'N' Such, so appropriated and infringed upon the trade dress of the national chain of restaurants known as Eggs 'N' Stuff as to demand immediate injunctive relief to prevent inevitable irreparable harm?"

The judge stared stonily at Derek, not as if he were an oral advocate, but as if he were an unusual kind of bug.

"In this case, Your Honor, the only possible answer to that question is: yes."

Ben had to admire Derek. His delivery was very smooth. Although he had never laid eyes on the script before, he did not seem dependent on it or tied to it. He managed to both read and establish eye contact with the judge.

"In every respect, be it color, design, or decor, interior or exterior, Eggs 'N' Such has intentionally mimicked Eggs 'N' Stuff for the express purpose of creating confusion amongst the Eggs 'N' Stuff clientele and unfairly diverting Eggs 'N' Stuff business. In the words of the great French existentialist—" He paused.

Ben realized there was a problem.

"—Albert Camus—" Derek got it entirely wrong. He pronounced the *t* in Albert and read Camus as if it were *came us*.

And then a miracle happened. The great Stone Face cracked. Schmidt tossed his head against the back of his chair and began to laugh, a loud, staccato clucking sound that reverberated throughout the keenly acoustic court-room.

The judge rubbed his hand against his forehead. "Came us," he murmured quietly, and then he began to laugh again.

Derek tried to continue, but stopped, realizing the futility of proceeding until the court had had its little joke. He turned and stared frigidly at Ben.

Ben received the chilling glance. He noticed Tidwell writing furiously in his notepad. Ben returned his attention to the table, shuffled some papers, and began formulating his future response. Inevitably, this was going to turn out to be all his fault.

* 20 *

"Okay, let's see what we've got here."

Sally Zacharias removed the documents from their envelope, extracted a pocket calculator from her purse, and began to scrutinize the five columns of letters and numbers.

Ben, Christina, and Sally, Christina's friend from the bookkeeping department, sat around a table at Angelo's. Christina had suggested that since Sally wasn't going to get paid for her services, she was at least entitled to a decent meal. Ben had given Sally the papers they found in Adams's office without telling her the name of the corporation to which he believed they referred. She stared at the mysterious documents for about ten minutes while Ben and Christina chitchatted over wine and garlic bread.

Eventually Sally announced her conclusions. "These appear to be summarizations of the annual financial reports of your unnamed, but apparently very rich, corporation over a number of years." She continued to scribble on her napkin and punch the buttons on her calculator. "I say *appear* because all the identifying labels in the left-hand column are either coded or abbreviated so that only an insider can read them. I can tell what the numbers are, but I can't tell what categories they represent."

"Why would anyone code their financial report?" Ben asked.

"It's not that unusual, especially with major corporations. They're always afraid of a hostile takeover or a shareholders' derivative suit or the fall of civilization as we know it. They're required to disclose some things to some people, but not all things to all people. Not unless the IRS or the SEC or the Justice Department forces them." She flipped through the papers. "This compilation was clearly not intended for public perusal."

"Is there anything in the report that anyone would want to hide?" Christina asked.

Sally reached for a slice of garlic bread and dipped it in

marinara sauce. "Hard to say. There is something unusual about the way this is formatted. See for yourself."

Ben leaned forward in an attempt to feign understanding. He hadn't the slightest idea what she was talking about.

"There seem to be three separate sources of income, or perhaps types of income, calculated independently. Then, on the final pages, the totals from each of the three sections are combined. And down here is the grand total. Over thirty-two million bucks."

Ben whistled. "Not bad."

Sally continued. "Now I can't be certain, but I'd be willing to bet that the figures in the middle right column represent the year's expenditures, and that this lower number reflects what's left over. In other words, how much money your mystery company made. Logically, this final page should indicate how those profits were distributed, but the numbers don't jibe. I haven't added it up but, oh, twenty thou and forty, fiftyish thou is about seventy, carry the five . . . let's call it twenty. Twenty million in expenses."

"That's a lot of expenses," Ben said.

Sally nodded. "We'll make a typical deduction for the inevitable tax losses, although this company probably has shelters built into the corporate structure to take care of a lot of that. We'll assume the impossible and suppose that no capital gains or depreciation skullduggery is going on. Subtract what appear to be line-item distributions and, oh, I'd say the difference is at least three million bucks. Just to give a ball-park figure."

Ben was totally confused. "Three million what?"

"Three million dollars made but unaccounted for in expenditures or profits."

"How could a mistake like that be made?" Ben asked. "Surely someone would notice."

"So it would seem," Christina said quietly.

"No one could divert three million dollars and get away with it."

"That depends on how many people had access to this summary," Sally said. "A lot can be hidden in annual reports and financial statements, especially if you keep your base financial data secret and can afford the cleverest accountants."

She tossed the papers on the table. "To most people, an annual report is just fifty pages of financial gobbledygook. Everyone looks at the bottom line and assumes the rest is accurate. Someone *else* has checked it, right?" She took another bite of garlic bread.

"Can you tell if anyone did anything . . . improper?"

"Not unless you can break the code in the left-hand column. Now, if I knew what company we were talking about . . . well, sometimes I hear things. So come clean. Who are you doing this for?"

Ben took the papers and placed them in his briefcase. "For a little girl with a lousy memory."

Sally's brow wrinkled. "I don't understand. What's this all about?"

"I wish I knew," Ben replied.

After lunch, Ben returned to his office and found a hand-delivered envelope waiting for him. Mike had sent over a copy of the MUD sheets from the phone company. The sheets listed every phone call made to and from Jonathan Adams's home and office phones during the seventy-two hours preceding his death. Next to the numbers, some staff person had written the name of each caller or callee and, frequently, a brief identification of the person named. There were no surprises. Several calls to other Sanguine executives and employees. Two calls to his wife. Four calls to franchisees in Michigan and Illinois.

Ben studied the names identified as Sanguine personnel. He pulled the Sanguine personnel directory out of the Eggs 'N' Such file and matched names to positions. Two of the interoffice calls, one on the day of the murder and the other on the day before, caught Ben's eye. The recipient of the calls was Harry Brancusci, a member of the Sanguine Enterprises accounting department.

Ben dialed the number.

"Hello?"

"Hello. Is this Harry Brancusci?"

A pause. "Who's this?"

Ben told him who he was. "I wondered if you could answer some questions for me regarding some Sanguine financial documents."

"I'm sorry, sir, but Sanguine accounting records are confidential." Did Brancusci's voice seem to quiver, or was it just a bad connection? "As a public corporation, we have to be very careful about revealing financial information. The SEC regulations are very complex—"

"I understand that," Ben interrupted. "I'm a lawyer. What's more, I'm *your* lawyer. At Raven, Tucker & Tubb. We represent Sanguine Enterprises. Anything you tell me is protected by the attorney-client privilege."

"Nonetheless," Brancusci insisted, "I'm afraid I can't provide that information unless I have express authorization from Mr. Sanguine himself. Shall I connect you with his office?"

Ben felt his blood pressure rising. "Can you explain

why Sanguine's annual expenditures and distributions don't
equal the total amount of gross profits?''

"I don't know what you're talking about," Brancusci
snapped. "Sanguine has over a dozen accountants here in
Tulsa alone, and I can assure you that every record is
checked and double-checked—"

"Why were you talking to Jonathan Adams just before
he was murdered?''

The voice on the other end broke. Brancusci sputtered
for a moment, then said, "It was business. Ours. And
none of yours.'' The receiver on the other end of the line
slammed down.

Ben sat motionless in his chair, listening to the dial
tone. I blew it, he realized. I should have gone over there
in person, so he couldn't blow me off so easily. Now he
knows everything I know. He'll find some way to explain
it away. And I'll be right back where I was before.

Nowhere.

* 21 *

Derek strode into his office and hung his jacket on the
brass hanger behind the door.

"Sorry I'm late, everyone. I've been at the clinic playing Stump the Surgeons. Damned idiots haven't the
slightest idea what's wrong with me.''

Ben and Christina sat in the chairs opposite Derek's desk. Maggie was sitting on the sofa parallel to both.

"Let me get straight to the point." Derek threw himself into the chair behind the desk. "I suppose you've all heard that we won the trade dress motion before Judge Schmidt."

There was a general chorus of congratulation.

"We've already received a written order of judgment. Receiving a written order from Judge Schmidt so soon after oral argument is truly amazing. I thought to myself, Schmidt must have really taken my arguments to heart. So I decided to reexamine our brief, to see what might've persuaded Schmidt so effectively."

Derek took a copy of the brief from his desk and began thumbing through the pages. "Upon rereading this brief, I found two misspelled words. One on page fourteen and another on page thirty-two." Derek ripped out the offending pages and slid them across the desk and under Ben's nose.

"It's a forty-page brief, sir."

"Yes, Kincaid," Derek said, his voice rising, "and it has two typos in it! This brief has *my name* on it! This brief is now part of the *public record*! And it's a public embarrassment. In the eyes of my peers—and, moreover, in the eyes of Judge Schmidt." The tone of his voice became increasingly nasty. "What is Judge Schmidt going to think when he looks at this brief and sees—" He pointed at the word *interim*, misspelled with a *u* between the *i* and the *m*.

"Inter-ee-um?" Ben offered.

Derek glared at him. "This isn't a joke, Kincaid. I hope you understand just how serious this is." Derek sunk back in his chair. "You wrote this mess, Kincaid. When was the last time you proofread it?"

Ben thought back. "On the Monday before the hearing. Then I gave it to Christina for cite checking."

Derek raised an eyebrow. "Passing the buck, Kincaid?"

"N-no, I was—I was just answering your question, sir."

Derek turned his attention to Christina. "What's your story, McCall?"

Christina shrugged. "I did all my checking vis à vis case citations, marked my corrections, and gave the red-ink copy to Maggie."

Derek turned and stared at Maggie. Her eyes were huge, and she looked as if she might burst into tears at any moment. "What about it, Maggie? You're supposed to do the final proofread on these things."

Maggie was so flustered she could barely speak. Her neck was covered with red blotches, and beads of sweat were forming along her hairline. "I . . . I'm sorry . . . I . . . you know how busy I am. I have to be at the phone in case you call, and . . . and now all the extra work for—" She jerked her head in Ben's direction.

The poor woman was melting like the Wicked Witch of the West. Ben sympathized. Maggie had been Derek's faithful servant for six years, and her reward was a public trip to the woodshed. A more merciful master might have interrupted her babbling, but Derek said nothing. He waited until she had thoroughly humiliated herself.

"Maggie, I want you to take this brief home over the weekend and read it, word for word, page by page. I want you to mark every typo, every miscitation, every misspelling—everything! Then, on Monday, we'll prepare a corrected brief and ask leave of court to amend."

Maggie nodded and took the brief.

"But, Mr. Derek," Ben said hesitantly. "If you ask the court for leave to amend our brief, the other side will do the same. We could end up reopening the entire motion. And we've already won!"

Derek raised his chin. "I'd rather lose a motion than live with this blight on my record."

Ben fell back against his chair. It was impossible.

"Maggie, you and Miss McCall may leave now. I'd like to speak to Mr. Kincaid in private about another matter."

Maggie found her feet and walked to the door. Her knees seemed weak and barely able to support her. Tears had finally sprung forth and were rolling down her cheeks. Christina quietly followed her out of the room.

"And shut the door behind you."

Christina shut the door.

Derek scrutinized Ben in silence. Ben wondered what his punishment would be. Copying dictionary pages, perhaps, or maybe he'd have to stay in during recess.

Several uncomfortable seconds elapsed before either of them spoke.

"How old did you say you are, Kincaid?"

"Twenty-nine."

"Mmmm." He sank back and stroked his chin. "I think I was older than you when I was twenty-nine."

Ben bit his tongue.

"You grew up in Nichols Hills, right? In the suburbs." Derek chuckled. "I'll bet your father never spanked you when you were a kid."

Ben kept on biting.

"I'll get to the point, Kincaid. I don't think you're going to cut it here. This isn't something that just occurred to me. I've been concerned about this since you arrived. I try to help the people I work with, Kincaid. I *care* about people. But I look across at you and I think: does this kid have the *fire* to be a successful litigator? And every time, I come up with the same answer: no."

Ben continued to stare back in stony silence.

"It's as if you don't know how to fight. You're not willing to be mean. I'll put it to you blunt, kid—in litigation, sometimes you have to be a bully, an out-and-out asshole. When you're a litigator, you've got to remember that every second of misery you can bring to the opposition is a second that will make them consider settling. Being an asshole is *always* in your client's best interest." He shifted positions. "But I don't see you doing that. You're too damn *nice*." He shook his head and formed a steeple with his fingers. "I guess I just don't see the *fire*."

After a few silent moments, Derek continued. "You know the adoption hearing is tomorrow morning."

"Yes."

"I want you to handle it. I don't mean just on paper. The whole shebang. Witnesses, argument, everything. Start to finish."

Ben's eyes grew to twice their normal size. "But, sir, I'm not prepared—"

"You see, Kincaid?" Derek sprang forward from his chair. "That's exactly what I mean. Most young associates would be chomping at the bit to do a hearing on their own. But not you. You hang back."

"It's not that, sir. It's just that it's an important matter and I haven't prepared—"

"So start preparing! You've got almost twenty-four hours. How much time do you need?"

Ben didn't say anything. He and Christina already had plans for the evening, but he could hardly reveal them to Derek.

"This is your big chance, Kincaid," Derek said, smiling. He propped his hands behind his head and stretched. "Prove me wrong."

* 22 *

Ben and Christina stood on the front porch and rang the bell. The sun was setting on the other side of the Arkansas, a spectacular pyrotechnic display that Ben barely noticed, much less appreciated. His mind was on the other side of the door, and on the next stop after this one.

No answer. Ben rang the bell again.

"Is this really necessary?" he asked.

"Yes," Christina said. "Don't be a wimp."

"Maybe we should wait a few more days."

"We've waited too long already. We need to go tonight."

Ben frowned. "We probably won't learn a thing."

"Probably. But we have to follow all our leads. Particularly the ones we risked life and limb to get."

"Yeah, yeah, yeah."

Inside the house, Ben could hear music playing at full volume. Something symphonic. Beethoven's Ninth, unless Ben was mistaken. He rang the bell again.

Someone had to be home. They probably just couldn't

hear the doorbell over the loud music. He tried the door; it wasn't locked.

No harm in poking my head in, Ben thought. He opened the door and stepped inside. Christina followed.

"Hello," he said loudly. Still no response.

In the center of the living room Ben saw Emily, sitting on the floor, eyes closed, listening to the music. Listening was an understatement; she was completely absorbed. It wasn't the pretentious, show-off absorption exhibited by snobs at the Philharmonic, Ben realized. She wasn't even aware they had come in.

The movement ended. Slowly coming out of her reverie, Emily opened her eyes, looked in Ben's direction, and screamed. The scream was uncommonly piercing, more than Ben would have thought possible from an eight-year-old girl.

Bertha Adams came running from the back room, her heavy legs thumping against the carpet, her right hand pressed against her chest. "Mr. Kincaid," she said, flushed and breathless. "I didn't hear you come in. Afraid I was napping again."

She saw Emily cowering on the floor. "It's all right, Emily. I'm here now. Remember me?" Emily responded to her voice by crawling across the carpet and clinging to Bertha's legs.

Ben crouched down to Emily's level. "It's okay," he said softly. "We've met before. I'm Mr. Kincaid. I'm your friend."

Emily looked pensively from Ben to Bertha. Bertha nodded and stroked the girl along her shoulders.

"You remember Mr. Kincaid, don't you, child?" She smoothed down the tiny girl's hair. "It's always hard when she comes back from the music. She's at her happiest when the music's playing. She's at peace. But when the music's over, it's like dragging the poor girl back from another world.''

Emily still clung tightly to Bertha's leg.

"We came for a specific purpose," Christina reminded Ben.

"We came," he said hesitantly, "because I need . . . a photograph."

Bertha looked at the floor and said nothing. Poor woman, Ben thought. I bring it all back to her.

"You mean of my husband," Bertha said quietly after a moment. "You can say it. I won't turn to mush. You want a picture of my dead husband."

Ben nodded. "For identification purposes."

Bertha's brow wrinkled slightly. "I already gave a snapshot to the police."

"Yes, I know. I need another one."

Bertha surveyed the living room. "I've always said this is the best picture he ever took." She removed a sepia-toned photo in a gold frame from a tabletop. In the picture, she stood next to her husband—she in a lace-covered white dress, he in a double-breasted brown suit. The picture was at least thirty-five years old. It was obviously their wedding picture.

Ben cleared his throat. "I think, perhaps, something more contemporary might be appropriate. . . ." His voice trailed off.

"Well, I have these wallet-size black-and-whites that were taken about a year ago. A photographer came to the office to take pictures for a Sanguine public relations brochure. Took a lot of personal photos while he was there."

She withdrew a photo from a drawer beneath her china

cabinet. "Not very flattering, but you can tell it's him."
She continued to stare at the photograph and seemed lost
in thought. After a moment, she passed it to Ben. "I do
miss him," she said simply.

Ben took the photo and thanked her.

"The hearing is tomorrow morning at ten," he reminded her. "Even though she probably won't be called
into the courtroom, you need to bring Emily."

Bertha nodded.

Ben crouched down and smiled at Emily. "Would you
like me to turn the record over?"

Emily nodded eagerly. Ben flipped the record on the
stereo.

The music swelled. Emily's eyes closed and once more
she was a part of the symphony. Ben's last sight, as he
and Christina walked out the front door, was of Emily,
the girl with no past, no future, barely a present, sitting
in the middle of the living room, joining the music in a
reverential symbiosis.

They walked silently down the sidewalk to Ben's Honda.

"You're not saying very much," Ben said to Christina
as he started the car.

"No."

Ben placed his hand on her shoulder. "She's quite a
girl, isn't she?"

Christina nodded. "How old is she?"

"Eight, we think."

Christina stared at the road straight ahead. "Is that
right?" She released a soft laugh. "That's how old my
little girl would be."

"You never told me you had a baby."

"I didn't," she replied. She pressed her fingers against

her left temple and stared out the passenger-side window
for the remainder of the drive.

* 23 *

The Red Parrot was not quite a cowboy bar, but then,
Tulsa was not quite a cowboy town. Tulsa did have equiv-
alents—transient oil rig hands, truckers, bikers, construc-
tion workers, miscellaneous unemployed, your basic
criminal element—and all of them apparently frequented
the Red Parrot.

Ben and Christina stepped into the smoke-filled bar.
Ben kept telling himself to be bold, but he knew he wasn't
convincing anybody, including himself.

They had both dressed down for the occasion, in blue
jeans, cotton western shirts, and boots. Ben even had a
western belt with BEN branded on the back. Something his
grandmother had given him that he'd never worn until now.
Ben thought Christina looked outrageous in her pink suede
cowgirl jacket, but then, he reflected, no more so than she
did in her daily work clothes.

Ben observed that the Red Parrot was roughly divided
into four quadrants. Quadrant one: the bar, where dirty
men and dirtier women stood shoulder to shoulder quaff-
ing longnecks and complaining about the day's events.
Quadrant two: the tables and booths, the intermediate step

between picking a woman up at the bar and taking her home for a quick but purposeful encounter. Quadrant three: the two pool tables, each with a trail of quarters on the side and men lined up waiting to play. Finally, quadrant four: the games area, where menacing-looking men tossed menacing-looking steel darts in the general direction of an oversized dart board. In the center of the bar was a multicolored Wurlitzer jukebox wailing some Hank Williamsesque tune about sixteen-wheelers and cowboys and the day "my mama got out of prison."

"This joint ain't big enough for the two of us, pilgrim," Christina said.

Ben looked at her blankly.

"Get it? Pilgrim? Sleazy western saloon, thugs, bad side of town. It just seemed to follow—"

"I understood, Christina."

"Oh. *Pardonnez moi.*" She looked hurt.

His lips turned up slightly. "Smile when ya say that, pardner."

She did.

Ben scoped out the clientele. The crowd looked seriously tough. Lots of muscle, tattoos, and stubble. Several men were wearing jeans jackets with matching emblems on the back. They were all members of something and Ben suspected it wasn't the Moose Lodge. At the table closest to the bar, two men were taking turns stacking upended shot glasses. The tower already rose above the level of their shoulders.

Meanwhile, over in the darts area, the game had taken a nasty turn—the dart board was replaced by human beings. It was a local variant on mumblety-peg; players alternated between standing against the wall and throwing the darts. Apparently, the object was to throw the dart as

close as possible to the sucker on the wall without touch-
ing him. Two throws, then the players switch places. Closest throw wins. Thrower's option as to what part of the
body to aim toward. Flinching was an automatic forfeit,
although striking the target body with the dart merely re-
sulted in a reduction in points.

"Well, I'm thirsty," Ben said. He and Christina wedged
themselves into a small opening at the bar. "I believe I'll
have an amaretto sour."

"Get a beer," Christina said curtly.

"What?"

"You heard me. Beer."

Ben looked confused. The bartender, a burly musta-
chioed fellow in a red-checkered shirt, walked up to
them.

"What kind have you got?" Ben asked him.

"Just say *beer*," Christina whispered.

"Beer," Ben obeyed. "Two."

The bartender nodded and moved toward the taps.

"An amaretto sour," Christina muttered. "These guys
would use you for a dust mop."

The bartender brought two mugs of beer and set them
in front of Ben and Christina. Ben tossed a five onto the
bar.

A thin, wiry man with a red steel wool beard and a cap
saw the five go down. "Were you in the service?" he
asked. His voice was like gravel.

"I beg your pardon?"

The man's teeth were tightly clenched, even as he spoke.
"Don't beg my pardon, man. Don't *ever* beg my pardon.
I hate beggars, man. Fuckin' hate 'em."

He pounded his fist against the bar so hard that Ben's
beer wobbled and bounced. "I asked if you were in the

goddamn service!" He was shouting. The smell of beer and booze and tooth rot was thick on his breath.

"Uhhh, no," Ben said quietly, not looking him in the eye. "Were you?"

"Damn right I was. Damn right." He pounded the bar again. "I don't suppose you fought in the war?"

"N-no—"

"Hell, no. Too goddamn good to be in the war!"

Ben had the distinct feeling he wasn't handling this very well. "I spent a year in the Peace Corps," he said softly.

"You think that's an *excuse*?" The man spat as he yelled. He emphasized the last word by knocking over his beer with his fist.

"Let's go," Christina whispered in Ben's ear. She tugged at his sleeve. "Pronto."

Ben took a step back from the bar.

"You know what I ought to do with you? Do you?" The man followed Ben. They were practically nose to nose. Ben took another step back. The wiry man followed.

A few others at the bar turned around to watch the fun. The man who had been standing to the right of Redbeard jabbed a friend and pointed.

"Leave him alone," the bartender said as he popped the lid off another longneck. "He's too young. He doesn't know. Here, have a beer on me."

God bless the bartender, Ben thought. But the bartender's offer didn't seem to make any difference. The man kept coming. Ben kept backing up.

There was a sudden, loud smashing sound. Ben whirled. He had backed into the nearest table and knocked over the tower of upended shotglasses. The supreme effort of the combined lifetimes of the two bikers lay dashed and broken into a million pieces on the floor.

"Sonovabitch!" the larger of the two men exclaimed. He was wearing a jeans jacket with a skull-and-crossbones appliqué on the back and had silver chains looped around his waist. He threw his chair back and stood up, pounding one fist against his hand. A dark-haired woman from the back of the room came forward and laid her hands on his shoulder. Ben couldn't see either of them clearly in the dark haze of the bar.

"Oh, God," Ben mumbled, trying not to sound too pathetic. "I was just backing up. I—I—"

"He didn't mean it," Christina said, stepping between the larger of the two thugs and Ben. "This brain-dead bully over here was forcing him backward."

"This *what*?" Redbeard echoed. "Whaddas that mean?" He shoved Christina aside, not gently.

By this time, most of the people in the bar were rubbernecking for a better view of the show. Ben had nowhere left to maneuver. Opposing hands clamped down on both his shoulders. He knew he was finished. What Redbeard didn't do to him, Skull-and-Crossbones surely would.

"All right, nobody moves," Ben said, swallowing hard.

Skull-and-Crossbones laughed heartily. "What the hell?"

"Nobody moves," he repeated, taking a deep breath. "I'm an undercover cop. Kincaid, Tulsa PD, Vice. Badge number 499."

The two men looked skeptical. "Yeah?" Redbeard said. "So show us your badge."

"Can't you see I'm in disguise, idiot?" Ben muttered. "Undercover cops don't carry badges."

Skull laughed. "The one that busted me last year did.

Nice try, though." He snapped his fingers. "Hey, guys, I got an idea. I think it's time for a game of darts."

He dragged Ben into the darts quadrant and shoved him against the wall. Two other thugs wearing matching jeans jackets held Ben in place in the target area.

"I don't play darts," Ben protested. "I wouldn't be a challenge for you."

"Not true," Skull said as someone handed him a fistful of darts. "I haven't played in years." He aimed a dart at Ben's face.

"Ben!" someone squealed. It seemed to come from the dark-haired woman hanging on Skull's shoulder. "It's Benjy!"

Ben squinted his eyes and peered into the darkness. *"Mona?"* he whispered.

It *was* Mona. It wasn't a face he was likely to forget. The current spouse of the senior partner in his firm was there, at the Red Parrot, with this biker. She was dressed in a dark-blue denim jacket and a black, hip-hugging, leather miniskirt, with some cheap metal jewelry dangling from her ears and wrists.

Skull asked, "You know this weasel?"

"Yes, yes," Ben said quickly. "I know her. We go *way* back."

"You been with my woman?"

Ben stuttered. "Buh . . . well, no . . . I mean, not—"

"Hell, what do I care?" A deep and scary laugh erupted from Skull's lips. "Who hasn't been? She's older than this bar!"

Mona's face seemed to melt. The product of hours of skillfully applied cosmetics disintegrated in an instant.

"I do know him," she said softly. "You'd better leave

him alone. He *is* an undercover cop.'' She winked at Ben.

"Really? Christ. Why didn't you say so?'' He turned halfheartedly toward Ben. "I thought we knew all the narcs around here. No hard feelings, huh? Just having some fun.''

"Right,'' Ben said, nodding.

Christina appeared behind his right shoulder and whispered in his ear. "Show him the picture. While we're buddies.''

"Oh, right.'' Ben saw that most of the bar's attention was fixed in his direction.

"Look,'' he said loudly, "I'm going to pass around a photograph and I want to talk to anybody who knows anything about this man. And I mean *anyone*.'' He cast a mean look in the direction of his former adversaries.

"Don't press your luck,'' Christina whispered.

Ben passed the picture to Skull, who accepted it without saying a word. Mona's identification of Ben as a cop seemed to have seriously altered the degree of respect he was receiving.

"He's been here,'' Skull said after examining the picture a moment. "Not recently, but he's been here.''

"Do you remember if he was here Monday night, last week?''

"Yeah. That sounds right. He sat in one of the back booths talking to some other guy. I guess it was a guy—I never actually saw a face. Was wearing a long white overcoat with one of those high collars. They both left together. That's all I know.''

Why is it, Ben wondered, other strangers come here and go unnoticed and unmolested, but I'm here maybe ten minutes and practically a dead man? He circulated the

picture throughout the bar. A few people remembered seeing Adams the night he was killed, but no one had anything to add to what Skull (whose actual name turned out
to be Marvin) had said. No one had seen the face of the
person he talked with.

Ben returned the photo to his wallet and started toward
the door. He saw Mona and stopped.

"Thanks," he said.

She placed her right hand against his cheek. "I've
missed you, Ben. Ever since the night of the party. It meant
a lot to me. I think about you all the time. You haven't
been returning my calls."

Ben smiled uncomfortably. He couldn't tell whether
Christina was hearing this.

Mona twirled her finger through a lock of his hair. "You
don't have to run off, you know. The night is young."

Ben took a step back. "Thanks, but I have a court hearing tomorrow morning."

"Hey," Marvin said, stepping beside Ben, "I'm sorry
about everything, man. I mean, the darts and the rough
stuff. I've been drinking. I got a little crazy—you know
how it is. I didn't know you were friends of Mona's.
Maybe we could all get together sometime and double date
or something."

Ben swallowed. "Yeah, or something."

"Yeah, it'd be fun, huh?" Marvin put his arm around
Mona, then slapped her on the backside.

Mona gave him a chilly smile. She clearly had not forgotten his earlier remark.

Ben waved, and he and Christina left the bar. The cool
night air was bracing. "I feel like I just crawled away from
the edge of a crumbling cliff," he said.

Christina smiled. "You know, that Marvin dude was

kind of scary at first, but when you got to know the real
man inside, he was all right. Kind of cuddly, actually.''

Ben didn't say a word.

* 24 *

Ten after ten. The judge was late.

Probably reading the briefs at the last moment, Ben
mused. He hoped the waiting didn't last much longer. Bertha, sitting in the chair next to him at the defendants' table, was already so nervous Ben had serious misgivings
about having her testify. But he had no choice. She was
his only witness.

He had tried to calm her; he carefully described a domestic proceeding to her as a sort of miniature trial without a jury and most of the procedural hassles. Despite his
efforts, the idea of cross-examination and *Perry Mason*
tactics sent her into a quiet panic.

Not that Bertha had an exclusive on nervousness. Ben
felt a trembling in his knees he feared would not disappear
when he stood up to address the court. Derek, of course,
was no help at all. He had ambled to the courthouse and
now sat in the back row of the tiny spectators' gallery.
Earlier, Derek had opined that it would not be to their
advantage to have more lawyers sitting at their table than
the Department of Human Services did. The Raven firm

already had a reputation for being overpriced big shots—
the kind of lawyers state court judges, who typically
come from small firms or unsuccessful solo practices,
hate. They didn't want to seem to be overdoing it or
trying to strong-arm the judge. Therefore, Derek explained, he would not sit at counsel table with Ben and
Bertha.

Besides, Derek had told Ben, you have to learn to fly
solo sometime. Being in court is a long series of tough,
quick decisions made by the seat of your pants. It won't
do you any good to have me there to defer to when the
hard decisions come. This is your chance to prove you
have the fire of a litigator. So Derek sat calmly in the back
of the courtroom while Ben prepared to bring the experience of not quite two weeks of private practice to bear
before the court.

Ben checked his watch. Ten-fifteen.

What's taking so long? The trembling in his knees became more pronounced. He looked back at Derek. Derek
seemed to be in a perfectly wretched mood, even by Derek's standards. Rumor had it that he had separated from
Louise, was living by himself in an apartment on the south
side, and spending entire nights in high-class watering
holes. Great. Derek never struck Ben as being all that
stable even in the best of circumstances, which these evidently weren't.

Mercifully, Emily would be spared the full proceeding,
although she had to be available if either side wished to
call her as a witness. Not very likely. The DHS would
assume she wanted to stay where she was, and Ben knew
she couldn't help Bertha's case. She would not be called.

Ben tried to review his notes while he waited for the
judge, but it was impossible. His mind was racing. A

snippet of Gilbert and Sullivan kept running through his head: "The law is the true embodiment/Of everything that's excellent/It has no kind of fault or flaw . . ."

"All rise."

Everyone in the small courtroom rose. Judge Mayberry walked into the courtroom and settled himself in the thronelike, elevated black chair. Ben marveled at the amount of ceremony even the most low-level domestic disputes judge could insist upon. Mayberry enjoyed the pomp and circumstance, the black robe, the latinate phrases, the whole legal works. Ben made a mental note to be advocative, but with the most deferential attitude toward the judge possible.

The court's bailiff read the style of the case. "In the matter of the minor Emily X, case number FS-672-92-M. Two motions are presently before the court. The Department of Human Services has brought a motion to remove the child from her present place of residence to the custody and supervision of the DHS. In response, the court has ordered Bertha Adams to show cause why the child should not be so removed. Also, Bertha Adams has brought a motion to legally adopt the minor child Emily X."

"Are all the parties present?" Mayberry asked. He spoke slowly, with a hint of a drawl. Ben wasn't sure if it was the judge's background showing through or his desire to affect a folksy, good-ol'-boy persona.

The man sitting at plaintiff's table rose and began speaking.

"The Department of Human Services is present, your honor. My name is Albert Sokolosky."

Sokolosky was in his mid-thirties and wore round, rimless eyeglasses, probably to affect a lawyerly look and make him appear older than he really was. He was extremely tall and thin, as if he had been held at both ends and stretched.

In a sudden rush, Ben realized he didn't really know the protocol of the courtroom. *Should I stand now? Should I wait for the judge to look at me? Why the hell isn't Derek up here to tell me these things?*

He stood. "My name is Benjamin Kincaid, your honor. I represent—"

"Just a minute, son. Give the clerk a chance to get the first name down."

Ben waited as the woman sitting beside the bailiff painstakingly scrawled out her best guess at the spelling of Sokolosky. In domestic proceedings, true court reporters, able to silently transcribe testimony at the speed of light, were not used. Instead, a tape recording was made, and for a fee, the court would make a copy of the tape available to any party who wanted to pay a court reporter to transcribe the tape, at an exorbitant rate often exceeding the monetary value of the domestic dispute. Which explains why lawyers rarely had a transcript made of proceedings in domestic matters. Which the judges knew. Which had the unfortunate result of giving the judges carte blanche to indulge themselves in any eccentricity or petty bullying their hearts desired.

The judge at last looked up; he offered Ben a patronizing, frightening grin.

"All right, son, give us your name now."

"Benjamin Kincaid, your honor." He swallowed hard. "I represent Bertha Adams in regard to both motions." His voice shook a bit, but he managed to control it. He hoped.

"Gentlemen," Mayberry said, scanning the courtroom

without making eye contact with anyone, "I don't see any reason to drag this thing out and complicate what should be a simple, unified matter. If you will give me your basic positions in your opening statements, we'll hear from Mrs. Adams, and then we should be able to resolve the motions in short order."

Ben listened carefully. The subtext, he thought, is the judge has something else he wants to do today. Pressing golf game or an attractive piece on the side. Ben made a mental note to cut his presentation to the bare essentials.

"Opening statements, gentlemen."

Ben rose to his feet, then realized that Sokolosky was also standing. Sokolosky's motion was first on the docket. That meant he spoke first.

"I think it would be better if we spoke one at a time, son." The judge chuckled, then looked to his clerk for a response. The woman grinned.

Mortified, Ben sat down.

Sokolosky walked to the podium. "Your honor, as you say, this is an extremely simple case. It is also a textbook litany of wanton misbehavior, of disobedience to the laws and policies of this state, and a testament to the prudence of the judicial tenets announced by courts such as this one." He gestured deferentially to the judge.

"Your honor, Emily X is a foundling. Bertha Adams *found* the child. She did not report her discovery to the Department of Human Services, although she was advised to do so. She did not report the finding to any of several missing child agencies active in this state. She did not attempt to find suitable foster parents or to locate the child's biological parents. She simply took the little girl home, to lead a cloistered, secluded life. She lied to her neighbors and kept the little girl to herself.

"In this day and age, we hear many rumors about elderly people snatching children from shopping centers and forcing them to become domestic servants or . . . to adopt even more revolting roles. While we are not suggesting that anything like that has occurred—"

The hell you aren't, Ben thought.

"—there is something . . . unusual about Mrs. Adams's handling of this matter."

Sokolosky shuffled through a file. "The Department has prepared a report, your honor, based upon what little information is known about the woman who calls herself Bertha Adams. Although I do not wish to appear indelicate, the Department earnestly believes that she is not a suitable foster or adoptive parent for several reasons. She fails to meet many, indeed most, of the objective criteria established by the Department."

Sokolosky gave a copy of the report to the bailiff, who then handed it to Judge Mayberry. He gave another copy to Ben.

Ben quickly glanced over the report. It was a graph-style report titled "Parent Evaluation." Long graph lines indicated the areas of inadequacy. *Age* was the longest. The report also noted her lack of experience at child raising, the absence of any regular income of her own, and, without explanation, the fact that she was a single parent.

Ben closed the report folder, furious. The report was intentionally misleading.

"Your honor, we do not doubt that Mrs. Adams has formed some sort of attachment or"—he paused meaningfully—"dependence on the child she has kept for so long. But we have been charged by the state of Oklahoma to try to find the best home possible for each such ward of the state. We have an extensive list of ideal parents who would simply love to adopt a little girl, even one as old as Emily. We respectfully request that this court deliver custody of the child to the DHS so that we can assign her to a permanent home.'' Sokolosky collected his papers and sat down.

The judge evidently felt the need for some levity. "*Now* it's your turn to talk, son,'' he chuckled. He looked again to his clerk for a response, which she freely gave. How nice to have your own standing audience, Ben thought.

Ben rose, attempting to exude confidence. He placed his notes on the podium. He had meticulously planned his strategy for his opening argument. He couldn't possibly justify the way Jonathan and Bertha had kept Emily without telling anyone, so he was better off not dwelling upon it. Instead, he would emphasize Bertha's warmth and good nature, her nurturing of the child despite difficult circumstances, and the bonding that had taken place.

"Your honor,'' he began. His voice sounded scratchy. He cleared his throat and started again. "Your honor, I notice that, although the DHS complains that my client doesn't meet many of their generalized, preconceived qualifications, they have never stated that she is or would be an unfit parent. Emily has lived with Mrs. Adams for almost a year now, and yet the DHS has made no complaints whatsoever about the child's treatment during that time. Mrs. Adams may not have followed the proper procedures, but I submit that she nonetheless has earned the right to be considered Emily's foster parent in loco parentis. I understand that the Department has its rules and procedures, and that it likes to see that they are observed. But the dispositive legal question in a proceeding of this

nature is: What is in the best interests of the child? A
slavish devotion to administrative procedure is not more
important than the child herself, and I'm sure that this
court cannot be fooled into making a decision that holds
otherwise.''

"Don't underestimate me," the judge said. Again,
the chuckle, the quick glance to the peanut gallery.
Ben had the distinct feeling he was not making an impression.

"Thank you, son," the judge said suddenly. "I think
I've grasped your point."

Ben stammered, then fell silent. He wasn't half-finished
yet.

"It's pretty clear to me that these two motions are mu-
tually exclusive," the judge continued. "If I give the DHS
the girl, I can't let Mrs. Adams adopt her. And if I let
Mrs. Adams adopt the girl, then the DHS ain't gonna get
her. So I'm going to consolidate these two motions and
make a single decision at the conclusion of the hearing. If
the Department has no objection, I'm going to ask Mr.
Kincaid to call Mrs. Adams to the stand, 'cause it looks
to me like she's the only person I'm gonna need to hear
from to decide this one."

Sokolosky half rose with a little bow. "No objections,
your honor. We concur."

Consolidation. Cut straight to the key witness. Again,
the hurry-up treatment. Why was Mayberry so determined
to conclude this hearing?

Ben called Bertha to the stand. She took her seat at the
judge's lower left with relative ease, but it was clear to
Ben she was extremely nervous. Realistically, Ben knew
he couldn't count on her for much.

Slowly and methodically, Ben took Bertha through the course of her life with Emily. How her late husband brought her home. How they took her to the police, but no trace of a parent could be found. How happy Emily made their home. How, at the suggestion of Joseph Sanguine, they found a lawyer to help them legally adopt Emily. Following Ben's prior recommendation, she did not mention Emily's neurological condition. Bertha spoke in a flat, even tone of voice. Ben knew that her nervousness was affecting her voice, but he was worried that it might be making her sound disinterested or artificial.

The judge listened to her testimony without comment or expression.

"Mrs. Adams," Ben continued, "if this court allows you to adopt Emily, will you do everything in your power to raise her in the best possible way?"

"Yes," she answered simply.

Damn. Ben didn't know what to do. That leading question was her opening to expand on her testimony, to deliver a persuasive speech, to convince the court of her earnestness. Ben had prepared her for this before the hearing. In her nervousness, though, she had forgotten everything. She had given a dry, one-word, almost noncommittal answer.

"Let me ask you again, Mrs. Adams."

"Objection," Sokolosky said, rising to his feet. "Asked and answered."

"Sustained," the judge responded without hesitation. "Anything further, counsel?"

Ben couldn't think of anything more to do. "No more questions," he said.

Sokolosky rose and walked to the podium to begin his

cross-examination. Ben noticed that his long yellow legal pad apparently contained pages of canned questions. He hoped Sokolosky's plan was not to badger Bertha into saying something harmful by keeping her on the stand for an unbearably long period of time. He sensed that Bertha was already close to her limit.

"Mrs. Adams, you've kept Emily for almost a year now, is that correct?" Sokolosky was adopting a businesslike, just-the-facts-ma'am approach. Distancing himself and the court from the situation and its inherent emotionality.

"Emily has stayed with us, yes."

"You reported discovering her to the police, didn't you?"

"Yes, I've said that."

"But, Mrs. Adams, the police told you that you should contact the Department of Human Services, didn't they?"

Bertha hesitated. "Yes."

Sokolosky continued to drive his point home. "In fact, I think it's safe to say that they assumed you would do so, don't you?"

"Well, I don't know. Perhaps. Yes."

"Yes. Probably you even *assured* them that you would. But you didn't, ever, at any time, contact the Department, did you?"

Bertha looked downward. "No."

"No. You kept your little treasure to yourself."

Ben didn't know what to do. Nothing Sokolosky said was really objectionable. Obnoxious, yes. Prejudicial, sure, but a judge, unlike a jury, is assumed to be able to sort the prejudicial from the probative without help from counsel. Ben didn't see Mayberry as the sort of judge who would enjoy a lot of time-consuming objections, especially when he was so anxious to move things along.

"I expect Emily is quite a good little helper to have around the house."

Bertha's face changed slightly. "No," she said, with a soft laugh, "not really."

For the first time, Sokolosky smiled. At the judge, not Bertha. "Oh, now, Mrs. Adams, haven't you ever asked Emily to help you . . . oh, let's say, wash the dishes?"

"Y-yes, of course, but—"

"Maybe to take out the trash."

"Yes. Certainly—"

"Fetch you a drink. Do the ironing. Keep you company."

"It isn't *like* that," Bertha protested. Her voice rose in pitch with her agitation. Sokolosky had put her on the defensive; she sounded defensive. "You're trying to make it sound like—"

"Just answer the questions, Mrs. Adams." The judge cut her off in midsentence. "Your counsel will make the speeches for you, no doubt." He looked down disapprovingly at Bertha.

"But he's making it sound like—"

"I won't tell you again, Mrs. Adams." The judge looked away. Bertha held her tongue.

Sokolosky took a long pause, letting the awkward moment fester. "Just answer one question for me, Mrs. Adams," he said finally. "Just one simple yes-or-no question. In the entire time that Emily has lived with you, can you honestly say that Emily has developed a strong attachment to you?"

Ben looked up at Sokolosky. He *knew*.

Bertha hesitated. Ben could see her eyes watering.

"Objection, your honor!" Ben found himself on his feet before he had consciously formed the thought.

The judge looked at him with a raised eyebrow. "Really, son? Sounds probative to me. What are the grounds for your objection, pray tell?"

Ben stuttered and hemmed. He didn't have any grounds. And he didn't want to refer to Emily's disorder. "It just . . . it isn't fair, your honor."

The judge nodded his head with an exaggerated bobbing motion. "Oh, the ol' it-just-isn't-fair objection." He laughed, and Sokolosky laughed quietly with him. Opportunistic bastard, Ben thought. "I don't think I'm familiar with that one, Mr. Kincaid. Perhaps I need to reread the Oklahoma Rules of Evidence." Even Derek got a laugh out of that one.

After the courtroom settled down, the judge returned his attention to Bertha. "Overruled. The witness *will* answer the question."

"I don't remember it," Bertha said, in a trembling voice.

Sokolosky chirped in to refresh her memory. "I asked you if you can honestly say that Emily has formed a deep attachment to you. Unlike Mr. Kincaid here, I don't think it would be so outrageous to find that two people who have lived together for nearly a year are fond of one another. Has she ever told you she loves you?"

"No," Bertha said softly.

"I don't think the court heard that."

"No," she said, much louder, her head turned down. Tears were streaming from her eyes.

"Does she invite other children over to meet you?"

"No."

"Does she ever wake up in the morning and call your name?"

"Of course not," Bertha said. "She isn't able to—"

"Yes or no, Mrs. Adams."

Ben steeled himself. "Objection."

Sokolosky cast a downward glance at Ben. "Again, Mr. Kincaid?"

He knows, Ben thought, glaring across the room at Sokolosky. The bastard. He knows and he won't let her explain. "Your honor, the witness has a right to explain her answer. The court can't force her to answer yes or no."

The judge spoke, his voice tinged with irritation. Ben immediately realized it was a mistake to tell the court what it couldn't do. "This is cross-examination, Mr. Kincaid, not direct. You may recall some discussion of cross-examination in law school. Mr. Sokolosky has the right to ask yes-or-no questions, and when he does, she is obliged to answer them in a like fashion." He leaned back in his chair. "You've already had ample opportunity to develop the facts on direct, Mr. Kincaid."

Sokolosky didn't miss a beat. "Mrs. Adams, I repeat: Does Emily ever wake up in the morning and call out your name?"

"No," Bertha whispered. She was crying full force now. Her makeup was smeared hideously. She was totally broken.

Ben swore silently to himself. The fact was she looked guilty. And incompetent. Like someone who got caught. No one you'd trust a little girl to.

Sokolosky paused yet another significant moment, then said, "I think that's enough, your honor."

Judge Mayberry rustled a few papers in his hands. "I am prepared to rule."

"But, your honor," Ben said, rising to his feet. "My redirect—"

"Not necessary. I've reached a decision."

"Your honor, I have a right to rehabilitate my witness."

The judge's voice rose to a shout. "Son, you don't have a *right* to anything! This court sits in equity, and it can do damn near anything it pleases. It's time for you to cease this whining every time you don't get your way. You sound like a two-year-old, not an officer of the court." He mimicked Ben in a squealing voice. " 'I have a right, I have a right.' " He pointed his finger directly at Ben. "If you're going to practice law in my court, son, you're going to have to grow up."

Ben was frozen in silence.

The judge took a deep breath. "You have some nerve even protesting this decision, which we all knew damn well was inevitable. Your client has broken every regulation in the book. Feel fortunate I have decided not to issue sanctions, due to her advanced age. I think it's pretty clear what took place here. I don't like it a bit, and there's no law firm in the world big enough to make me think otherwise."

Bertha, still sitting in the witness box, had dissolved into uncontrolled sobs.

"The DHS motion is granted. Bertha Adams's motion is denied. The child Emily X is to be placed in the custody of the DHS immediately."

Immediately. Ben was stunned. Emily was practically being ripped from Bertha's arms.

"Your honor." A voice came from the back of the courtroom. "My name is Richard Derek. I also represent Mrs. Adams."

The judge nodded. He was obviously acquainted with Derek.

"Your honor, I understand that your decision is made, and I don't contest it. But this child has lived in Mrs. Adams's home nearly a year. All her belongings are there. All her acquaintances are there. Surely it would be more humane to give her a week to make her goodbyes."

The judge considered this for a moment. He obviously liked the part that implied he would *surely* act humanely. Derek had a talent for judicial manipulation Ben obviously lacked.

"Very well. The DHS will pick the child up at Mrs. Adams's place of residence one week from today, nine o'clock in the morning. But I hold you responsible, Mr. Derek, to see that she is there and ready."

"Understood. Thank you, your honor."

All parties rose, and the judge left the courtroom. Shakily, Bertha tried to stand and walk away from the witness chair. Ben knew he should help her, but he couldn't. He could barely help himself. Before Derek came to counsel table to speak to him, he raced out of the courtroom and into the nearest bathroom, where he was sick as he had never been sick before.

* 25 *

No one said a word as they walked back from the court-house to the Raven offices. Ben went directly to his office and closed the door. He sat in the chair behind his desk, lights off, not moving a muscle.

After several minutes passed, there was a knock on the door. Without waiting for a response, Derek came in, frowned for a moment, and turned on the lights.

"Don't worry about reporting to the client," Derek said. "I've already taken care of that."

"You talked to Emily?"

"I talked to our client, Joseph Sanguine," Derek answered evenly. "He was sorry we were unsuccessful, but he has realized from the outset that the case was a losing proposition. All in all, I don't think he was dissatisfied with our services."

"Well, that's a relief," Ben muttered under his breath.

Derek plopped a heavy brown file onto Ben's desk. "Here's your next assignment. Another Sanguine matter. I'll be supervising your work, but it's your baby. Take it and run with it. And feel privileged—this case is a gem. Lots of money at stake. It was originally going to Bryce Chambers."

Reassigned from Chambers? Ben glanced at the file.

Chambers was a senior associate. He'd been with the firm for five or six years. "Why would I get a good case originally designated for Bryce Chambers?"

Derek shrugged. "It was Sanguine's idea. Maybe he wants to make up for the dog you just tried."

"What about our appeal?" Ben asked.

"No appeal. What would we appeal anyway? The judge acted within his discretion."

"Due process violation," Ben said quickly. "Procedural errors. He denied us the right to redirect—"

"Forget it. You have a right to tell your story and a right to confront those who speak against you. The Constitution doesn't say anything about the right to *redirect*."

"But it's not fair." Ben's voice quavered. "The judge can't change the rules in the middle of the game. We anticipated the right to redirect."

"Ben. Let me give you some advice. Don't dwell on this case. It's in your best interest. In fact, it's in everyone's best interest to simply forget about it. Move on to something else. Better luck next time and all that." He paused. "And that includes all your cloak-and-dagger stuff. Don't think I don't know what's been going on. It would be different if our client wanted to press the issue. But he doesn't. He's ready to move on to something else, and we should be, too."

Ben didn't say anything.

"Ben, I know how you feel. Everyone eventually experiences their first loss in court and everyone hates it. But you have to face up to the facts, Ben—*you lost*." He waited a moment and let the words sink in. "And now you have to move on."

Derek walked toward the door. "You've got a second

chance here, Kincaid—a new case to prove yourself with. So don't blow it. And don't forget what I told you yesterday. I'll be watching you carefully.''

Just before he left, he stopped and added, ''You know, you really weren't bad in court today. It just didn't work out.''

After Derek left, Ben turned his chair and looked out the window, down thirty-eight stories to the city below. Somehow, Derek's condolences only made things worse.

He knew he had let Bertha down. And Emily. That beautiful little girl was going to be dragged away from a home where she was as content as she was capable of being, shuffled through a dozen foster homes, one after another, no one able to cope for long with this strange, brain-damaged girl. Each move would be more and more disorienting, especially for a girl whose only orientation is to the present instant.

Ben covered his face with his hand. He should have won. He should have stayed home last night and prepared more. He should have made the judge understand. He had only himself to blame.

Another knock on the door. A head poked through a slim opening. ''May I come in?''

Ben looked up. It was Alvin. Of all people. ''What is it?'' Ben asked.

Alvin closed the door and perched himself in the closer of the two chairs.

''If you've come to give me a pep talk,'' Ben said, ''or to tell me tomorrow is another day or something, forget it, okay? I don't want to hear it.''

Alvin's brow wrinkled. ''I don't know what you're referring to.''

''You didn't come to discuss the hearing this morning?''

Alvin's brow wrinkled again. "Did you have a hearing this morning? I didn't know. No, I have a problem of my own."

Ben pressed his fingers against his temples. He had to smile. The rest of the world had problems, too. He had almost forgotten. "What is it, Alvin?"

Alvin cleared his throat. "Remember the other night when we went out for drinks with the new recruit? The Yale guy?"

"At the Bare Fax? Yes, I definitely remember. How's your head?"

"Fine, thank you. While we were there, you may not recall, but—"

"I recall everything about that night, Alvin. Believe me."

"Do you remember the woman who . . . helped me out?"

"You mean the redhead with the uh . . ." Ben searched for the right word, then decided to reconstruct the entire sentence.

"She's a very nice lady," Alvin said, again clearing his throat. His face was turning crimson. "She was forced into . . . well, her career choice, I guess you'd say, by circumstances beyond her control. That isn't what she's like at all."

"Let me guess. What she really wants to do is go to college and dedicate her life to Christ."

Alvin's eyebrows raised. "That's exactly right. How did you know?"

Ben cast his eyes toward the heavens. "I could see it in her eyes."

"Anyway, we talked awhile that night and later she

came by my apartment for a visit. We had an excellent time.''

"Alvin, I don't want to seem impatient or insensitive, but I'm having what some people might call a very, *very* bad day. What is the point?''

Alvin spoke in a hushed tone. "I'm going to marry her, Ben.''

Ben's chin nearly hit the desk.

"I've asked her, and she's accepted. We've set a tentative date early next month.''

"Next *month*?''

"Well, we want to wait until her daughter is out of school.''

"Daughter?''

"Yes. Illegitimate, I'm afraid. But I'm going to change all that.''

Ben fell back into his chair. He didn't know where to begin. "But"—he waved his hands meaninglessly in the air—"your career! You were so concerned about your career, Alvin." He looked at Alvin sternly. "Did you sleep with her?''

"I don't see what that has to do with anything.''

"And you told me you were celibate. Probably a virgin.'' He exhaled slowly. "You know, Alvin, you don't have to marry the first girl you sleep with just because you slept with her.''

"I think you're way out of line, Kincaid.''

"Have you told Greg about this yet?''

Alvin looked uncomfortable. "I haven't told anyone else yet. I came to you first, though now, I can't imagine why. I didn't think Greg would understand.''

"You mean you thought Greg would make fun of you— and you were damn well right.''

Alvin grunted and walked toward the door.

"Look, Alvin, do yourself a favor. Don't tell anyone else about this for a while. Wait until the newness wears off a bit. Just to be sure."

"I don't see why—"

"Do it for me, Alvin. Buddy to buddy. Okay?"

Alvin bristled and threw his shoulders back. "Fine. Mum's the word." He opened the door, then paused. "I must say, though, I thought you would be different. Somehow, you seemed . . . I don't know, more *sensitive* than the rest of the guys. I hoped you'd understand about true love, about wanting to help a woman and a little girl." He pulled the door shut.

Ben stared down at his desk. He thought his head was going to explode. A little girl. A little girl. I hoped you'd understand about wanting to help a woman and a little girl.

Almost in a daze, Ben began dialing the telephone. Seven rapid clicks, some static, and two rings. Someone lifted the receiver on the other end.

"Hello?"

"Look, you sonovabitch, I know damn well you and Adams spoke the day he was killed. I want to know what you discussed. You don't want to open up to the police— I can understand that. But not talking to me is a whole goddamn different ball game. I'm sure you're scared for your own skin and you don't want to end up like him. I'll tell you something—I don't give a damn. People are depending on me, so I'm depending on *you* to level with me. So *talk*!" His words reverberated in the phone receiver.

There was no reply. Silence. Static.

"I said, I want you to fucking talk to me! *Now!*"

A long pause. Then, at last: "I don't know what it is you want to know."

"What did Adams discover in the financial records? Or what did *you* discover in the records and tell him about?"

Another pause. "I can't talk here," he said at last. "Can we meet somewhere?"

Ben fell back into his chair and closed his eyes. He felt such a sense of release that he nearly teetered onto the floor. "Yes," he said. "We can meet *now*."

* 26 *

The River Parks are probably the most scenic parts of central Tulsa. Attractive greenery, nature walks, exercise parcourse, bike trails, playground equipment, picnic tables, and hot dog stands—it all can be found between the Arkansas River and Riverside Drive. The park performed a variety of important civic functions. It was where harried parents brought their children to get them out of the house, where housewives came to aerobicize their way to personal fulfillment, where homosexuals congregated in search of companionship.

It was also an ideal place to have a private conversation in public, Ben decided. Harry Brancusci, Sanguine's accountant, had agreed to meet Ben there during his lunch break. They talked as they walked slowly upriver along the jogging trail, their voices dropping to a hush whenever someone passed nearby.

"So Jonathan Adams suspected that money was being diverted out of the Sanguine corporate gross profits. Why did he need you?"

"For proof," Brancusci said quietly. He was a thin, dark-haired man, probably in his mid-thirties. He had the disconcerting habit of shutting his eyes whenever he looked at Ben and opening them again whenever he looked away.

"Somehow, Adams learned a slush fund existed. Don't ask me how. But he needed proof. So he came to me. Only Sanguine accountants and top executives have access to Sanguine financial documents. In the case of accountants, we have them only briefly. And no one accountant has access to all financial documents. Sanguine Enterprises is divided into three divisions, financially speaking. The first division is composed of franchises that pay a percentage of their monthly gross profits; the second division is composed of franchises that pay a straight fee and keep their profits. The third financial category involves nonfranchising activities, administrative costs, office expenses, leases, executive perks—that sort of thing."

His eyelids closed as he turned to face Ben. "Sanguine has three accounting staffs, each corresponding to one of the three divisions. I'm in the franchise straight-fee department. So I never saw more than one-third of the Sanguine financial data."

Ben wiped his brow. It was a hot day, and unlike those trotting past him on the jogging trail, he didn't enjoy sweating. "Why the elaborate cloak-and-dagger approach to something as simple as doing the corporate books? That must have made people suspicious."

"Not really. It's pretty standard corporate operating

procedure. It's a nasty world out there. A lot of people would be interested in knowing how Sanguine is doing from quarter to quarter.''

"At some point, though, someone must have access to all three sets of data. Someone must compile all the financial information so that Sanguine executives can see the big picture and judge how the corporation is doing, plan for the future, pay the taxes—whatever it is executives do.''

Brancusci nodded his head. "Sure, someone. Some officer of the corporation or vice president or secret conclave of accountants. But not me. And not Adams.'' His thin face turned away. "Adams wanted me to follow the paper trail and find out who had access to, as you say, the big picture.''

"And?''

"And?'' Brancusci raised his eyebrows and shrugged. "And I did. Follow the trail, that is. With the assistance of a blonde, teenage office messenger who was not altogether unfriendly to me—'' He paused doubtfully, as if unsure whether this was a conquest of which he should boast. "I monitored the flow of interoffice mail throughout the two-week period prior to this year's annual meeting in Nashville. One day a thick report with numbers that didn't come from any of the three standard accounting departments was circulated among the upper echelon. So that night . . .'' His eyes stretched out across the water. ". . . what do you know, I had to work late. Walked into Sanguine's office under the pretense of delivering something he needed, unlocked his desk with a paper clip, and swiped the report. Photocopied it, returned it, and no one was the wiser.''

Ben decided the less said about that the better. Given

recent events, he was in no position to criticize. "What did you learn from the report?"

"I learned that Adams was right. A large amount of money was being diverted from the gross earnings of the corporation."

"How large?"

"Difficult to say for certain, but it's in the millions. I'd guess about three million dollars, over a number of years."

Ben nodded. It was the same ball-park figure Sally Zacharias had derived.

"The diversion of funds has been concealed by a series of false invoices. Each accounting department was told that another department was receiving the missing money. A perfectly covered trail. The money is accounted for on the books, but nobody not-in-the-know knows where it's really gone."

"So what are the coded papers I found?"

"That was a summary I generated. Based on the information in the report I swiped from Sanguine's desk."

Ben paused a moment and let a black-leotarded woman, shielded from the world by a Walkman and earplugs, pass by. Then, he decided, it was time to ask the $64,000 question. "Who was getting the money?"

"I can't say for sure. But I can tell you who wasn't. The corporate shareholders. That was the reason for the entire elaborate deception, unless I'm greatly mistaken. Sanguine is a public corporation, you know. Based on provisions in its corporate charter, it has an obligation to pay annual dividends to shareholders when the corporation generates large gross profits. Or to report its decision not to pay dividends and explain why. But if you reduce the corporate gross profits enough, nobody expects dividends to be paid. More money for the slush fund."

Ben took a deep breath of fresh air. All this corporate bookkeeping stuff was really over his head. At the D.A.'s office, he had avoided white-collar crime whenever possible. But, he supposed, the details weren't important. He followed the gist of the matter. Someone was ripping off millions of dollars, and Adams found out about it.

"Why was Adams so determined to track this down?" Ben asked.

"You tell me," Brancusci said. "I'm no shrink. But I can tell you this. Sanguine and the rest of the upper management types—they always treated Adams like dirt. He was old guard, definitely not one of the boys. Adams was with the company when Sanguine bought it and brought in his own management crew. Adams stayed on as a condition of the buy-out agreement. Evidently, it was cheaper to keep him and bear the nuisance than to pay him off. But that didn't mean they had to like him. It didn't mean they had to treat him like a human being."

Brancusci bent down, lifted a small rock, and flung it into the river. It skipped on the surface four times before sinking. "Don't be fooled by his job title. Adams was a vice president in name only. They never gave him anything important to do, and they paid him accordingly. Sanguine and his cronies were getting rich; Adams never even got a raise. No one said anything, but the fact was they were trying to hound him into quitting the job he didn't really have anyway. I mean, this whole slush fund is a perfect example. By title, Adams was one of only five vice presidents in a multimillion-dollar public corporation. He should've had access to all important financial papers. But he didn't. He didn't know what was going on. They kept him locked out."

Ben wiped his brow again. The weather was uncommonly hot, and the air seemed thin and hard to breathe. "Adams was going to blackmail Sanguine, wasn't he?"

"Yes. Maybe. Hell, I don't know. He was going to do something with the information, that's for damn sure. Something to improve his current station in life."

"And what about you? You seem to have incurred a great deal of risk in this business. What was in it for you?"

Brancusci gazed out at the river. Then he said quietly, almost under his breath, "Let's just say I have a strong distaste for injustice. And poverty."

Ben pulled the summary out of his jacket pocket. "There's a coded notation in the left-hand column on the second page." Ben pointed to the line on the ledger. "It's marked *Ca-Em*. Is that a reference to Emily?"

"I don't know. I copied it like I found it. Could stand for anything. Obviously, it's in code, and I wasn't privy to the key." He scrutinized the summary. "It appears to be grouped with other corporate real estate holdings in Tulsa. I'm almost certain this item three lines above is the office lease payment for our Tulsa headquarters. I recognize the amount."

He continued to study the summary. "Ca-Em. Four hundred and seventeen dollars and forty-six cents. The same every month. Might be a mortgage payment or installment payment on some property. Kind of small, though. I'd bet it's a rental or lease payment."

"You may have to testify, you realize."

Brancusci stopped walking. Although he faced the river, Ben could see the panicked expression in his eyes. "No way in hell I'm going to testify. I've already spilled everything I know. Personally, I liked Adams and felt sorry for him, and I want to see his killer caught as much as anybody. Maybe more. If I didn't care about the old man, I wouldn't be talking to you now. But I can't testify. If anyone even finds out I've spoken to you—"

"If you'll produce the report you based the summary upon, a personal statement may be unnecessary. But if you don't, I guarantee you that either I or the police will slap a subpoena on you. And if you lie under oath, I'll see that you do time for perjury. Your choice. The penitentiary in McAlester is a nasty place."

Brancusci grimaced. "My choice, huh? Yeah, right. I should've expected to get screwed again." After a moment, he resumed walking down the jogging trail. "I'll give you the damn report. Give me your phone number. I'll call you when I'm ready. We'll arrange another meeting. Nothing personal, but I don't want you to be seen at my apartment."

Ben pulled a business card out of his wallet and gave it to the accountant.

"One more thing before you run off," Ben said. "Who was in a position to know about this slush fund and profit from it?"

"Hell, I bet they all knew about it. All the vice presidents, except Adams. The only way to keep them quiet would be to, well, share the wealth. But only one person could have authorized it. The one person it would be absolutely impossible to leave in the dark. Sanguine."

He turned to look at Ben and, for the first time, his eyes opened. "Your client."

* 27 *

"You think he knew more than he was telling?" Christina asked.

"I don't know," Ben answered. "He told a hell of a lot."

Christina and Ben sat behind closed doors in Ben's office. Ben had told her everything he'd learned from Brancusci.

"He should have called me back by now," Ben muttered. "I wonder what's taking him so long?"

"Probably can't find his papers. You know how accountants are. Offices always a mess. Desks cluttered with papers and slide rules and IRS regulations. Don't worry. Probably spilled coffee on the documents and had to blow-dry them in the bathroom."

Ben sank back into his chair. "Look, Christina, I know you're trying to be cheery, and I appreciate it, but really—don't bother. I'm not in a good mood."

Christina fidgeted with the papers in her hands. She was wearing a black leather skirt with offsetting burgundy hose. Her strawberry hair was pulled back and twisted in a strange cross between a French braid and a librarian's bun. "I was told the hearing wasn't all that bad, and that you displayed a certain . . . *panache.*" She paused. "I heard it wasn't your fault."

"You heard wrong. I should've told the judge about Emily's condition in the first ten seconds of opening statement. But I didn't. I was afraid that if the judge thought she was handicapped, he would insist that she be placed in an institution." He rubbed his hand against his forehead. "I made a judgment call. And I was wrong."

"You did your best."

"My client didn't ask me to do my best. She asked me to make it possible for her to adopt a child."

"Well, anyway. *Comme çi, comme ça.* What can I do for you now?"

"Find out what that Ca-Em item represents. Maybe I'm wrong, maybe Em is short for Embassy or Emmanuel or Empire State Building. But I don't think so. Somehow all of this has to tie together."

"You want me to call every apartment complex and condo rental property in town?"

"Well, start with the apartments and duplexes in the metro area. Do it systematically. I think one of the legal assistants in real estate could come up with a list of Tulsa rental properties."

"Raven has an ongoing business relationship with the Jeanne Graham realty agency," Christina said. "We use them to find apartments and houses for summer clerks and new lawyers. I bet they can help."

"Good." A tiny light was returning to Ben's eyes. He'd been hesitant to assign this chore to Christina because it seemed impossibly large. Christina, however, already made it seem not only possible, but easy. "Use them. If anybody hesitates to provide rent information over the phone, give them some song and dance about being with the Tulsa Credit Union. Or maybe the IRS. Nobody wants to irritate the IRS. Tell them you need this information to complete your audit of one of their tenants blah blah blah. Of course, sir, if you'd rather, we can just audit *you*. . . .''

"I get the picture, boss."

"Go to it."

"Oh, I almost forgot. Maggie gave me this phone message on my way in. Your mother would like you to return her call."

Ben took the pink memo slip from Christina and crumpled it in his hand.

"Must be important, huh?" Christina said. "She's called several times since you've been here."

"I'll take care of it," Ben said abruptly.

Christina's eyes narrowed. "What are you doing while I'm playing Nancy Drew on the telephone?"

"I'm going to visit Joseph Sanguine again. I think this new case assignment will give me a perfect excuse."

"Shouldn't you okay that with Derek first?"

"Can't. He's not in the office. Maggie says he had an acute asthma attack. Had to be taken to the hospital."

"Couldn't happen to a sweeter guy."

Ben allowed himself a small smile. "Anything else?"

"I guess you've heard about Alvin."

Ben sighed. "Yes, I've heard about Alvin. How did you find out?"

"Ben, you should know by now that you can't keep secrets from me."

"Do him a favor, Christina. Don't spread it any further than it's already gone."

"Why? Oh, you just don't want anyone to find out the firm has another ruthless seducer of women, right?"

Ben looked at her stonily.

"Well," she said, quickly rising to her feet, "I can't sit around all afternoon making small talk. I've got a couple thousand people to call, give or take a few slumlords—"

"Christina," he said, stopping her. "Thanks. I mean, for everything. This, and the other night and, well, everything."

Christina touched him lightly on the shoulder. "My pleasure. Just don't let me catch you at the Red Parrot with any other chicks."

"No danger there."

"One question, though. Who do I bill my time to now? The adoption hearing is over. That billing matter is closed."

Ben arched his neck and loosened his shirt collar. "It's not over till I say it's over," he said. He was embarrassed at having said something so trite, but he meant every word of it. He couldn't just give up. There had to be something else he could do. Something he could do right.

* 28 *

As he passed through the double doors into the main lobby of Sanguine headquarters, Ben noted that new high-tech, double-bolt locks had been installed. What could have prompted that? he wondered. He smiled. Of course, even high-tech, double-bolt locks are of little value when the thieves have keys.

He gave his name to the receptionist, who instructed him to go on upstairs. He entered the elevator and punched the second-floor button.

He was surprised to have gotten an appointment to see Sanguine so easily. Before he left the office, he asked Maggie to call ahead and tell Sanguine he was coming. He expected to have a long wait. Perhaps Maggie saves all her charm for telephone conversations, he mused. Or did Sanguine have some reason for wanting to see Ben?

Tidwell met Ben as soon as he reached the second floor.

"Mr. Sanguine has penciled in some time for you starting in just a few minutes. You're lucky to see him at all. Mr. Sanguine is a very busy man. I've already reported to Mr. Sanguine regarding the . . . uh, adoption hearing," Tidwell added, clearing his throat.

"Tattletale," Ben muttered.

"So if you've come to discuss that with him . . ."

"No," Ben said firmly. "Haven't you heard? I'm working on a new Sanguine matter now. Big lawsuit in Vancouver."

Tidwell was visibly taken aback. He ran a hand across his balding scalp. "Vancouver?" he said. "I thought Bryce Chambers was handling that."

"Nope. Seems Sanguine just can't get enough of me."

"Hmm." Tidwell seemed lost in thought. "Say, you know why New Jersey has all the toxic waste dumps and Washington, D.C., has all the lawyers?"

"No. Nor do I care."

Tidwell sniffed. "New Jersey got first choice."

A loud buzzing noise sounded within Sanguine's office. "Mr. Sanguine will see you now."

Ben walked quickly to the door, cutting Tidwell off. Ben entered the office first and, without waiting to be invited, seated himself in the mahogany chair he had occupied on his prior visit.

"I have some papers that require your signature," Tidwell said as he walked behind the huge desk and stood beside his mentor. Although he was speaking to Sanguine, Ben noticed that his eye never strayed far from Ben. "Final drafts of the shareholder prospectuses. I've already proofread them."

Sanguine glanced at the papers for a nanosecond, signed each in two places, and handed the papers back to Tidwell.

"Also," Tidwell added, "I believe I've found a suitable location for our prospective Fort Smith franchise."

"We'll talk about it later," Sanguine said dismissively.

After Tidwell left, Ben and Sanguine stared at one another in silence for several moments.

"Mr. Sanguine," Ben said at last, breaking the ice.

"Call me Joe."

"Joe." The first-name address was instinctively uncomfortable to Ben, but it would be even more uncomfortable to refuse after receiving such a gracious invitation. "There are a few matters regarding this Vancouver matter I wanted to discuss with you. You could take the offensive and sue DeAmato here in Tulsa. Based on the *Burger King* v. *Rudzewicz* precedent, the court will have personal jurisdiction over the parties. If we wait and he sues us first, he'll almost certainly sue in Vancouver, and you'll be stuck with the difficult choice of law questions, venue problems, and the necessity of hiring Canadian lawyers to act as local counsel. The whole operation will probably double in cost.

Fighting a case out-of-state, much less out-of-the-country, is always more expensive."

Sanguine leaned back in his chair and lifted his feet onto his desk. "I sense an *on the other hand* approaching."

If nothing else, Sanguine understood lawyers. "On the other hand, all DeAmato probably really wants is out of her franchise license agreement. All this stuff about fraud and Sherman Act violations and punitive damages and so forth is just smoke. She just wants out."

Ben opened his briefcase and removed a manila file folder. "Taking this thing to the trial stage would consume large amounts of money and time, and even if you won at trial, you wouldn't get much in damages. I believe you should consider cutting your losses, saving the litigation costs, and giving the woman what she wants. Set her free. Cancel the franchise agreement and start a new operation with someone else. There must be jillions of would-be breakfast food entrepreneurs in Vancouver."

Sanguine shifted his weight in his chair. "You must realize though, Ben, that with an operation like ours, costs aren't everything. We have over six hundred franchises scattered across North America. Where would we be if all our franchisors suddenly decided to quit operating their franchise and start operating a competing business under a different name? We'd be up the proverbial creek without a paddle."

Sanguine dropped his feet to the floor and leaned forward across the desk. "Sometimes you have to maintain discipline. Set an example. Tell them in unequivocal terms that if they walk out on Sanguine Enterprises, there'll be hell to pay." His eyes met Ben's. "Nobody messes around with Sanguine. That's my credo."

Ben shuffled the papers in his hands and looked away. Propped on the edge of Sanguine's desk was a flashlight, *Ben's* flashlight, standing on end. The flashlight he and Christina had left in Adams's office the night they broke in.

"Let me shed some light on that," Sanguine said. He laughed at his own little joke. "I found that in Jonathan Adams's office a few nights ago. The window was open. Evidently there was a break-in, but no one could find any sign of a forced entry. Or theft. We called the police, but . . ." He shrugged with an unconvincing lightness. "You don't know what a prowler would be doing in poor Jonathan's office, do you?" Sanguine was staring directly at Ben. "I remember you were very anxious to poke around in there."

Ben squirmed uncomfortably. This was not the direction he wanted the conversation to take. "You were very close to Mr. Adams, weren't you, sir?" Ben said. "His death must have come as a terrible shock."

Sanguine cocked his head to one side. "You really want to know the truth? No, we weren't close at all. I didn't like him, and he didn't like me. He didn't belong here. He didn't belong in this *world*. I encouraged him to quit when I bought the company, but he resisted. He wanted a job, he said, not a pension. He had a contract; it was part of the deal. Part of the take-over agreement. I couldn't make him go. But I could sure make him pay the price of his own stubbornness."

Ben tried not to react. He had hoped to uncover a motive, but he didn't expect to have one served to him on a silver platter.

"That's right," Sanguine continued. "Look astonished. You're young. What the hell. Someone dies and everyone's supposed to act as if he were a saint. Well, Adams wasn't a saint. Where I came from, we didn't have time for that kind of hypocritical crap. Where did you grow up, Kincaid?'' He quickly corrected himself. ''Ben.''

''I grew up in the suburbs of Oklahoma City. Nichols Hills, to be exact.''

''Ah, such a trying childhood. Like something out of David Copperfield. You must have emotional scars through and through.'' He leaned forward, pointing with his pencil. ''Let me tell you where I grew up. On a Sioux Indian reservation in South Dakota.''

Ben scrutinized Sanguine's face. His first impression was right. That would explain the kachina dolls and the other scattered Western relics in Sanguine's office.

''Yes, I'm an Indian. Excuse me, we're supposed to be called Native Americans now. I keep forgetting. And no, to answer your next question, Sanguine isn't the name I was born with. It's Bloodhawk. At least that's the anglicization. Joseph Paitchee Bloodhawk. My mother was white.'' He chortled quietly. ''I guess she contributed the Joseph part.''

''I didn't realize there were Indian reservations anymore.''

''There aren't any in Oklahoma. Tribal lands, yes, but no reservations as such. Still exist in other states, though. For the most part, still just as dirty and debasing and poverty-blighted as when I grew up. You have any idea what it's like to grow up in a place like that? Over sixty percent unemployment? Average income about three thousand a year? You have any idea what the odds are against making anything of yourself after a childhood like that? No, of course you don't. How could you?''

His voice rose in volume. ''You don't know what it's like to grow up knowing people think you can't do any-

thing more complicated than running a bingo parlor because you're just a dumb Indian. And the worst of it,
knowing that you really *are* just a dumb Indian, and that
there's not a damn thing you can do about it.''

Just at the edge, Sanguine caught himself. He exhaled
and fell back into his chair. "But of course," he said,
"you don't know anything about that. They probably didn't
have any Indians in Nichols Hills, did they? They probably
don't allow such riffraff.''

Ben couldn't see the point in saying anything. This
stream-of-consciousness soliloquy was giving him far more
information than he could ever elicit with questions.

"My point is this," Sanguine said. "I worked very hard
to become successful. Against damned near impossible
odds. And that's no exaggeration—I had no breaks, no
connections, no education, and no money. But I have been
successful. I'm rich. Sanguine Enterprises is in the Fortune Five Hundred and I'm on the list of the hundred
richest men in America." Sanguine's full attention seemed
focused on the pencil he held in his hands. "And I've used
that success. I've tried to make things a little easier for the
next Indian in line. And I'm making a difference. Maybe
in the next generation, there'll be more than one Sioux
crossing the poverty line. Maybe the next one will be able
to do it without changing his name.''

The pencil in Sanguine's hands suddenly snapped. "But
the adversity does not stop, no matter how successful you
are. Just when you've got a company that seems to work,
here comes this man who's too mired in yesteryear to even
consider a change for the better. Every opportunity to di-
versify, he's against it. Every idea for increasing efficiency
or productivity, he's against it. That's why I made Adams
vice president of new developments. Sort of a private joke.

He knew it was, too, and it stuck in his craw. That's what I liked best about it."

Abruptly, Sanguine shifted his gaze to Ben. The pencil pieces fell to the desktop.

"I suppose in your eyes there was something admirable—in a perverse, futile way—about the old geezer's tenacity. A latter-day Don Quixote. I can almost see it myself. But I would not let him bring down my business. I would not let him tear down everything I had accomplished. I would *not*." He pounded his desk to emphasize the final word.

Ben sensed that the conversation was going no further in that direction. "I guess you've heard about the adoption hearing," he said.

Sanguine seemed startled, as if brought out of a trance. "What? Oh, yes. Of course, I bear no malice against the *widow*. Tough break for her." For some reason, he laughed quietly.

Ben began to organize his papers and put them back into his briefcase. "Well, I just wanted to make sure you had been informed."

"What about being a grandparent?"

"I beg your pardon?"

"So the court thinks Mrs. Adams is too old to learn how to be a mommy. No big surprise there. How about getting her appointed as a foster grandparent? Courts do that now; I was just reading about it in *Time*. It's supposed to be good for the kid and the elderly person. She wouldn't get to see the girl every day, but she would get some reasonable visitation rights." He shrugged his shoulders. "Better than nothing."

"I hadn't thought of that," Ben admitted.

"You hadn't? Geez, what am I paying you guys those

outrageous fees for? You lose on impossible theories and don't even consider arguments you might actually win.'' He paused, savoring the moment. ''I thought of something you didn't. Hell, I think I'm a better lawyer than you, Ben. This dumb Indian. A better lawyer than you.''

* 29 *

Ben stepped out of the elevator on the fourteenth floor and walked toward his apartment. Shifting his briefcase into his other hand, he fumbled around in his jacket pocket. After a moment, he found the right key and shoved it into the door.

The door was already unlocked.

Ben set down his briefcase. If this were a movie, he thought, the audience would be screaming ''Don't go in, you fool!'' But then, Ben mused, if I didn't go in, there would be no movie. Slowly, he turned the doorknob and pushed the door open.

The lights were on. A medium-size woman with long chestnut brown hair was sitting on the floor in a pretzel-like configuration resembling the lotus position. She was munching on cheddar-cheese-flavored potato chips and french onion dip.

''About time,'' she said, wiping the back of her hand across her mouth.

"Julia," Ben said. "How did you get in?"

"I told the super I was your sister. Some wild story, huh?"

"Those potato chips will make you fat again," he said.

"If I want Weight Watchers counseling, Ben, I'll go to the meetings. Besides, it's not as if you have anything nutritious to eat here."

"I just moved in."

"No kidding." She glanced around the room, still only furnished with cardboard boxes and a sleeping bag. "When are you going to buy some furniture?"

"Sometime after my first paycheck and before I die." He shut the door. "Mind if I come in?"

"Be my guest."

Ben tossed his jacket on the floor and sat down opposite Julia. She was still his pretty baby sister. A little older, a bit too plump, but still very attractive. Although the wrinkles surrounding her eyes seemed a bit more pronounced than when he had seen her last. Time marches on, he supposed, even for baby sisters.

"I thought you were living in OKC," he said.

"I am. I came here to talk to you." She rolled up the potato chip bag and replaced the lid on the dip.

"About what?"

"About why the hell you're dodging Mom's phone calls. Don't you know she's worried sick about you?"

"Jesus Christ," Ben said. He pressed his fingers against his forehead.

"Don't give me that," she said angrily. "Personally, I don't care whether you ever talk to your family, but Mother does. I can't believe the way you've been acting! First, you get a new job, then you move to a new city, all without saying boo to anybody. You don't give anybody your phone number or address—it's as if you're deliberately trying to isolate yourself. I had to act like a frigging private investigator just to find your apartment."

"Julia, I'm really not up to a scolding right now. I've had a really horrible week. You can't imagine—"

"I don't *care!*" she shouted, cutting him off. "I'm tired of you bumbling along feeling sorry for yourself just because—"

Ben's face tightened and he cut her off with a fierce, stony look. After a moment, she started again, a little slower and softer. "It just isn't fair, Ben. It's not fair to Mom or—"

"Stop!" Ben's face was reddening. "You want me to call Mom, I'll call Mom. It's just that I've been very busy—"

"With what? Taking over something? A corporate merger, maybe?"

Ben sighed. "I'm not a business lawyer, Julia. I'm in litigation—" There was a loud knock at the door.

"I'm closer," Julia said. "You catch your breath. Wimp." She walked to the door and turned the knob.

It was Mike.

Julia's mouth opened, then slowly closed again. She took a step back, and Mike entered the apartment. He'd been caught in the rain; water on his overcoat was dripping onto the floor. Mike and Julia stared at one another for several seconds, then Julia turned to her brother.

"So, Ben, you've been running around with Morelli. That explains a lot."

Mike just stood there; rain droplets plopped from the hem of his overcoat. "I need to talk with you, Ben," he said at last.

Julia chuckled, a quick, bitter laugh. "That's it, Mike. Act like I'm not even here. Come to think of it, that's what you did the whole time we were married."

Ben leaned back against the wall. *Here we go again.*

"That's really not fair, Julia. You know I worked very hard—"

"At some things, yes," she interrupted. "At others, no."

Mike took a deep breath, then released it. There was really no point in playing the scene out again. "You're looking good," he said. "I'm glad to see nursing school hasn't turned you into a drudge."

"If it hasn't, it will," she said, her teeth set tightly together. "It isn't the way I planned to be living my life at this point."

"I see you still blame me for your having to pursue a career." He shook his head back and forth. "You know, you didn't have to choose one of the hardest professions in the world—unless maybe you were still trying to punish me."

Julia's eyes and nostrils flared. "I wanted to be supported in the manner to which I was accustomed. You promised me you'd take care of that, Morelli."

"Morelli is your name, too, Julia," he said.

"Not anymore," she snapped. "Not anymore and never again."

"You *guys*," Ben said, in a slow, pleading tone. "Come on. Don't do this."

"I really do need to speak with Ben," Mike repeated.

"Fine." Julia lifted her coat off the floor, then walked to the door. "But don't forget, Ben—"

"I'll call Mother as soon . . ." He hesitated. "As soon as I can."

Julia nodded. "See that you do. Goodbye, Ben." She closed the door behind her.

Mike took off his coat and sat down on the floor next to Ben. "You know, I haven't seen her for three years. Isn't that weird? You see someone every single day, every single night, for so long, then you don't see her at all for the next three years." He shook his head. "Weird."

"If I were you, I'd wait another three years before your next reunion." Ben straightened up and tossed Mike one of the throw pillows. "What did you want to see me about?"

"I've got a little more evidence to share," he said cryptically. "First tell me what you've been up to lately."

Ben sat forward eagerly. "I've talked to Sanguine, Mike, and you won't believe everything he said. This was as close to a flat-out fourth-act *Perry Mason* confession as anything you're going to hear in your lifetime." Ben quickly recounted the high points of his conversation with Sanguine.

"Did he say he killed Adams?"

"No, but he admitted everything but that. He practically fed me a motive."

"Oh, a motive. Well, that settles everything." He tossed the pillow behind his head and leaned back against the wall. "Didn't they teach you anything in law school?"

"I know, I know. Motive isn't an element of proof for establishing a prima facie case of murder. Or any other crime, for that matter. But it will go a long way toward getting a conviction from a jury. You know it as well as I do."

Mike hesitated. "Well, perhaps I should visit Mr. Sanguine again."

"Do it tomorrow morning. Or maybe we should go now. What if he skips the country?"

"Give me a break, Ben. The man heads a multimillion-dollar corporate empire. He's not going to skip the country. If you've *really* put the fear of God into him, he *might* hire a lawyer. A slick lawyer can keep him out of prison longer than he could hope to stay hidden. Come to think of it, he'll probably use your firm. Come to think of it, he may hire *you*. He seems to have such a high opinion of your work these days. Wouldn't that be a knotty problem? If R T & T agrees to represent him, you won't be able to testify against him."

"They can't do that. They'd have to check for any conflicts of interest before accepting the case, and I'd speak up. If a lawyer expects to be called as a witness, he can't agree to act as a lawyer in the case. And that goes for his entire firm."

"And so Raven, Tucker & Tubb would lose one of its most profitable clients, perhaps its *most* profitable client, perhaps permanently. Any idea how that would affect your standing with the shareholders?"

Ben had to stop a moment at that.

"Look, Ben, give us a few days to finish the physical-evidence analysis. Then, if we're sure we're right about Sanguine and the evidence matches up, I'll drop in on the esteemed president of Sanguine Enterprises."

Ben nodded his reluctant acceptance of the plan. "So what have you got now?" he asked.

"More forensic evidence," Mike replied. "The hair and fiber team found several dark coarse male hairs on the inside lining of Adams's overcoat. They match the ones I told you about before that we found on Adams's body."

Ben's eyes widened. "Dark hair. That could be Sanguine."

"Yeah, it could be, but is it? Adams could've picked them up from someone at the bar beforehand, or at his home, or office, or anyplace else for that matter. But the distribution of hairs on the inside of the coat and their proximity to blood splatters makes the fiber boys think they came from the killer. They think it happened while the killer struggled to get the body into the Dumpster." He paused. "And I think they're right. That would explain, for instance, why the hairs are all on one side of the body."

Mike studied a small notepad that he withdrew from his coat pocket. "I sent the hairs and a sample of the blood we think came from the killer away for a special test. A DNA fingerprint."

Ben looked impressed. "I've read about that. How does it work?"

"Well, they analyze nuclear rather than mitochondrial DNA—"

"Ahh," Ben said. "Thank you for making that distinction clear."

Mike continued unperturbed. "They use restriction enzymes as scissors, cut the DNA into segments and arrange the segments into patterns that resemble the Uniform Product Code labels you see everywhere now. They're easier to compare than fingerprints. And, unless our man has an identical twin, no two are alike."

"Isn't there some question about whether the results are conclusive?"

"Yeah. But at this point, any evidence is better than none."

"Brrrr," Ben said, hunching his shoulders and rubbing

his arms as if he'd caught a chill. "Genetic IDs. Sounds like something you'd hear about on the Big Brother telemonitor."

"Do you want to catch this guy or not? I should get the test results by telephone tomorrow afternoon or the next day. Then I'll ask Sanguine for an exemplar of his hair and blood. If the hair samples match—"

"We'll know he's the killer."

"We'll know he saw Adams within the last twenty-four hours before he died," Mike corrected. "Since he told the police otherwise, that might be enough to bring him in for some pointed questioning. And if it's Sanguine's blood under Adams's fingernails, we'll have an airtight case."

Ben hated to admit it, but sometimes the law did move too slowly for ordinary human beings to bear.

"You know what the really funny thing is?" Mike said slowly. "I still don't know what I did wrong. In my marriage, I mean. I worked hard. I worked night and day. You know I did. I tried to do the right thing. I tried to make her happy. If I could do it all over again, starting today, I don't have the slightest idea what I should do differently."

Ben gave Mike a fraternal punch on the shoulder. "Let's call up Julia," Ben said. "I'm sure she'd be happy to tell you."

The two men looked at one another and then, with some regret, burst into laughter.

* 30 *

Washroom protocol was a peculiar feature of the law office life-style. The washrooms were perhaps the only communal meeting place for persons from all echelons of the firm. Everyone went there at one time or another, excepting the three named partners, each of whom had his own private washroom that could only be entered with a special key. In the general public men's rooms, however, the partners and associates alike enacted a complex ritual, from greeting all present by name upon entrance to the vigorous washing of hands on the way out. Associates went to ostentatious lengths to demonstrate that they had no latent uneasiness about urinating in the presence of others, and every one of them, Ben suspected, would have preferred to remain silent and be left in peace in a private stall while they took care of business. The office washroom, however, might be the only place a junior associate ever saw most partners. Ergo, bizarrely enough, it became a place to try to make an impression.

Ben met Greg on his way in.

"Long time no see," Greg said, pushing the door open. "Boy, have people ever been talking about you."

Ben was reflexively defensive. "I don't want to hear about—" Greg silenced him by raising a finger to his lips in the hush position. He rubbed his thumb and forefinger across his lips, then flicked his fingers, as if to throw away the key. Greg crouched down and checked to see if there were any feet visible beneath the stall doors. Evidently there weren't.

"Can't be too careful," Greg said, turning back toward the urinals. "Partners are everywhere."

Ben rolled his eyes. "Don't you think you're overdoing this firm intrigue routine?"

"Hey, I've planned to be a lawyer all my life," Greg said. "It's all I ever wanted to do. I'm not going to blow it now by being stupid. Loose lips sink ships."

What a great place to work, Ben thought.

"I understand your first court appearance was an unmitigated disaster," Greg said. For some inexplicable reason, he seemed to be grinning.

"Glad everyone's heard about it," Ben muttered. "Saves me the bother of sending out announcements."

"Ah, well," Greg said, "that's why you've made those connections in high places, right?" He flashed his perfect smile. "A wise associate hedges his bets."

"I don't know what you're talking about, Greg. You're starting to sound like Alvin."

Greg's smile became something like a patronizing leer. "You didn't really think you could keep something like that secret, did you, old boy?" Greg zipped up and walked over to the sinks. "Don't be so secretive. Your fellow associates were very impressed. *I* was very impressed. I hadn't pegged you as the one to make the smooth career moves. You seemed a smidgen too busy being noble to me. But you outflanked your entire class. And in a very masterly fashion, too, I might add. How can Raven fire you now? It can't happen. It's perfect." He wiped his hands on a paper towel. "I guess I should have realized you were on the fast track after that stint with Mona Raven."

Ben stared blankly at him. "I don't know what you're talking about."

"Right. That's your story, and you're sticking to it. I don't blame you. Did Mona have something to do with this? I was in Chambers's office when he found out. Was he ever pissed! He was counting on that Vancouver case reassignment to keep his billables above the freezing point. Wait till he hears this latest news." He slapped Ben on the shoulder. "Pretty impressive for someone whose only court experience was . . . what was the phrase, an unmitigated disaster?"

Deep furrows crept across Ben's forehead. "I don't understand," he said. "What has Mrs. Raven to do with the Vancouver case?"

"Come on, Ben—this is part of the act, right? Are you serious? Mona Raven and Sanguine are lovers. Were lovers, anyway. Before her marriage to Arthur Raven. Mr. Raven is evidently an amazingly understanding husband. Of course, at his age, he'd have to be."

Ben was stunned. "Where do you *hear* these things?"

Greg beamed. "A good lawyer has many sources." He winked and sauntered out of the washroom.

All roads lead back to Sanguine, Ben thought. No matter what startling new development I come across, Joseph Sanguine is always involved.

He stopped suddenly. What *was* Greg's latest news?

* 31 *

Ben walked back to his office, stifling a yawn. He hadn't slept at all the night before. Too much was happening, pulling him every which way at once. Derek, Julia, Sanguine. Emily. Too much. Too much concern, too much guilt. He began to wonder if he would ever sleep peacefully again, if the gnawing in his stomach would ever subside.

Just as he had nearly made it to his office, he was stopped by Maggie. "Two messages came in for you, Mr. Kincaid," she said, in an unnecessarily loud tone of voice.

"Thanks, Maggie." He lifted the message memos from his spindle.

The first was from Christina. It read: *No luck yet. Still hard at it—probably conducting more audits than real IRS. Why does Tulsa need so many different places to live?*

Ben smiled. Now there's a good woman. This was probably part of the cosmic karma, he mused. In exchange for getting to work with Christina, he had to tolerate working with Derek and Maggie.

The second message informed Ben that Mr. Derek wished to see him. Ben crumpled that message in his fist and, taking his own sweet time, strolled into Derek's office.

"Good to see you, Kincaid."

Ben blinked. Derek actually seemed cordial, all smiles. "Where have you been hiding yourself?"

Ben was startled by this sudden outburst of friendliness. This wasn't the Derek he had come to know and be repelled by. Something had changed radically.

"Take a chair, son. I'd come around, but my trick knee is acting up again."

Ben sat as instructed.

Derek looked into Ben's eyes, but it seemed more a friendly scrutiny than the usual dissection. "Well, now, you've been a busy boy, haven't you?" He squinted his eyes into impossibly thin slits, then laughed. "Just got off the phone with Joseph Sanguine."

Oh, great, Ben thought. I pushed Sanguine too hard, and he's ticked off about it. I'm history. Finished. Fired. Impoverished. Destitute.

"We've been after Sanguine for years to appoint someone to act as in-house liaison counsel for Sanguine Enterprises, and we wanted it to be someone from our firm. To solidify the relationship between our business and his." He paused meaningfully. "Do you realize that Sanguine Enterprises paid over four million dollars in legal fees to Raven, Tucker & Tubb last year alone? Incredible. Needless to say, we don't want to lose this client."

Derek uncrossed and recrossed his legs manually, using both hands to lift the legs into place. He winced as he bent his right knee. "Sanguine wants you to be his in-house counsel, Kincaid. He asked for you by name and made it clear he would accept no substitutes. Frankly, we thought he'd go for someone with more legal experience, someone who'd been here ten, maybe fifteen years, rather than ten, fifteen days"—he waved his hand absently in the air—"but who are we to judge? The client always knows best. Sanguine says he wants to train someone fresh, someone who will learn to transact business his way from day one. And frankly, Sanguine knows damn well we'll give him whomever he wants."

Ben stared at Derek in disbelief. His mind was frozen in the mental equivalent of a gaping jaw. "I . . . I—don't see how . . ."

"I don't see how you did it either, Kincaid. You've been involved in two minor cases, you've only been on the Vancouver case for one day, and suddenly, you're in-house counsel. Sanguine said something about admiring your aggressiveness and spunk. I don't know what you've been doing during your visits to his office, but whatever it was, it worked like a wet dream. You've taken a giant step ahead of your peers."

He paused, then decided in favor of another of his characteristic blasts of brutal honesty. "Frankly, Kincaid, I didn't think you'd be the one to take a giant step ahead of the wolf pack. You struck me as too meek and mild for Raven, and especially for Sanguine. I guess I was honest with you about that. Well, I suppose it's Sanguine's decision."

"What would in-house counsel do?" Ben asked hesitantly.

"Oh, find out what's going on, first. They're so disorganized at Sanguine, they've got cases pending that they've lost track of or totally forgotten about. Sanguine's got local counsel working for him all over the globe, but no one back home looking over their shoulders and supervising the work. Before long, I expect you'll start building your own staff of in-house lawyers. You'll be in charge of other people, lawyers older than yourself, probably. They could

hardly be much younger, could they? You'll also take care
of the day-to-day legal minutiae that comes to an operation
the size of Sanguine Enterprises on a regular basis. Of
course, litigation matters, especially the big money cases,
you'll still want to refer out to Raven, Tucker."

"But—" Ben found himself sputtering like an infant.
Something was wrong, but he was unable to express that
to Derek. "I never wanted to be an administrator. I wanted
to litigate. I wanted to try lawsuits."

Derek waved his hand in the air. "Kid, you can make
this job whatever you want. It's your blank check. Speaking of checks, you'll maintain your firm salary, and *in
addition*, you'll be receiving a sizable stipend from Sanguine. Eventually, they'll take over your entire salary. Plus,
you'll receive a signing bonus and various corporate benefits. Kincaid, you've been working here less than a month,
and you're *rich!*"

Ben fell back in his chair. It sounded too good to be
true. Much too good.

"All you have to do is play your job right and keep
Sanguine happy. Remember," Derek added, the expression in his voice changing somewhat, "we're *all* counting
on you. Sanguine asked for you and you alone. If you fail,
there's no guarantee he'll choose someone else from this
firm to take your place."

Derek paused to let his words sink in. Then his face
suddenly brightened. "Now, congratulations, you wild
man. Get out of here. Go celebrate. Take the rest of the
afternoon off. We're going to have a reception this evening
at my house for some key Sanguine people you'll need to
meet, and some of our attorneys who work on Sanguine
matters. You'll be the guest of honor, Kincaid."

Without another word, Derek returned his attention to

the tall stack of papers on his desk. In a daze, Ben managed to find his feet and make his way back to his own office. Too much. Too much.

* 32 *

Ben had to concede that Derek's home could not be faulted for failing to reflect the personality of the owner. The house itself, a huge rectangular, white-brick affair that might have passed for a mausoleum, towered in the foreground. The cabana beside the Olympic-size swimming pool, also in white brick, looked like a miniature of the house.

The highlight of the patio area, however, was the pool itself. On the bottom of the pool, shimmering beneath the surface, was a mermaid, her head in the deep end, her tail in the shallow. The mermaid was not merely painted on; she was sculpted, in three-dimensional splendor. Best of all, the mermaid was painted with anatomical accuracy and detail. Each green scale on her tail could be discerned; the pink nipples on her ample breasts were visible from any point in the backyard. The voluptuous sea maiden seemed to rise from the surface of the pool and beckon the innocent to a watery doom.

As if this wasn't enough, a clear acrylic screen was built into the wall of the deep end of the pool. From a staircase outside, guests could descend into a sunken room and, without getting a toenail wet, observe the merlady and her court. The potential uses of this architectural wonder staggered Ben's imagination.

Ben was trapped in a conversational clique with Derek and Sanguine. Derek seemed perfectly at home; had he moved back in? Maybe Louise had gone somewhere else—home to Mother, perhaps. Derek was talking about himself, Sanguine was listening, and Ben was bored. Tidwell was also there, but he wasn't saying much. He seemed to be out of sorts. In fact, he had yet to tell a single lawyer joke. Perhaps, Ben hypothesized, he's concerned that the presence of in-house counsel will diminish his influence with his boss.

"Speak into my good ear," Derek said, amid a chain of reminiscences about an antitrust case Derek had litigated for Sanguine several months before. "I don't like to admit it, but I might as well tell you, Joe, I've got some hearing loss in my right ear. When I was in the Coast Guard, I spent a miserable winter night doing swimming drills on Chesapeake Bay. The wind was so cold it could freeze your eardrum shut. Total aural paralysis. My poor ear has never recovered."

Out of Derek's eyesight, Sanguine winked at Ben.

"That explains a lot of the things I've heard you say in oral argument," Sanguine said to Derek. "I've always suspected you couldn't hear the judge's questions."

Derek took a sip from his martini. "Remember the oral argument in Charleston?" he said. "The personal jurisdiction question?"

A misty-eyed expression crossed Sanguine's face. "That was a classic. Were you in on that, Tidwell?"

"No, sir," he said politely. He smoothed the few hairs

stretched across his bald head. "I was checking out a potential location for the Phoenix franchise that week."

"Well, you missed a classic," Sanguine continued. "This poor legal assistant kept trying to pass Dick a note while he was speaking, but he didn't notice her, and she kept whispering and *psst*ing till finally the judge himself rose from the bench and told Dick to turn around and take the damn note!"

Derek and Sanguine laughed heartily. Ben did the best he could.

"She was a cute little redheaded number," Sanguine said after he calmed down. "What was her name again?"

"Christina," Derek said, smiling. "Christina McCord or McLaine or something like that."

Ben considered correcting him, then thought better of it.

"We ought to work with her again, Dick," Sanguine said, winking. He nudged Derek with his elbow. Derek's drink spilled onto his hand, but he didn't seem to notice. "I liked her."

Derek countersmirked. "Would you like that, Joe? I think I could make her available to you. If you catch my meaning."

This was more than Ben felt able to hear. Boring nostalgia trips and macho posturing he could handle, but he drew the line at snide remarks about a woman who was currently performing a hellatious task for him as a personal favor. "If you'll excuse me," he said, "I need a fresh drink."

"Sure, kid," Derek said, still ha-haing to himself. "Drink up. This is your night."

Ben walked toward the bar table. The whole party gave him the creeps. Especially Derek. Derek has been nothing but antagonistic and arrogant since the day I came to the firm, Ben thought, but today, he's hosting a party in my honor. Not forty-eight hours ago, Sanguine was hostile, suspicious, and barely civil to me, but today, we're old drinking buddies.

Marianne and Greg were standing in the bar line chatting. Greg saw Ben approaching, threw his arm around Ben, and squeezed his neck tightly in the crook of his arm. "My old buddy!" he screamed. "Ben! How's it going, big guy?"

Ben wasn't sure if Greg was drunk or if this was just his boisterous way of maintaining his status as the prince of party animals. "I'm fine, Greg. Nice coat, by the way."

"What, this old rag?" He flashed his lightweight cashmere jacket. "You like the way it hangs?"

"Well, I like it better than that white *Brideshead Revisited* number you wore the first day of work."

"Yeah, I thought it was time for an image revamp. This makes me look more like a regular guy, don't you think?"

"Greg . . . that's *cashmere*."

Greg glanced at his jacket. "Huh. Yeah, I guess it is. Hey, this is some party, isn't it? I bet Marianne had no idea the perks would start perking this soon, huh?" He jabbed Marianne in the side. "And I guess we've got you to thank for this one, Ben-man!" He gave Ben another squeeze around the shoulders. "You're some kind of animal, big guy."

Ben nodded pleasantly.

"Hey," Greg said, his eyes suddenly growing as wide as his smile. "Remember that time at the Bare Fax, you and me? Was that awesome or what?" Greg laughed heartily enough for both of them, which was fortunate, since Ben wasn't laughing.

"Yeah, those were the days," Ben said. He couldn't believe they were reminiscing about an event from last week as if it were a golden memory from yesteryear.

Greg took a gin and tonic from the bartender. "Well, I better move on. More flesh to press and shareholders to *im*press." He socked Ben on the side of his arm. "But I guess you know all about that, huh, big guy?" Greg turned away and blended into the crowd.

Ben and Marianne looked at one another. "What the hell was that all about?" Ben asked.

Marianne smiled thinly. "I think you just got promoted from fellow associate to big guy," she answered. She took her rum and Coke from the bartender.

"I guess he heard the announcement about in-house counsel."

"Apparently," Marianne said. "Especially the part about how you'd be assigning Sanguine work to attorneys of your choice."

"Really?" Ben responded. "I didn't know that."

Marianne stared at him. "Talk about the way of the world. If you're a woman, you can bust your butt your whole life and never get a decent job. If you're a man, they fall into your lap so fast, you don't even know what you've got."

Ben took his Seven-Up from the bartender. He noticed that Marianne had changed her hairstyle. Her straight black hair was pulled back in a tight bun.

"I guess that's intended to make you look more professional?" Ben asked.

"What? Oh, the hairdo. Yeah, well . . ."

"At least you're not still worrying about your name," Ben said.

"I'm not," Marianne said, "but that reminds me. Have

you met my date?'' Ben shook his head. "He's around
here somewhere. Tall, good-looking fellow. Thick mustache. His name is Kevin. Actually, his full name is
Charles Kevin Bryant. He's an architect. But I can't decide
whether I should introduce him as Kevin or Charles. You
know, to make the right impression." She reflected for a
moment. "Maybe C. Kevin."

C. Kevin? Ben tried to keep a straight face. C. Kevin
walk. C. Kevin run. "Not very conversational, is it?"

"I suppose not. But Kevin sounds so little-kiddish. I
want people to understand that he, too, is a young professional. I don't want anybody to get the idea that I'm going
out with a bum." She took a drink from her rum and
Coke. "What do you think, Ben? I trust your judgment. I
want to do the right thing."

"I'm sure you will," he murmured.

Marianne adjusted her glasses and peered over Ben's
shoulder. "Oh my *God*, Ben," she said slowly. "You're
not going to believe this."

Ben turned to look in the same general direction as Marianne. Alvin was just arriving—and Alvin had brought a
date.

Ben started to look away, but before he could, Alvin
caught his eye. He started walking in Ben's direction.

"I suppose you know who she is," Ben said under his
breath.

"Do I look like a hermit?" Marianne responded. "Of
course I know."

Alvin walked up to Ben, all smiles, and thrust his hand
forward. "Shake, partner." Marianne received the same
jovial treatment. "I'd like you both to meet my fiancée,
Candy Cordell. Candy, this is Ben Kincaid and Marianne
Gunnerson."

It was her, all right. As little attention as Ben had managed to pay to her face on that fateful night, he nonetheless recognized the multitalented dancer-waitress from the Bare Fax. Her red hair was gathered up and separated into two pigtails, which seemed to remove at least five years from her age. The low lighting on the patio also seemed kinder to her than the harsh, no-secrets lighting of the Bare Fax. She was wearing blue jeans and a white blouse with a plunging neckline and small holes throughout. It was a blouse that would make her very popular with the men at the party and very unpopular with the women.

Ben yanked Alvin by the arm and pulled him aside. "What are you *doing*?" he asked in a harsh whisper. "This is professional suicide."

Alvin looked at him gravely. "If she's going to be my wife, Ben, *and she is*, they're going to have to meet her sometime. Besides, they don't have to know about . . . you know, the past."

The subject of their conversation interrupted them before Ben had a chance to rebut. "Oh, I remember you," Candy squealed, as if finding a long-lost friend. "You were there in—"

"Yes, that was me all right," Ben said, cutting her off. "What madcap days they were."

"Excuse me. Can I cut in?"

Ben jumped, startled. It was Derek again, with Sanguine hanging on his shoulder. They both looked hours drunker than they had when he left them a few minutes before.

Derek spotted Candy and leered at her in a not-very-subtle manner. Oh well, Ben thought, I suppose she's accustomed to it.

"Introduce us to the young lady, Mr. Hager," Derek said, grinning obscenely.

"With pleasure, sir," Alvin said, rising to the occasion. Introductions were had all around. Alvin placed heavy emphasis on the words *my fiancée.*

Derek edged closer to Candy. "I hope you won't think me sexist if I say, in all candor, that you are a beautiful woman."

"Not at all. Call 'em like you see 'em, that's what I always tell my customers." She laughed boisterously.

Derek's eyebrows arched. "What do you do, if you don't mind my asking?"

Ben covered his eyes and held his breath.

"Well, I'm going to college now," she said.

Ben exhaled quietly.

"At least I am at the start of the fall semester. Alvin's treat." She slid her arm around his waist and squeezed. "He's my little sugar daddy."

"Is that right?" Derek said loudly. He seemed to find this very amusing.

Suddenly, music began to swell from the chain of speakers built into the outside walls. A Fifties rock 'n' roll tune was starting. "Sounds like it's time to boogie," Derek said eagerly. "Anybody here dance?"

"I dance all the time," Candy said.

"No!" Ben and Alvin shouted simultaneously.

"I mean," Alvin added, "her first dance should be with her fiancé."

"Quite right," Ben seconded. "Quite right."

Alvin took Candy's hand and led her to the area reserved for dancing. Derek and Sanguine walked the other way. "Hell of a woman," Ben heard Derek say as they walked away. "Didn't think Hager had it in him. Knockers out to here."

Ben heard a new voice behind him. "And just as the music begins, who do I find but my all-time favorite dancing partner."

Ben swirled. As if the nightmare wasn't bad enough already, there, standing behind him, was Mona Raven, hanging on the arm of her illustrious husband.

"Mona!" Ben cried, and he really felt like crying. She was dressed in casual chic, a gold lamé blouse flowing seamlessly into a tight leather skirt. Unlike Candy, the low lighting did her no favors.

"I believe we've met," Raven said, in his creaky, tremulous voice.

"Yes, of course we have. It was a pleasure," Ben said, shaking hands. He wondered which meeting the old man remembered.

"And *we've* had the pleasure of a dance, as I recall," Raven said, turning his attention to Marianne. Apparently his memory functioned best in relation to pretty younger women. "That was a tradition I think we should revive." He offered Marianne his arm. Marianne smiled and walked to the dance floor with Raven.

Mona placed her hand on Ben's shoulder and pressed close. "I thought you were very manly at the Red Parrot the other evening. Almost heroic."

"Kind of you to say so." Ben looked out the corners of his eyes to see who was watching.

"I want seconds," she said. She contorted her mouth in strange undulating ovals and growled.

"Forget it, Mona. It just isn't going to happen."

"If you don't, I'm going to tell Joseph about some of the nasty skeletons in his new in-house counsel's closet."

"Yeah," Ben said, "I've heard you and Sanguine have a few old bones rattling around, too."

Mona drew back a step. "I don't know what you're implying." Her smile faded. "I don't think I like your new attitude, Benjy. I may have to have a little discussion with my husband. He always likes to know which associates are poking his wife."

"Fine," Ben said. He looked the woman straight in the eyes. She just didn't scare him anymore. Somehow, he thought, after you've seen a woman in a faded jeans jacket hanging on the shoulder of a 250-pound biker, it's hard to take her seriously. "You tell him what you want, and then I'll tell him who I found slumming at the Red Parrot the other night."

Mona laughed. "He'll never believe you."

"I have pictures."

"You do not!"

"Don't I, though? We undercover cops never leave home without our bow-tie cameras."

Mona's eyes fluttered. The energy seemed to drain out of her face. "It's because I'm old, isn't it?" Ben saw water forming into the wells of her eyes.

"No," he said softly. He put his hand on her arm. "It's not like that. It's just not right for me."

Before she had a chance to respond, a scream shot out from the area near the shallow end of the swimming pool.

"You're a contagion! A goddamned bubonic plague!" It was Louise Derek, railing at her husband. What was she doing here? Her face looked tired and drawn, even worse than it had that morning in Judge Schmidt's courtroom.

"I thought they split up," Ben said, staring at the feuding couple.

"They did," Mona said as she watched the spectacle. "They got back together again. He begged her to let him come back. Think of the good times, think of the kids, all that rot. I told her not to go back, but . . ." Mona sighed. "After he tried to kill himself, she gave in."

"What?"

"Ran a hose from the exhaust pipe on his Jaguar. Tried to asphyxiate himself. Had to be rushed to the hospital."

"I heard he had an acute asthma attack."

Mona looked at him and smiled. "My, you really *are* young, aren't you?" She turned back to watch the Dereks. "I suppose she hasn't made his life a picnic these past few years. It would be easy to feel sorry for him if he weren't a totally selfish, unfaithful, egomaniacal son of a bitch."

"You're the Typhoid Mary of infidelity!" Louise screamed, easily loud enough for everyone at the party to hear. Her voice was a strange amalgam of shrieking and sobbing.

"Come on, honey," Derek said. "You're making a scene. Don't get upset." He reached out toward her.

"Don't tell me not to get upset!" she said, slapping his hands away. "I have every right to get upset!" She took a giant step backward, which brought her to the edge of the shallow end of the pool.

"Get her away from the pool," Ben said, not loudly enough. "Someone needs to get her away from the pool before this tragedy turns to farce."

"I want you out of the house!" Louise continued screaming. "I want you, and all your belongings, and every filthy microbe of your being out of my house!"

"Honey, be reasonable." Again Derek reached out to her.

She swung wildly at his arms, missed, and slipped. She waved her arms in desperate circles, trying to regain her balance, but it was too late. With a loud shriek, she plummeted into the shallow end of the pool.

Ben hoped Derek would at least have the decorum not to laugh. He was seriously overestimating Derek's powers of self-control. Derek virtually exploded with glee. "It's too rich!" he said, between drunken laughs. "Too perfect."

"Well, that's the limit," Mona muttered. She threw down her purse, stomped over to the swimming pool, and, with a single shove, pushed Derek into the pool. He screamed, then started splashing wildly.

Ben noticed several people looking anxiously toward the front gate. The show was over, he supposed, all but the mopping up of the blood. He decided it would be a good time to join the exodus.

As he headed toward his car, he saw a shadowy figure standing in the street, pacing back and forth beside the curb.

"Ben?" the figure asked. It was Brancusci.

"What are you doing here?" Ben asked.

"Looking for you. Your office told me where you were. Eventually. What a snotty secretary you have." He stepped into the beam of the streetlight. "I've got all the papers you wanted together. They're at my apartment now."

Ben sighed. It had been an exhausting day. He couldn't possibly focus on financial reports tonight. "I think tomorrow morning will be soon enough."

Brancusci's brow creased. "I thought you said you were in a hurry? Besides, it isn't just the financials. I figured out who—" He froze in the middle of the sentence.

"What? What is it?"

"My God," Brancusci said, almost imperceptibly. "I didn't know *he'd* be here."

Ben turned and saw Mona walking out with a tall, good-looking fellow with a mustache. He realized it was Marianne's date, the notorious C. Kevin. Poor Marianne— evidently, he wasn't as professional as she thought. Or maybe he was.

"Did he see me?" Brancusci whispered. He ducked behind one of the cars parked on the street.

"Did *who* see you?" Ben asked. "C. Kevin?"

More people were coming through the gate. Brancusci began skittering away.

"Call me tomorrow," Brancusci whispered. He disappeared into the darkness.

The guests were dispersing. After a few moments, Derek and his wife emerged from the front of the house. Ben ducked into his Honda.

Derek had both arms around his wife's shoulders. He was patting her dry with a bath towel. "I'm so sorry, sweetheart," Ben heard him say, in a soft, purring tone. "I'll try to be better. Let's get you to the hospital and see about that nasty bump on your head." He opened the passenger door of the Jaguar parked in the driveway, and she stepped inside. Derek crawled behind the wheel and drove the car down the street.

What an incredible night, Ben thought, driving away. His headlights flashed on the front porch, and Ben saw someone standing in a dark corner beside the door. He looked in his rearview mirror. He couldn't see anyone. A trick of the light? If not, how long had the person been there? Is that who Brancusci saw?

He turned his car around and flashed his brights on the front of the house. There was no one there, now.

Ben made a U-turn and headed home. He rolled up the car window, trying to shake off a distinct chill.

PART THREE

*   *

If Bees Are Few

* 33 *

"Success!" Christina announced. She held her yellow legal pad over her head triumphantly. "We're lucky the entry on that ledger was for such an odd amount. If it had been an even four or five hundred, I'd have a thousand possible locations for you. As it is, I have one."

"One what?" Ben asked, looking up from the brief he was writing.

"One apartment. Well, two floors of an apartment complex, to be exact. The Malador Apartments, the tall round building just south of downtown. They have three sizes of apartments—efficiencies, one-bedrooms, and two-bedrooms. And the monthly rent for a one-bedroom apartment is—yes, you guessed it—*exactly* four hundred and seventeen dollars and forty-six cents, tax and bills included."

"Incredible!" Ben said. "You're a gem and a half, Christina."

"Well, yes," she said, fluttering her eyelids.

"I suppose we can't be certain the payment was for an apartment rental. Even if Brancusci is right about it being some kind of real estate payment, it might be for a private home or even undeveloped real estate."

"I don't think so. If Sanguine was setting up some kind

of pied-à-terre on the sly, he'd want as much anonymity as possible. An apartment complex would be ideal. He could send one of his many minions over to rent the place, then just drop the rent check in the mail once a month. But the *pièce de résistance* is the amount of the monthly rental, Ben. It's an exact match.''

"That's got to be it," Ben said. "At any rate, it's definitely our best lead. Let's go."

Ben and Christina sat in the front seat of Ben's Honda, parked halfway down the street from the Malador apartment building. On the way, they had stopped at Christina's apartment so she could change into less eye-catching clothes. An ordinary blue jeans skirt and a white blouse. No leotards.

Ben filled her in on everything he had learned during his last visit to Sanguine. She particularly enjoyed the news about the new double-duty locks on the front doors of the office building. Once Christina was up-to-date, they began to plan their strategic assault on the Malador Apartments.

"Why *me*?" Christina exclaimed. "I thought we were a team."

"We are a team, but it's your turn to run with the ball. It will seem more credible coming from a woman. And besides, I have to stay free for the follow-up. I can't do that if they've already seen me claiming to be a pollster." He ran through his mental checklist to see if he could come up with any more excuses. "And what if I got caught? I could be disbarred. Legal assistants can't be disbarred."

"No, but we can be fired, imprisoned, ridiculed, and impoverished." She took the clipboard from the backseat. "Yes, I can see it now. It is better that I go."

Ben smiled.

Christina brushed her golden-red hair away from her face. "Maybe I should change clothes again."

"Stop stalling. You look fine. Very professional. Just tell them you're with the city of Tulsa. You're taking a survey of apartment dwellers on behalf of the Chamber of Commerce in order to formulate plans for a large-scale downtown renovation project lah-dee-dah-dee-dah." He paused. "And Christina. Lay off the French."

"Got it," she said. She pushed open the car door, then stopped. "Shouldn't I have a badge or ID?"

"Will you get out of here already?" Ben shoved her out of the car. "Don't worry, you'll be great."

"Great," she muttered, closing the car door. "You'd better be damned appreciative when this is over."

"I will be. Honest."

"Hmmmph." Christina rearranged her clothes, placed the clipboard under her arm, and began marching down the street.

"Why do I agree to do these things?" Christina muttered to herself as she rode the elevator to the seventh floor. I'm a thirtysomething adult divorcée, not a stupid college kid. I'm too old and too smart to be playing cops and robbers. As if breaking and entering and nearly being caught wasn't enough. As if I didn't do him any favors in that sleazoid bar where we both could've been killed.

The elevator doors parted. Christina canceled her interior monologue and tried to concentrate on the task at hand. She stared at the door to apartment 701. Well, she thought, I suppose this beats doing document productions in Shreveport.

Almost immediately after she knocked, the door swung

open. A short, wide man in a white T-shirt bearing the logo of a domestic beer company stood beyond the portal. He shamelessly surveyed Christina from top to bottom.

"Yeah?" he grunted.

Christina felt a flush of heat rush through her body. "Hello, sir. My name is Christina Crockett and I'm with the City of Commerce taking a survey for the Chamber of Horrors. I mean—" Christina's hand passed across her forehead. "Oh, God, let me try that again."

The man in the doorway stared at her. He took one hand off the doorjamb and rubbed his stubbled chin.

"You know it's always harder to pick up again after lunch," Christina said. "I've got to stop eating Mexican." She laughed self-consciously. God, what a nightmare.

"I wouldn't know," the man said. "I work nights. After work, I usually just grab a coupla beers and crash."

"Oh, really," Christina said, scribbling meaningless shapes on her clipboard. "That's very interesting. What kind of work are you in?"

"Security watchman over at the Williams Center. For now, anyway. It's not what I really wanna do, but times are kinda tough. What's it to you?"

Christina smiled reassuringly. "Just something I need to know for this survey. Tell me, do you live alone?"

He snorted. "Don't I wish. Yeah, other than my wife, three brats, and a brother-in-law—yeah, I live alone."

"I see, I see." More furious scribbling on her clipboard.

"I tell you what, Miz Crock, or whatever, none of 'em gonna be home for at least an hour. You wanna step in for a bit?" His eyebrows danced suspiciously. "I got some beer in the fridge."

"Oh, I don't think so."

"I could get some grass, if you're into that."

More self-conscious laughter. "Oh, thanks, thanks, but no . . ." You'll pay for this, Ben, she swore silently. "Now, I'm going to read you a list of major businesses headquartered in the Tulsa area, and in order to gauge the effectiveness of their promotional campaigns, I'd like you to tell me if you're familiar with them. All right, how about . . . uh . . ." Come on, Christina, she thought, don't blank out now. "Uh . . . the Williams Companies?"

"I said, I work at the Williams Center. You think I'm some kinda moron?"

"Oh, no, no. Far be it for me . . . How about the Bama Pie Company?"

"They make those little bitty pecan pies, right? I like those. Damn wife never brings those home anymore. Moron wife."

"I see, I see. How about Sanguine Enterprises?"

"Mmm . . . never heard of it. Any reason why I should?"

"No, not at all." Somehow, Christina sensed that lying was far beyond this man's capabilities.

"Look, I'm tireda standin' in the doorway. You comin' in or not? I'll make it worth your while."

Christina let loose her loudest laugh yet. "Tempting, tempting. But totally against regulations. Thank you for your cooperation. Be seeing you."

"What are you, some kind of religious freak or something?"

"No . . . no . . . but, thanks again. . . ."

She beat a hasty retreat down the corridor.

* 34 *

By the time Christina reached apartment 724, she was convinced that the entire Tulsa populace was comprised of fundamentalists, housewives, soap-opera addicts, and the unemployed. The hardest to shake were those determined to see her born again before she finished her survey; the hardest to rouse were those mesmerized by the thrilling exploits of *All My Children.*

With a weary hand, she knocked on the door of apartment 724.

The woman who opened the door wore the unflattering solid white cotton uniform that unmistakably identified her as a nurse. She was a large woman, though not a fat one; she had an imposing, big-boned figure.

"Are you affiliated with one of the hospitals in the Tulsa area?" Christina asked after running through her preliminary patter.

"I was," the nurse said emotionlessly. "I'm retired now." The woman was tight-lipped and uncommunicative. Nothing but the facts.

"I see. Are you now working for a private employer?"

"Yes."

"How long have you been employed in this capacity?"

"Almost two years now."

"May I ask who your employer is?"

The woman hesitated. "That information is confidential."

Christina tried to keep the conversation moving. "I see. Well, I don't think it's important that I know the name. I think the Chamber of Commerce would, however, appreciate knowing if your employer is affiliated with one of the major corporations in the city, such as . . . oh, the Memorex/Telex Corporation, or Sanguine Enterprises."

The woman's reaction was unmistakable. "Who *are* you?" she asked. Her face tightened up, as if drawn in by invisible strings.

"As I said, I'm just a surveyor for the Chamber of Commerce. I take it you do not live alone . . . ?"

The woman's irritation visibly increased. Her eyes fixed upon Christina's. "My *patient* lives here, not me. I look after her nine-to-nine each and every day, including holidays. And I should be tending to her now, so, if you'll excuse me—"

"And what is the patient's name?" Christina asked, but it was too late. The door closed in her face midsentence.

"She's the one, Ben, I guarantee it. When I said Sanguine's name, she looked at me like a trapped Nazi war criminal."

Ben stroked his steering wheel. The sun was beginning to fade behind the horizon.

"You checked the rest of the apartments in our price slot anyway?"

"Of course. No one else seemed at all suspicious, though at three of the apartments there was nobody home. But she's the one, Ben. I guarantee it."

Ben stroked his chin thoughtfully. "Yeah, she's the

one—but what is she? I don't see the connection. An old nurse and her patient. How does that tie in with Sanguine?'' He drummed his fingers on the dash. ''Do you know what's wrong with the patient? How old she is?''

''No, Ben. Those questions all came after she slammed the door in my face.''

Ben sighed. ''Then we move to Plan B. It's time for me to follow up.''

''Do it fast, Ben. I think she was suspicious. She might talk to her mysterious employer or someone else. Then who knows what might happen. I don't want you to get in any trouble.''

Ben saw the genuine concern in Christina's eyes. Something about the nurse had really spooked her. ''I'll be all right,'' he said, trying to sound confident. ''I'll wait a few hours, so she won't be too suspicious. Besides, before I go in, there's something I need to see Mike about.''

''Why not get Mike to investigate this? He's a cop. Cops are supposed to do things like this, not baby lawyers.''

''What grounds would he have for going in there? How could he establish probable cause? We don't have anything nearly concrete enough to get a warrant. *Well, your honor, that nurse seemed real suspicious.* Forget it.'' He started the car. ''If we get the cops involved in the seizure of illegal evidence, it may become impossible to nail Sanguine.''

Christina brushed her fingers against the side of Ben's head. ''Be careful, Ben. Promise.''

''Oh, yeah? Why?''

Christina folded her arms across her chest. ''Because you still owe me dinner, and I don't want you to weasel out of it. Jerk!''

* 35 *

Ben knocked softly on the door. Then, remembering his role for the evening, he knocked again, with a solid insistent pounding.

The nurse opened the door a few inches. She was exactly as Christina had described her. Formidable, like a slab of granite. Ben felt his confidence dripping away like water from a wrung washrag.

"Yes?" the woman said. Her body language was a neon sign saying DON'T MESS WITH ME.

Ben reached slowly into his inside jacket pocket. Do it fast and smooth, Mike had said, like you do it every day. Don't let her get a close look. It is a fake, after all. I can't risk sending you out there with the real McCoy. I might get into trouble.

"Lieutenant Kincaid, Tulsa PD." Ben flashed his badge with a quick fluid motion, barely giving the woman time to focus on the glinting metal. "Detective. Larceny. I'm investigating a series of robberies in this apartment complex."

The woman did not open the door. "I haven't heard about any robberies."

"Lucky for you," Ben bluffed. "Don't you ever read the papers? Talk to your neighbors?"

"No," she replied.

"May I come in?"

The woman peered at him. Her internal deliberations were almost visible. After a moment, with evident regret, she allowed Ben to pass through.

The apartment was sparingly decorated. The furniture had a higgledy-piggledy quality to it, as if it had been randomly collected from a variety of garage sales with no view toward the whole. A manteled fireplace with no grate, no screen, and no ashes. A round white acrylic dining room table, perfectly clean. Sheets draped across the bay window in place of curtains.

The nurse gestured toward the sofa. As Ben walked in that direction, he glanced down the main hallway jutting off to the left of the fireplace. At the far end of the hallway, in another room, he saw a woman sitting in an upright wicker chair, staring back at him.

She was wearing a long blue overcoat, or perhaps a bathrobe—Ben was too far away to tell for certain. Ben guessed her to be somewhere in her late thirties or early forties. Her legs were crossed at the knee and her arms were drawn tightly across her chest, each hand clinging to the opposite arm. She was barefoot.

Her features seemed pleasant enough from Ben's distance, but her facial expression was pensive. Her skin seemed untouched by sun—a radiant, glowing ivory. It was a glow Ben thought he had seen before.

"That is Catherine . . . Catherine Andrews, my patient. This is her apartment. I care for her."

Ben nodded. The woman down the hallway didn't seem to acknowledge the introduction. Her eyes were glassy, and her gaze fixed.

As an afterthought, the nurse added, "My name is Harriet Morrison. I'm a nurse."

Ben continued to look at Catherine. Something seemed wrong. So wrong that this tight-lipped nurse was spontaneously offering helpful information to divert his attention.

The nurse led Ben further into the living room, where his view of Catherine was obstructed.

Ben removed a small notepad from his back pants pocket and began to scribble disinterestedly. "Forgive me for prying," he said, "but for security reasons, I have no choice. Do I understand that Miss Andrews is here alone at nights?"

"That is . . . correct," the nurse said haltingly. "I leave after I see that Miss Andrews is settled for the night."

"Are you here every day?"

"Yes." Her left eyebrow rose.

Being too nosy, Ben thought. Slow down and play the game. "Do either of you have any valuable jewelry on the premises?"

The nurse sat down in the love seat facing the sofa. "Miss Andrews has a few pieces. Nothing of great value, I'm sure."

Ben continued to make notes on his pad. Then, on the pretext of surveying the apartment, he stood up and paced around the living room. "No TV or stereo. Just as well. Burglars love electronic equipment. Easy to take, easy to pawn. Do you have any drugs on the premises?"

The nurse hesitated. "Of course, being a nurse, I have some medications here."

"What kinds?"

"Nothing of interest to prowlers."

"You'd be amazed what a dope-starved junkie might be interested in, ma'am. What do you have?"

"Sedatives, tranquilizers, sleeping pills, that sort of thing." She paused. "Catherine sometimes requires . . . calming. Nothing illegal, I assure you."

"I'm sure. Do all the doors here have dead bolts?"

"I'm afraid not. Just ordinary push-button door locks."

"Unbelievable," Ben intoned gravely. "I'll have to make a note. The manager really ought to do something about that. A burglar could be in here and out again with all your valuables in sixty seconds. Piece of cake."

The nurse shrugged. "There's not much to take, really."

Ben continued to pace around the apartment until he had positioned himself in front of the hallway. He raised his voice. "I wonder if I could ask *you* a few questions, Miss . . . Andrews, is it?"

The nurse stood immediately. "Could I speak to you privately, Lieutenant?"

Ben strode over to the nurse.

"Lieutenant, Miss Andrews is . . . not well. Not physically *or* mentally. I'm sure you've surmised the reason she requires the constant care of a nurse. She is not . . . lucid. She is in a continual depressive state, paranoid, probably schizophrenic. It would be difficult to have a conversation with her and impossible to learn anything. And it could cause considerable trauma to her, you not being a trained professional."

Ben looked back at the woman in the wicker chair. Asleep with her eyes open, as far as he could tell.

"I understand. I probably have everything I need. But do call the police station if you see anyone or anything suspicious, will you? Ask for Lieutenant Kincaid."

The nurse nodded her head, not smiling. "I will. What's that number?"

There was a pause. Ben stuttered. "It's . . . it's in the book. Or dial 911."

The nurse stared intently at Ben. "You're very young to be a police lieutenant, aren't you?"

"I went into the force as soon as I got out of the army," he said, thinking off the top of his head. "I've done my time."

"I see," the woman said, without breaking eye contact. "What was your badge number again? In case I should want to contact you."

"Not necessary," Ben said, steadily edging toward the door. "Just ask for me by name. Thank you for your time, ma'am."

* 36 *

There was no moon. Ben would have wished for a moon—not a full moon, just enough to see and breathe and feel like the night wasn't swallowing him whole. Times like this, Ben almost wished he was a smoker. Not for the flavor—just so he would have something to do while waiting. Besides waiting. And waiting.

It began to rain. Not a lot, just a fine mist. He rolled the car windows up, but left a small crack in the window closest to him so he could hear. The windows began to fog, but there wasn't much he could do about it. He couldn't turn on the engine to power the windshield wipers or defogger without drawing attention to his parked car. Ben pulled his shirt-sleeve over his hand and wiped clear a circle on the side window. He had to be able to see.

How did that line go? Like sands through the hourglass, these are the days of our lives. No kidding, Ben thought. Seven o'clock passed, then eight. Ticktock, ticktock. A mixture of recollection, analysis, and daydreaming trickled through Ben's head. Maybe the nurse lied. Maybe she stays there all day and all night. Maybe it's a trap. Maybe she's the killer. Ticktock, ticktock. Nine o'clock.

At a quarter to ten, the nurse stepped out of the elevator feeding the sunken parking garage of the apartment complex. Her feet clubbed the pavement. She walked through the garage, then stepped into a yellow Nova and started the engine.

Ben waited a full five minutes after she had driven away before he stepped out of his car. A matter of caution, he told himself, but he knew he was really just drumming up the nerve. He hopped a brick wall, walked into the sunken parking garage, and punched the elevator button. He rode the elevator to the seventh floor.

Quietly, taking care not to attract attention, he walked the short distance to apartment 724. He knocked sharply on the door. He knew she wouldn't answer, but the suburbs in him made him try, just to be polite. He knocked again.

No answer.

He had examined the simple lock earlier, when he was inside. Later he'd driven to a pay phone, called Greg, and had a brief conversation about push-button door locks. It sounded simple enough.

He withdrew the Citibank MasterCard from his wallet and slid it between the edge of the door and the wall, just below the lock. He wedged the card beneath the lower end of the tongue. One sharp slice, and a quiet popping noise told him the lock was sprung. Simple. Most bathrooms were better protected. He stepped into the apartment.

"Hello?"

The apartment was dark except for the light of a single lamp burning in the room at the far end of the hallway. He saw a dark figure moving in the shadows and then, a moment later, she stepped into the hallway.

Ben flipped on the lights. Catherine could not have reacted faster if he had hit her knee with a hammer. She fell back, clutching the wall with one hand. Her eyes expanded to three times their previous size. She breathed with sharp, painful gulps of air.

And yet, she did not scream. She did not run. She stared at him with uncomprehending eyes. She did not seem to recognize him but, after a moment, she did not seem afraid of him either.

Ben took a step closer. He had not meant to startle her. He had to do something fast to put her at ease.

"I'm here to help you," he said quickly. He wished he could take it back. Sounded like something out of a fairy tale—knight in shining armor here to save the damsel in distress. He took another step closer.

"Daddy?" she asked. She had a high-pitched, uncertain voice, the voice of a child. Ben wondered how many times she used it in the course of a day. Or a week. Or a year. She was wearing a dingy blue bathrobe, tattered and pocked with holes and dried food stains. She pulled the robe tightly around her body.

"No," he answered quietly. "I'm not Daddy. But I'm

your friend—I want to help. I knocked on the door, but no one answered, so I let myself in.''

She stared at him, puzzled, as if he were speaking in a foreign language. Her initial rush began to fade; her eyes seemed droopy and tired.

"I was here this afternoon. Remember?'' He was standing directly in front of her now. Her dark hair was stringy and matted; it hadn't been washed for weeks. Her pale face was smudged and dirty.

She continued to stare at him. "Are you Harriet's helper?'' she asked.

"Yes,'' Ben said quickly. "That's it. I'm her new helper.''

"Harriet told me to sleep. But I couldn't sleep. I was afraid.'' The pained look crept back into her eyes. "Daddy might come for a visit.''

Ben sat down on the love seat next to the sofa. He gestured for her to sit on the sofa, but she hung back in the hallway, clutching her bathrobe.

He knew he needed to gain her confidence or he would get nowhere. "Do you like poems, Catherine?''

She nodded slightly.

"I do,'' he continued. "Do you know this one? 'To make a prairie it takes a clover and one bee/One clover, and a bee/And reverie.' ''

" 'The reverie alone will do,' '' Catherine said slowly, " 'if bees are few.' ''

I was right, Ben thought. "Catherine, I know Harriet was very busy tonight—maybe she didn't get to do everything you wanted her to do. Is there anything I can do for you?''

"Can I have a bath?'' she asked quietly, without looking at him. Although Ben sat only a few feet from her,

her eyes couldn't seem to focus on him. "Harriet left, but I didn't get a bath." Her voice dropped to a conspiratorial whisper. "She almost never lets me anymore."

"Of course you can have a bath. I'll run the water." Ben stood and walked toward Catherine and the hallway. She did not move away from him. Her expression was of almost palpable sadness. Sadness and exhaustion.

He took a wisp of her straggly black hair in his hand and brushed it away from her face. Then he walked into the bathroom, flipped on the light, and started running the water. After a few moments, Catherine timidly followed him into the bathroom.

"How hot do you like it?" he asked. She looked at him as if he were speaking gibberish. He adjusted the knobs for a medium-warm temperature.

"That's enough," she said. She reached past him and turned off the faucets. The tub held perhaps three inches of water. "I'll need a towel."

"Are you sure that's enough?" Ben asked. Catherine did not answer. She began to remove her bathrobe. "I'll go out and . . . find you a towel," Ben said, embarrassed. He stepped out of the room, leaving the door slightly ajar.

Ben found the linen closet and removed a white towel. He stepped into the bedroom and checked the dresser drawers. No panties or bras—no undergarments at all. No ornaments or photos or any other indication that a person actually lived there. On the nightstand next to the bed, Ben found a small book of poems by Emily Dickinson and four large bottles of pills, two of them about half empty. He read the labels, but it was all pharmaceutical Greek to him. Sleeping pills, he guessed, or maybe tranquilizers. Four different kinds.

He carried the towel back to the bathroom door. On the

floor, outside the door, he saw Catherine's bathrobe tossed in a heap, next to a brown towel. He bent down to pick them up, then stopped. The towel stank abominably, like the worst smell from the worst sewer from Ben's worst nightmare. The towel was knotted on both ends, like a diaper.

"Don't you have any"—he paused, searching for the right word—"undergarments?"

"No," Catherine said from inside the bathroom. She was still whispering. "Harriet couldn't buy any. It would attract attention. Daddy's spies are everywhere. Making sure I'm good."

Ben glanced through the crack in the door and saw Catherine's reflection in the mirror. She was standing naked in the tub. The water barely covered her ankles.

"Is the water too hot?" he asked through the door.

"It's fine, thank you."

"But . . . why are you standing? Why don't you sit down?"

"Oh, no. No, no, no. I could fall asleep and drown and die. It happens every day. Daddy says."

Ben looked away from the bathroom. "My God," he murmured under his breath. "What have they done to you?"

"I'm ready to get out now." Ben heard the sound of water splashing as she stepped out of the tub. He handed the clean towel through the door and, a moment later, handed through her bathrobe.

She stepped outside. The smudges on her face were still there, perhaps smeared, perhaps a bit faded. Her eyes were red and bloodshot and tired. Ben held her by her upper arms and, to his surprise, she did not shrink away.

"Look, Catherine," he said, "I'm going to take you out of here."

"No!" she cried, horror-struck.

"For God's sake, why not?"

"He'll find out! He'll find out!" She was breathing heavily again, punctuating her words with desperate gasping noises. "He'll kill her! I have to stay here and be good. I have to prove it's safe for him to bring her back." Her hands pushed against Ben's chest.

"Who is *he*, Catherine. Who is *he*?"

"If I'm good, he'll reward me, he'll bring her back. If I'm bad again, it'll be worse than before."

Ben held her tightly. "Bring who back, Catherine? Your baby?"

"My *baby*!" She was screaming, protracting each syllable. "My baby! God, please don't take her away! Please! I'll do anything. I can't live without my baby!" She tried to say more, but there was no more left in her. Her chin dropped.

Ben took a red handkerchief from his jacket pocket. "Here. Wipe your eyes."

She stared at it. "I can't use that. It's too pretty."

"No, really. Take it. It's for you."

"For me?" She seemed amazed. She held the handkerchief against her face, then placed it in her bathrobe pocket.

Ben held her firmly in his hands. She pulled herself against him, and they hugged one another tightly. Her tears washed against Ben's face.

"Will you help me?" she pleaded.

"I'll do anything you want," he said. Gently, he moved her to the bedroom and lowered her onto her bed.

"Stay with me," she said. She touched him lightly on the arm.

He pulled the covers over her. "I really can't. It wouldn't be—" He stopped. Her eyes were beginning to well up again.

"Perhaps for just a little while," he said. He lowered himself to the bed and cuddled next to her. He knew that he shouldn't be doing this, but at the same time, knew that he should. She had asked him to help her and he would, damn it, he would do anything she wanted. It was time for him to do something right, and he would. He would.

* 37 *

Ben eased off of the bed, careful to create as little disturbance as possible. Without turning on the light, he found his shoes. As he stepped toward the door, his foot fell on something sharp. He started to cry out but caught himself. He reached down and plucked the object from his foot. It was a syringe. He wasn't surprised.

He crept into the hallway, pulled on his shoes, tiptoed out of the apartment, and locked the door behind him.

The sun was just beginning to rise; the first orange rays were seeping over the horizon and surrounding the broad outlines of the Williams and Bank of Oklahoma Towers. The fresh morning air felt invigorating, cleansing.

Ben walked briskly, then began to jog, down the street to his Honda. He drove back to his apartment, thinking he would shower and change his clothes before calling Mike.

He rode the elevator to the fourteenth floor, reached for the doorknob to his apartment, then froze. His mood took a sudden, crashing, downhill turn.

The door was not shut.

Ben stared at the door, listening intently. He always shut and locked his door before he left. *Always.* And it was way too early for another visit from Julia.

Ben steeled himself. He kicked the door open and pressed himself up against the outside wall.

There was no sound inside.

After a moment, he stepped into the apartment. Records, books, pillows, and boxes were scattered across the floor. The television was shattered; shards of gray glass lay on the floor beneath the broken box. The stereo cabinet was upset and lying on the floor; the turntable cover was crushed. Ben saw what little he owned smashed and broken into pieces.

The kitchenette was just the same. Everything was upside down and out of place—pots and pans on the linoleum floor, plates broken, refrigerator door wide open. In the bedroom, clothes were scattered, and his sleeping bag was thrown in a heap in the corner. Either a hurricane had blown through during the night, or someone had ransacked Ben's apartment.

Someone, it suddenly occurred to Ben, who might still be there.

Ben ran out of the apartment and stood outside the door. This is ridiculous, he told himself. I've been in every room. No one is there. Somehow, logic didn't make him feel any better about going back inside.

While Ben deliberated, his telephone rang. After three rings, he decided to brave it. Once inside, it took him three more rings to find the phone, buried under a pile of heavily starched and now thoroughly wrinkled white shirts.

"Who is it?"

"Where the hell have you been all night? I've been calling since three in the morning." It was Mike, and he sounded hostile.

"Mike, thank God. I was just about to call you. Someone searched my apartment. Tore the place apart."

"Yeah?" Mike sounded decidedly unsympathetic. "Maybe if you spent more time there these things wouldn't happen. I mean, I understand, a guy's been in town not quite two weeks, he starts to get a little lonely—"

"Look, Mike, I need help—"

"Sounds like you're doing okay to me, lover boy. But that's not why I called. I've got another stiff on my hands."

Ben felt the gnawing sensation in the pit of his stomach intensify. "Who?"

"Don't know. No identification." Then he added: "It's like before."

"What do you mean, like before?"

"Like why the hell do you think I've been trying to call you? I've got another corpse bearing your business card! Clenched in his rigor-mortised fist!"

Ben began to breathe rapidly. "What does he look like? It is a he, isn't it?"

"Yes, it's a he. He's about five foot eight, short dark hair, probable Italian descent, no chin, beak nose."

"My God. It's Brancusci. The accountant. Mike, this is very important. Did he have any papers on him?"

"Nothing. I told you—he's been stripped clean."

The gnawing sensation was like a knife. Ben began to feel light-headed. "Got any suspects?"

"Just the usual," Mike replied. "You."

Ben and Mike stood in an alleyway in the heart of old downtown Tulsa, a few blocks north of the river, wedged between Ernie's Pool Hall and a tiny Greek restaurant. Both were closed; their Fifties-era neon signs were dark. Diagonally across the street, the scuzziest Safeway in town was just beginning to open for a new business day. The street people huddling over the sidewalk vents began to awaken, stretching and urinating and brushing the night's grime from their clothes.

For the first time in his life, Ben considered whether déjà vu was more than a cliché. The weather was misty, wet, and unpleasant—just like before. He and Mike stood in a filthy alley—just like before. Again, he watched paramedics lift a broken corpse onto a stretcher with considerable difficulty and stash it in the back of an ambulance. Again, he knew that the only thing sparing him from a grueling police interrogation was a former relation by marriage to the investigating detective.

There was one difference, though, Ben told himself, one key difference. This time, it was probably my fault. He had promised Brancusci he would call, but in the excitement of locating the apartment at Malador, he had forgotten all about Brancusci. Even after seeing how anxious and afraid he had been at the party, Ben had forgotten. And now Brancusci was dead.

"This Brancusci guy had your business card clenched in his fist," Mike said. "Any idea why?"

Ben told him about his meetings with Brancusci. He

also revealed the details about the apartment at Malador and his chat with Harriet. He declined to tell Mike about his return visit.

"Something is going on in that apartment," Mike murmured. "I'm going to send out a couple of uniforms to check it out."

"Not yet," Ben said quickly. "Any bust now would tip off the man in charge. If we wait, we might be able to use the apartment to track down our killer."

Mike exhaled wearily. "Perhaps you're right."

"Do you know how Brancusci was killed?"

"Same as before," Mike said, with a sort of a grunt. "With a big knife. It's too early to tell, but it looks like it could be the same knife that was used on Adams. We've found no trace of a weapon. I've got men searching the general area, but I'm willing to bet we won't find anything. The killer's smart enough to take the knife home and stick it back in his roast beef."

"Who found the body?"

"We're not sure. We got an anonymous phone call about two in the morning. I'd guess it was another street person, except they probably wouldn't have a quarter for a telephone call. Did you get a look at the knife wounds?"

Ben swallowed hard. "No," he whispered.

"Unfinished business," Mike said. "I'm making a big guess, based on what happened to the Adams corpse and the evidence that the two killings are connected. I'm guessing that our killer got caught in the act. I think he'd made the fatal slice and was just beginning the sicko mutilation when someone cut in. So to speak."

Ben ignored the morbid humor. "Who could have seen them?"

Mike shrugged. "Anyone. Drunk. Prostitute. Street

person. You'd be amazed how many people are running around Tulsa late at night, particularly downtown. Most of them have nowhere else to go. I've got guys interviewing to see if anyone saw anything significant."

"Think you'll have any luck?"

"Who knows?" Mike thrust his hands in his overcoat pockets. "The homeless aren't really renowned for their sense of civic obligation. Most of them don't like cops much, either. Cops are always pushing them around, telling them to get off the streets. As if they could." Mike paused. "There is one thing in our favor, though. I can't believe the killer chose this place. My guess is Brancusci lives around here and insisted on meeting somewhere nearby. The way I see it, the killer calls Brancusci up, they agree to meet somewhere, and Brancusci gets knifed. Killer drags the body into the alley and begins to slice."

Ben rubbed his throbbing temples. "It doesn't make any sense. When I saw Brancusci last, he was totally on edge. Why would he agree to meet the killer out on the street in the dead of night?"

"The killer probably didn't identify himself as such," Mike answered. "Maybe he pretended to be you."

The churning in Ben's stomach seemed to explode, like a firecracker in the duodenum. Of course. It made sense. Ben was long overdue. Brancusci would be waiting for him to call so that Brancusci could give Ben the financial records Ben had bullied him into providing.

"Excuse me," Ben said. He walked down the alley, turned around the corner to the back of the building and fell to his knees to be sick. He retched a futile retch. He realized that he had not eaten since—when? He could not remember his last meal. He had been busy. Busy forgetting about Brancusci.

Slowly, Ben rose, wiped his mouth, and walked back to the alleyway.

"We've got to go see Sanguine, Mike, and you've got to make him talk."

Mike guffawed. "Right. Just like on TV. He'll break down, whimper, and confess."

"Then scare him. Teach him the fear of God and the criminal justice system."

Mike fidgeted with his pipe. "I don't even know what it is we think Sanguine has done. I don't understand how it all fits together—the fraudulent records, the apartment at Malador, Adams, the little girl. What do we charge him with? Corporate fraud? We can't tie him to either murder, and it's not against the law to rent an apartment."

"Sanguine has to be the killer, Mike."

"Think you've got it figured out, huh, Sherlock?"

"Yeah, I think I do."

"Know who trashed your apartment? And why?"

"I think Sanguine was looking for the stolen records. Maybe Brancusci wasn't stupid enough to carry them with him when he got killed. Or maybe Sanguine wanted to see if I had copies."

Mike looked at Ben and held his gaze firmly for a moment. Then, with an air more of resignation than confidence, he opened the door of his car and slid behind the wheel.

"You'd better be right," Mike said simply.

"Let's take separate cars," Ben said.

Mike nodded. "I hope one thing has occurred to you, though," he added. "Whoever the killer is, he's apparently killed to lay his hands on misappropriated financial records. That killer may also believe *you* have the same records."

"So?"

"You know what Shakespeare said, kemo sabe. 'The first thing we do, let's kill all the lawyers.' ''

Ben's body suddenly turned cold. "Christina knows about the records, too," he said.

Before Mike had a chance to answer, Ben ran down the street to his Honda, gunned the engine, and pulled out into the street.

* 38 *

Ben bolted out of the thirty-eighth floor elevator, jogged around the corner, and ran down the corridor to Maggie's station. Maggie was reclining in her secretarial chair and thumbing through a fashion magazine.

"Have you seen Christina yet this morning?" Ben asked breathlessly.

Maggie raised her head slowly and peered at him, squinting her eyes. "I haven't seen her."

"Call her at home."

Maggie shook her head. "Mr. Derek told me to keep the line open—"

Reaching over her typewriter, Ben picked up the phone receiver and shoved it under Maggie's chin. "Call her!" he shouted.

Maggie's eyes narrowed. Then, after glancing at the list

taped to her desk, she dialed the number. "No answer," she said after a moment.

Ben pounded his fist against her desk. "Damn, damn, *damn!*"

Maggie exhaled slowly. "She's in the library," she said at last.

"What?"

"She left a note on my desk this morning. She's in the library."

"Why didn't you say so?"

Maggie looked down at her magazine. "You didn't ask if I knew where she was. You asked if I had *seen* her."

After two weeks of wondering, Ben suddenly understood how a man could be driven to kill. Suppressing his temper, he ran down the corridor and into the library.

Christina was standing in the stacks beside the Supreme Court reporters, wearing her green Robin Hood outfit.

"Christina!" Ben shouted. Several associates sitting at the reference table looked up. "Thank God you're here."

"Ben! How did it go?"

"Fine." He walked over to her. "Just fine."

"I called your place late last night but you weren't there."

"Yeah, I was—"

"Is something wrong? You look really strung out."

"I was just worried."

Christina's brow knitted. "What's happened, Ben?"

"Brancusci is dead."

Christina's hands slowly dropped to her side. "My God," she whispered. "Did you get the—"

"No. I think that's why he was killed."

Christina looked at him but didn't say anything.

"Look, Christina, I need your help."

She nodded. "Serving you always gives me that special *joie de vivre*."

"Then find out where Brancusci lived. Go there and wait for the police to arrive. *Don't* go in until they get there. It's not safe. I want you to help them search. Mike will okay it. You know more about this case than they do; you'll know what to look for. See if you can find those records or anything that might tell us who Brancusci met last night."

"Got it. Then what?"

"Then go over to apartment 724 at the Malador and wait for me. You know the way. And"—he paused, unable to think of a diplomatic way to put it—"bring some women's clothing. I don't know the exact size. She's a little shorter than you, and about the same weight. Just take some stuff that doesn't have to fit too well. Everything—from the undies out."

"Got it."

And thanks for not asking, Ben thought. "I want you to call Maggie every half hour, on the half hour. Instruct her that if you don't call on the half hour, she's to call the police immediately. Understand? Immediately."

Christina's lips turned up slightly. "You were worried about me, weren't you?"

"I just . . . If the killer knew about me, he could know about you. Be careful, okay?"

"You got it," she said, smiling.

Ben turned and dashed back into the corridor.

As he passed Maggie, she announced, "Mr. Derek wants to speak to you."

"It'll have to wait."

Maggie was insistent. "He wanted to see you as soon as you came in."

"Tell him to stick it in his bad ear," Ben said. "I have something else I have to do."

<h1 style="text-align:center">* 39 *</h1>

The four men sat in Sanguine's office and stared at one another; Ben and Mike were in the chairs facing Sanguine's desk, while Tidwell stood faithfully at his master's side. The atmosphere was thick and heavy. No lawyer jokes today.

"Perhaps you misunderstood one of your professors in law school, Mr. Kincaid," Sanguine said. "You see, in-house counsel is supposed to be an advocate *for* the corporation and its employees, not against them."

"I never accepted that job," Ben replied bitterly.

"God knows everyone at Raven thinks you accepted it," Sanguine countered. "You still work for the Raven firm, don't you? You go where the firm tells you to go and do what the firm tells you to do, right?"

"I never accepted that job."

"Pity," Sanguine said, glancing at Tidwell. "You may need a job soon." He put his hands behind his head and leaned back in his chair. "I'm going to have to have a chat with Dick Derek. Promises were made; gifts were exchanged. God knows I've done enough for Derek in his time."

He crossed and uncrossed his legs, with an exaggerated air of ease. "Well then, gentlemen, let's see the evidence. I'm not going to try to obstruct justice. Show me the proof. Show me this corruption festering in the bowels of my company."

Ben clenched his teeth. The man knew damn well they didn't have the financial records. At best, they had a coded summary that could be interpreted by Sanguine flunkies to say anything. Sanguine was just playing games with them.

"We're not prepared to preview our case at this time for your amusement," Mike replied. "But I can assure you that I wouldn't be here if I didn't think the evidence against your company and against you personally was substantial."

"In other words, no evidence," Sanguine said, making a check mark with a pencil on his desk blotter. "Got any witnesses?"

Ben could not restrain himself. "There's no one left who can testify against you, you bloodsucker. You've taken care of that. But you won't stay lucky forever. We've found Catherine."

Sanguine displayed no outward emotion. "Catherine?"

"Yeah, we've found that disgusting little hovel at the Malador where you've been keeping her. She's in pretty pathetic shape. She's scared to death—afraid to go out, even afraid to talk. You did a fabulous job on her." Ben took a deep breath. He had gone too far to stop. "It won't last, though. We're going to trace the rental payments on the apartment back to you, if we have to subpoena every check you've ever written. We're going to work with Catherine, too. She'll recover—I know she will. And when she does, she'll start to talk." Ben pushed himself forward in his chair. "Then where will you be, Mr. Sanguine?"

Sanguine went through the motion of stifling a yawn. "Tidwell," he said, drowsily, "get me the file on rental properties maintained by the corporation."

"Certainly." Tidwell scurried out of the office.

Sanguine returned his attention to Ben. "Do you have any idea how much real estate this company owns?" He paused. "Well, you should. Your firm secured most of it for us. And a lot of that property *is* rental property. We use some of it for storage, some for branch office space, some for staff support and low-cost staff residences. I employ over three thousand people in Tulsa alone, Mr. Kincaid. Maybe we do rent some space at the . . . what is it? . . . Malador Apartments. Frankly, I haven't the slightest idea. Do you really suppose that I know who's living at every single property?"

"I think you know who's living in this one," Ben said quietly.

Sanguine stretched out his arms and propped up his feet. "You really should have become in-house counsel here, Kincaid. It would have yanked you out of this caped-crusader mindset and given you a strong dose of reality, something you sorely need."

"I think this is getting away from the point," Mike said. "Mr. Sanguine, two of your employees have been murdered in a two-week span. Surely you can understand our concern. One man was slain just as he was about to provide documentary evidence to the police—"

"Is Kincaid here with the police now?"

Mike hesitated. "He's . . . working as a special investigator. Doesn't the coincidence strike you as the least bit suspicious, Mr. Sanguine? Two of your employees in one month? Victims of very similar murders?"

Sanguine shrugged his shoulders. "As I said, Lieutenant Morelli, I employ over three thousand persons. I'm sorry two of them have died, but I hardly think it's evidence of a gigantic conspiracy. And I don't see how you became convinced the trail leads back to me. I barely even knew this last man, this . . ." He searched his memory for the name unsuccessfully. ". . . the accountant. And I can't help it if Jonathan Adams liked to hang out in chain-and-leather biker bars."

Ben felt his blood beginning to boil. "Someone lured Adams to the Red Parrot," he said evenly. "Someone set up a meeting there. Someone with dark hair."

Sanguine laughed heartily. "Oh well," he said, wiping his eyes. "That proves it was me."

"Mr. Sanguine," Mike said coolly, "I suggest you take this matter seriously."

"Why should I take this seriously? You barge in here in the middle of the working day, making the most outrageous accusations with a straight face, and you haven't got the slightest shred of evidence. And no witnesses. You haven't got anything but one snot-nosed kid who's supposed to be on my payroll who doesn't know what the hell he's talking about!"

He pointed angrily toward Mike. "I'll tell you what, Lieutenant. I'll give you what you want. I will take this seriously, and deal with it like I would any other threat to my business. I'm calling my lawyers in now, and they'll spin you and your gang of civil servants around so fast you won't know what hit you. A lawsuit for harassment, just for starters, with maybe some civil rights claims thrown in for good measure. Your department will wish you'd never been born.''

He jerked his finger in Ben's direction. ''And you! I'm going to file a bar complaint against you, Kincaid. You've been acting as my lawyer and trusted counselor and at the same time using my privileged confidences to nail me to the wall. I'd call that a serious conflict of interest and I think the committee will, too. You'll never practice law again, kid.''

He returned the threatening finger to Mike. ''Which reminds me, Lieutenant. I'm registering a formal complaint against you with your superior officer. That would be Chief Blackwell, right? Guess what? The chief and I are old fishing buddies. We play golf together at Southern Hills several times a year. You may be on permanent traffic duty real soon, pal. Or walking the beat with the street cops. And I have friends on the streets. They'll be watching for you.'' He reached into the humidor on his desk for a cigar. ''This might be an advantageous time for you to consider another line of work. Maybe you could get into law school, Lieutenant.'' A quick look at Ben. ''They're evidently not too particular these days.''

Ben closed his eyes. How in the name of God did this happen? They came in here from a position of strength to force Sanguine to talk, but it was clear that Sanguine had the upper hand. He was twisting them around like Silly Putty.

A beeping noise emerged from the telephone on Sanguine's desk. Still washed with fury, Sanguine punched a button on the phone and turned up the volume on the intercom. ''What the hell is it?'' he shouted.

A female voice emerged from the speaker box. ''Uh . . .

I have the report on the Phoenix franchise you requested, sir.''

Ben sat upright in his chair. A sudden chill shot through his body.

''My God, we've got to get out of here,'' Ben said, rising to his feet and grabbing his coat.

''What are you talking about?'' Mike asked. ''We can't leave now. Don't be such a—''

''I can't wait,'' Ben said, already halfway out of the office. ''It may be too late already.''

* 40 *

In his mad dash from the office, Ben neglected to have his parking ticket validated by the receptionist. As a result, he wasted nearly ten minutes before the parking guard would let him out of the Sanguine parking lot. He drove crosstown like a lunatic. Heavy lunch-hour traffic was just beginning to clog the main streets. Every light seemed to turn the wrong color at the wrong time and sometimes Ben even stopped for them. He raced through the intersection of Sixty-first Street and Riverside Drive and sped north onto Riverside. He heard an angry cacophony of horns and squealing tires behind him. He didn't look back.

He drove his Honda beside the parking garage of the Malador Apartments and swerved sideways, blocking the only exit from the garage. He leapt out of the car, hopped over the brick wall, and ran toward the elevator shaft. How long had he and Mike been at Sanguine's office? Almost an hour now. Damn. He pushed the UP button and waited, barely able to hold still. *Come on!* He would have shouted if he'd thought it would help.

A bell sounded, and the elevator doors swung open.

Tidwell was in the elevator, in front of a large, middle-aged woman with a beehive hairdo and an enormous purse. Tidwell saw Ben and froze. Ben stepped into the elevator. The woman standing behind Tidwell did not understand. Finally, when Tidwell didn't move out of the way, she tried to move around him.

Tidwell stretched his left arm across the elevator, blocking her path.

"Let her off," Ben said evenly.

Tidwell dropped his arm, and the woman stepped around him. Suddenly, Tidwell grabbed the woman by her right arm and, placing his foot at the base of her spine, kicked her toward Ben. Ben fell backward but braced himself by stretching his arm across the opening of the elevator. Tidwell tried to rush out under his right arm, but Ben grabbed him by the shoulder and shoved him back into the elevator. Tidwell's head banged against the wall, and his body fell. The elevator bell rang again, and the doors closed, trapping the three of them together.

"Please don't hurt me," the woman said, her face washed with fear. She was crouched in the corner, trying to hide behind her purse. "I just want off."

Ben pushed the button for the seventh floor and turned to face Tidwell, still lying on the floor next to the wall. "What have you done, you son of a bitch?" He grabbed Tidwell by the collar of his jacket and shook him.

In one smooth continuous motion, Tidwell reached into his inside jacket pocket and withdrew a large kitchen knife. The woman screamed. It was *the* knife, Ben realized. Ben grabbed Tidwell's wrist with both hands and slammed it against the wall of the elevator. Tidwell's grip held tight.

Once more the elevator bell rang, and the doors opened. The woman screamed and bolted out of the elevator. "Help!" she screamed. The couple waiting to get in saw the two men wrestling in the elevator and, after a second, hurried away.

"Call the police!" Ben shouted, trying not to lose his grip. His knees were beginning to buckle under the strong downward pressure. Tidwell was a hell of a lot stronger than he looked.

Tidwell tightened his free hand into a fist and smashed it against Ben's right ear. Ben cried out. His grip involuntarily loosened. Tidwell twisted his wrist free and brought the blade of the knife down into the soft underside of Ben's upper right arm. Ben screamed in pain. Light bulbs seemed to flash in front of his eyes, and he felt himself falling. He fell backward, as if seating himself on the floor of the elevator. Tidwell stepped toward him and pulled back his knife to strike.

At that moment the bell rang, and the elevator doors began to close. Tidwell turned his head and, stretching his knife hand between the doors, he slapped the safety bumper and reopened the doors.

Ben didn't waste a second. Pulling himself up by the metal rail, he rose to his feet and, while Tidwell's hand was still outside the doors, he swung his fist into Tidwell's nose. Tidwell yelled. Blood began to spurt from his nostrils. The elevator doors opened, and Ben raced through.

Holding his bleeding arm close against his body, Ben

ran to the closed door of apartment 724. The door was unlocked. Ben ran inside and tried to bolt the door, but before he could, the full force of Tidwell's body slammed against the other side of the door, knocking Ben back into an end table next to the sofa. A large brass lamp fell onto the floor with a crash.

Ben ran backward into the living room, combing the room for a weapon. He remembered how, years ago, Mike had tried to teach him some rudimentary jujitsu and how Ben had laughed at the macho pretense of it all. Times like this he could use some macho pretense.

Tidwell came through the door, his knife poised above his right shoulder. His face was wet and transformed into a grotesque death mask. Sweat was dripping from the thinning hair on the sides of his head. Tidwell wiped the blood from his face with his sleeve, but it continued to trickle out of his nostrils. Dark shadows were forming beneath his eyes. If Ben had not already known who he was, he would not have recognized him.

Ben grabbed the brass lamp from where it had fallen next to the sofa, yanked the cord out of the wall and pulled off the shade. He smashed the end of the bulb against the table, leaving cut and jagged pieces of glass and tungsten exposed. He held the base with both hands and swung the lamp between Tidwell and himself. His right arm was weak with pain and could barely support the weight.

He gritted his teeth and held tight to the lamp. As stupid as he felt brandishing a lamp, Ben realized that the lamp had more reach than Tidwell's knife.

Tidwell stopped creeping forward and smiled. "I could throw the knife," Tidwell said, smiling grotesquely, with blood-smeared teeth.

"You'll have to kill me on your first throw," Ben said. "Because if you miss, you're a dead man." He realized how heavily he was breathing and tried to control it. "Where's the nurse?"

Tidwell continued to smile. "I gave her the day off."

"Catherine!" Ben shouted. "Get out of here!" There was no response.

The two men stared at one another across the room, both breathing with loud, heaving gasps. Tidwell ran his palm across his face again, wiping away the excess sweat and blood. The blood was beginning to dry and coagulate beneath his nose; it was turning a sickening black color.

Ben was suddenly aware of the steady flow of blood from his own upper right arm. The blood had saturated his shirt sleeve and was beginning to drip onto the carpet. His right arm was tingling and becoming numb. He knew he wouldn't be able to hold the heavy lamp in midair for long. All Tidwell had to do was wait.

And then, the sound of footsteps in the corridor broke the stalemate. A hand pushed the door open a little wider. "Ben?" a timid voice asked.

Christina stepped into the room carrying a bundle of women's clothing. In less than a second, she had noted the overturned furniture, the bloodstained faces, the weapons. She turned, but before she had a chance to run, Tidwell had his free arm wrapped around her throat and the sharp end of his knife pressed against her face.

Christina screamed. Tidwell slapped his hand across her mouth to stifle the noise. The clothes in her arms fell to the floor. "Shut your mouth or I'll cut it off," he growled into her ear.

Christina obeyed. The loud screaming was replaced by a soft whimper. Her wide eyes looked desperately at Ben.

Ben took a step forward, still brandishing the lamp. "Let her go," he said. His head felt light and dizzy.

"I don't think so," Tidwell said. Again he flashed the sickening smile. "Drop the lamp."

"Not a chance."

Tidwell tightened his choke hold on Christina's throat. "Drop the lamp or I kill her."

Ben's eyes locked with Tidwell's. "How do I know you won't kill her anyway?"

Tidwell's eyes and nostrils flared. "Drop the lamp or I'll kill the fucking bitch!" He shook Christina's body back and forth, still pressing the knife close against her face. Ben saw a thin line of red emerge on her cheek.

Christina began to cry. She tried to stifle the noise, but the sobs still came out, in short, choking gasps. Tears were streaming from her eyes.

Slowly, keeping his eyes fixed on Tidwell, Ben lowered the lamp and set it on the floor in front of him. He couldn't have held it up much longer anyway.

"Bad mistake," Tidwell said, chuckling. He yanked Christina's body backwards and placed the knife horizontally across her neck.

Outside the door, Ben heard the clatter of heavy footsteps. The unidentified feet ran down the hallway corridor and stopped outside the front door.

Tidwell's head jerked to the side. "Drop it!" he shouted through the door. He twisted Christina's body around so that it stood between him and the doorway. "I'll kill her!"

Christina's eyes closed tightly.

"I'll kill them both!" Tidwell screamed. His face was jerking spasmodically, looking outside the door, then at Ben, then outside again. "Drop it or I'll kill them both!"

Ben heard the sound of two soft clumps on the carpet in the corridor outside.

"Now we're comin' out!" Tidwell shouted, his face pressed close behind Christina's. "Me and the bitch! And you're gonna let us, or I'll cut her fucking throat!" Shoving his knees against the back of her legs, he forced her through the doorway.

As Tidwell inched his way into the doorway, the inner wall began to block his view of Ben. Tidwell was concentrating on the people outside. As soon as Ben was certain Tidwell couldn't see him any longer, he picked up the lamp, this time holding the base end away from him. In two steps, Ben was across the room and turning the corner to face the doorway.

Tidwell saw Ben in the corner of his eye as soon as Ben stepped into the doorway. Tidwell whirled and pulled the knife away from Christina toward Ben. He was too late. Ben swung the lamp like a baseball bat. The base of the lamp smashed into Tidwell's head, and he fell in a crumpled heap onto the floor.

The two uniformed policemen standing in the outer corridor rushed forward and took hold of Christina. They gently lowered her to the floor.

Ben brushed the matted hair away from Christina's sweaty, tear-streaked face. "Are you all right?" he asked.

She looked up at him and, after several seconds, nodded her head faintly.

Ben stepped over Tidwell's body and rushed across the apartment to Catherine's dark bedroom. He flipped on the lights. Catherine lay naked and motionless on the bed, the sheets twisted around her feet, her face staring up at the ceiling.

"Catherine?" He moved to the side of the bed closest

to her. He saw two empty pill bottles lying on the bed, the same two bottles he had seen half-full on her bedstand the night before. He touched the side of her neck. No pulse. She was stone cold.

Ben was faintly aware of the sound of footsteps in the living room. One of the policemen had Tidwell on his feet and was pushing him into the bedroom. Tidwell's arms were handcuffed behind his back. Blood was trickling from his nose and his left ear.

Tidwell saw the milky-white figure frozen on the bed. He made a soft, choking noise. "Don't stand there leering," he said, gasping for air, ". . . at my daughter."

"Daughter?" Ben stared at the bloody man silhouetted in the doorway. "I thought she was your lover."

Tidwell stared back at Ben, then averted his eyes. In that instant, Ben realized he had been right.

Ben's eyes began to swell, and he found it difficult to breathe. He gazed at the pale porcelain figure, now transfixed, like a statue. He noticed she had something clutched in her right hand. He pulled her fingers apart slightly. It was his red handkerchief.

Ben heard the pounding of footsteps outside, and realized that reinforcements, probably led by Mike, were finally making their appearance. In two quick steps, he walked toward Tidwell, took aim, and swung his fist directly into Tidwell's face.

PART FOUR

*   *

The Fixed Moment

* 41 *

Ben sat on the sofa in a living room that looked like a page out of *Architectural Digest*. At one end, a beautiful brick fireplace with an antique wooden mantel served as a Victorian focal point for the entire room. At the other end, an ornate wooden entertainment center held all the necessities of twentieth-century life. Behind the sofa were a black grand piano, several tables bearing ceramic knick-knacks, and family photographs.

The woman sitting on the sofa facing Ben had in fact just turned sixty, although she looked at least ten years younger. Her fresh, ruddy complexion and her perfectly styled hair, dark brown with scattered, dustlike particles of gray, evinced the care and attention she had exercised to preserve herself.

"I don't think I understand," the woman said carefully. "So Emily is Catherine's daughter by . . ." Her voice faded, and her face suggested an unpleasant expression.

"That's right, Mother," Ben said, nodding. "The moment I saw Catherine, I knew she had to be Emily's mother. They have the same eyes, the same complexion. The same quiet beauty." He paused reflectively. "And, of course, the poetry was the clincher. I think Catherine named Emily for Emily Dickinson." He rubbed his arm in the spot where it was still sore. "Even after I realized the killer was Tidwell, though, I never guessed the rest."

Ben's mother rubbed her hands against one another. "It takes something like this to make a person realize just how lucky she is. That sort of behavior never happens in Nichols Hills."

Ben smiled.

Mrs. Kincaid lifted a demitasse from her saucer and sipped her tea. "I don't know how you ever figured it out."

"The light finally dawned when Sanguine mentioned his franchise property in Phoenix. Tidwell had mentioned Phoenix before, and Fort Worth and some other cities, and indicated that he was in charge of securing real estate for the franchisees. Adams was just a puppet vice president; Tidwell found the properties and told him where to go. Tidwell was the only one who could have arranged for Adams to arrive at a vacant lot at just the right time to find Emily. It was all part of his sick master plan.

"I realized that Tidwell had left Sanguine's office as soon as I told him I had found Catherine, the only witness who could possibly testify against him. He'd been gone fifteen minutes and hadn't returned. It wasn't difficult to imagine where he'd gone." Ben pressed his forefingers against his temples. "If only I'd realized sooner."

"Benjamin, you have to stop blaming yourself for everything. Everything is not your fault."

Ben gazed out the immense bay window.

"Benjamin, I think I know why you feel that way. . . . I want you to know—"

"Mother, I don't want to go into this."

"I want you to know," she insisted, "that your father

did not dislike you. If he was hard on you . . . it was for a reason.''

The two of them sat for a moment without saying anything, neither looking directly at the other. Ben's mother took another sip of tea.

''I guess you know I was . . . upset when you stopped calling,'' she said, maintaining an even tone. ''You're the only son I have. It seems as if you haven't been the same boy since Toronto and Ellen—''

''Mother—''

''I *worry* about you, Benjamin.''

Ben stared at the ceiling. ''Mother, I've had a lot to deal with.''

''Such as?'' she said. A slight edge crept into her voice. ''Switching jobs and cities and making a mad scramble for whatever you imagined might make your father happy?''

''It wasn't like that. . . .''

She leaned back against the sofa, obviously unconvinced. ''Tell me what happened, Benjamin, that last day you saw him.''

Ben shook his head. ''I don't think I can. It's too hard to remember. . . .''

Ben stepped into the hospital room. The walls were a bleak green, made worse by the low lighting. The television tilting from the ceiling flickered with a rapid spattering of black-and-white images, but no sound emerged. The serving table next to the bed held a cold luncheon plate, barely touched. Ben wondered if there was a thermostat somewhere in the room. It seemed very cold.

Ben's father lay on the hospital bed beneath two crisp white sheets. One plastic tube was patched into his right nostril, another was feeding his arm. His cheeks sagged with age and exhaustion, ending in jowls that rounded the underside of his chin. His eyes were closed. Ben had seen his father in the hospital before—this was his fifth visit—but he had never looked like this.

"Dad?" he said quietly.

His eyes opened. They blinked aimlessly for a moment, then lighted on Ben.

"You came," he said, in a raspy whisper. Obviously, it was difficult for him to talk.

"Of course I came," Ben said, leaning over the guard-rail on the bed.

"I know you're busy at school." He tried to push himself up by the palms of his hands.

"That's all right, Dad. Stay where you are."

He relaxed. His voice seemed to regain some of its strength. "You learning anything up there?" The strong, slow drawl was a constant reminder of his farmhouse roots. "They taught you how to sue doctors for their life savings yet?"

"Dad, please." Ben gripped the guardrail tightly. "It isn't like that. In law school, we learn legal *concepts*. It's an intellectual pursuit."

Ben's father chuckled softly, as much as the tube in his nose would allow. "Then you should be good at it." He sighed. "In med school, we had to *work*."

"I know, Dad. I've heard."

"I don't know why you couldn't just go to med school and be respectable."

"I don't know, either, Dad. I guess I just didn't want to spend my entire life sticking my fingers in people's bodily orifices."

The older man's voice became stronger. "Make fun if

you like, but you'll never make the kind of money working for the district attorney you could make as a doctor.''

''No doubt.''

''So what else goes on at school, besides learning legal concepts?'' His eyelids fluttered up and down. ''Getting any?''

''*What?*''

''You heard me. I'm sure you're familiar with the phrase. I'm asking you about girls.''

Ben cast his eyes skyward. ''I'm not dating anyone at present.''

''That's not exactly what I asked. I bet you get laid all the time. God knows your sister does.''

''*Dad!* Come on—''

''It wasn't like that when I was in college. Students didn't act like that. Well, *I* didn't. Hell, people were probably banging each other right and left. I wouldn't know.'' He inhaled raspily. ''Your mother was the only one for me.''

He seemed to rest for a moment, then suddenly his eyebrows knitted. ''You didn't do it with Jenny Jacobson, did you?''

''*Who?*''

''Jenny Jacobson. That skinny girl you dated in high school.''

''In high school? Of course not.''

He exhaled. ''Well, thank God for that. She was a nice girl. Her father and I have been in the Rotary Club together for twenty-five years.''

Ben rested his chin on the guardrail. The two of them remained silent for several moments.

''So give me a report card, son,'' he said. He reached under the sheets and scratched himself. ''Tell me how I've done as a father. Tell me what I've done right and what I've done wrong.''

"Dad . . . I don't know what you mean.''

"No, of course not.'' A smile came over his face. "Whatever you lacked in drive, whatever your other undesirable qualities, you were always *nice*.'' He paused. "Assuming niceness is a desirable quality.''

He looked up at his son. "It's kind of hard to tell your father he's been a son of a bitch when he's about to die, huh?'' And then he laughed, a loud, abrasive laugh that turned into harsh coughing and sputtering. Ben reached out to him, but he waved Ben away.

After a few moments, he regained control of himself. His eyelids seemed very heavy.

"Mother said you wanted to talk to me about something,'' Ben said.

"Yes, I did. There's a package waiting for you at home. Something I had Jim Gregory's firm prepare. A portfolio.''

"A portfolio?''

"That's right. Detailed information on all my various holdings and investments. I'll be kind and just say that you've never expressed much interest in the family business. But you're going to have to now.''

"You shouldn't talk like that. You'll be fine.''

"Don't be a pansy, Ben. I'm dying. This is it. Like it or not, you're going to have to take over the family finances. I've made a pile of money, and I want you to see that your mother and sister are taken care of.''

"Dad, wouldn't it be better to hire someone to do this?''

"That's so like you, Ben. Get someone else to do it.'' He pushed himself up in the bed. "Look, it's not like I'm asking you to actually *make* some money. All I'm asking

you to do is take care of what I've made for you. You're
going to be the head of the Kincaid family, and I expect
you to act accordingly.''

"So that was it?" Ben said. "You asked me to come
here so we could talk about money?"

Ben's father made a choking, snorting noise. "Yeah,
what's wrong with that? I guess you were expecting some
profound philosophical deathbed advice." He lowered
himself back into his sleeping position. "Fine, I'll give
you some advice. Don't get old. It isn't worth it, it isn't
fun, and it isn't fair. You spend your whole life going from
one moment to the next. A happy moment here, a sad one
there. Working hard, living clean, starting a family, hoping you can stack two or three, maybe even four of the
happy moments together. Trying to freeze time. Trying to
fix the moment. But it can't be done.''

His pace slowed and his eyelids drooped lower over his
eyes. "And then you're old, and your life is like a book
you read too quickly. All you can remember are a few
scattered images and random thoughts. No sense of the
whole.''

He exhaled deeply. "I think I'm going to sleep for a
while now, Ben.''

"I'll go.''

"No, stay. If you leave, your mother will insist on coming in, and she needs rest, too.''

"All right. I'll stay.''

He smiled slightly, and his eyes closed. His hand raised
and almost touched Ben on the cheek, then fell back to
the bed. After a moment, he was asleep, and deep within
the dream from which he would never awaken.

* * *

The clattering of the demitasse in the saucer made Ben look up. His mother was staring at him.

"How's your arm?" she asked.

"Oh, fine. Several stitches. I'll probably have a scar, but"—he shrugged his shoulders—"people rarely admire my upper arm."

"What do you think you'll do now?" she asked.

"I don't know," Ben answered. He was being honest.

"Well, there's no need to hurry your decision. It's not unusual for a man to change occupations several times before he's thirty. Even in Nichols Hills."

"I like the law," Ben said. "I like the potential it has for helping people, even if the potential sometimes goes awry."

"Well, Benjamin, if you're certain you know what you want to do, you should do it." She hesitated a moment. "The only concern your father ever had was that you wouldn't live up to your potential."

"I'm afraid I can't agree with that statement."

"It's true. You needed your father to push you to try harder."

"You make him sound very altruistic."

She sighed. "Are you going to be all right?"

"I think so," he said slowly. "I don't know. Something about this whole mess. I believe I'm starting to feel better." He brushed his hands against his lap and stood up. "Well . . ."

"Stay in touch this time."

"I'll try, Mother." He walked toward the front door, then stopped. "Mother?" he said.

"Yes?"

"It's nothing against you. I mean . . . you know. I love you."

She picked up a home-decorating magazine from the coffee table. "I know you do, dear."

* 42 *

The tall, thin woman with the stringy blonde hair was not dressed like a nurse or any other identifiable authority figure, but she seemed to be the one in control. Ben told her that he was an attorney, careful to suggest, without actually stating, that he was Tidwell's attorney. The woman bought it; she was probably used to seeing junior attorneys sent out to do dirty duty like this. The woman gestured toward a chair, and Ben sat down.

The chair faced a wall that, from about four feet above the floor on up, was made of a thick, clear acrylic. A metal speaker in the center allowed communication from one side to the other. Apparently, Tidwell was still considered dangerous. Ben rubbed his arm and decided that he was in no position to disagree.

A door in the room on the opposite side of the glass opened, and a heavyset male guard escorted Tidwell into the room. Tidwell was wearing a loose-fitting orange jump suit. Ben was reminded of the outfits his father used to wear when he was working in the yard. The guard led Tidwell to the chair opposite Ben's on the other side of the acrylic, then positioned himself against the wall next to the door.

Tidwell stared contemptuously through the acrylic barrier. "Know why lawyers are always buried at least *twelve* feet underground?"

"Forget it. That's not why I came."

"Because deep down, they're really nice people," Tidwell growled, obviously disappointed. "What do you want?"

"I came to see for myself."

"See what?"

"See if you really *are* crazy."

Tidwell started to smile, then caught himself. After a moment, apparently deciding there was no harm, he allowed himself a full grin. "Of course I'm crazy," he said. "I'm in the loony bin, aren't I?"

"Under observation," Ben said slowly. "So the shrinks can decide whether you're capable of comprehending the charges brought against you."

Tidwell continued to smile. "I must be crazy," he said. "How else could I do all the horrible things I've done? I couldn't distinguish between right and wrong."

"Save it for the jury," Ben muttered.

"I was controlled by an irresistible impulse. I didn't comprehend the nature and quality of the acts I was committing."

"Christ!" Ben said, pounding his forehead. "Your lawyers have even briefed you on the M'Naughten test for insanity."

Tidwell smiled but said nothing.

"And you're just smart enough to pull it off," Ben muttered, shaking his head.

Tidwell stared back at Ben. His beady green eyes

seemed yellow through the distorting ripple of the acrylic panel.

"Can you tell me one thing?"

Ben waited for a response and got none.

"I've almost deciphered this puzzle, but there's one piece I don't have. After I was stupid enough to tell you I'd found Catherine, and you ran back to the apartment, what did you do to her?"

"I didn't do anything," Tidwell said, smiling contentedly.

"What did you *say*, then," Ben said. "Let me guess. I think you told Catherine that Emily was dead, that you'd killed Emily to punish Catherine for being bad. That would do the trick. That would push her over the edge."

Tidwell's grin widened appreciatively.

"You sick son of a bitch," Ben said. He felt he needed to stand. He began to pace back and forth before the acrylic screen. "You killed Catherine just as surely as if you had crammed the pills down her throat."

"What's it to you, anyway?" Tidwell asked.

"I—" Ben started, then stopped. There was no way he was getting into that. "I got to know Catherine, a little bit," he said simply.

He walked to the door and opened it.

"I hope they fry you, you sick bastard," Ben said. "I hope they draw and quarter you and drag your entrails through the streets of the city."

Tidwell's smile spread from ear to ear. "I do, too," he said. "Isn't that crazy?" And he laughed and laughed and laughed.

* 43 *

"If you don't have any more questions, I'll leave the two of you alone to read the documents," Ben said.

Ben was standing beside the long conference room table; Bertha Adams and Emily were seated on the other side. Emily seemed calm and detached. All the tragedy of the past month has centered around her, Ben thought, and what little of it she ever knew she's entirely forgotten. That's life in the fixed moment.

"After you read through them, sign each place I indicated and leave the papers with my secretary," Ben said.

Bertha looked up and nodded. She seemed more at ease than she had at any time since Ben first met her. "Thank you, Mr. Kincaid."

"Sure." Ben left the conference room and walked back to his office.

Christina was waiting for him. She was wearing her brown miniskirt and the familiar yellow leotards.

"So you decided to come back to work?" he said, smiling. "How are you?"

"I'm going to be fine. *C'est la guerre.*" She brushed her golden hair away from her eyes. The thin black scab on her right cheek was still noticeable. "*You're* the one we should be worrying about."

"Well, this is cozy. Got room for a third?"

Mike was standing in the doorway.

"Come on in," Ben said. "What have you and your squad of law-and-order zealots turned up?"

"Not a lot," Mike admitted. "We've searched Tidwell's house and come up with a birth certificate. Catherine was his daughter, all right. And we've found a marriage license. Tidwell was married some twenty-eight years ago, when he lived in Flagstaff. Catherine was born soon after. Real soon, if you know what I mean. Catherine's mother died when Catherine was about six and apparently, sometime not too long after"—he hesitated for a moment—"Tidwell let Catherine take her mother's place in his affections. Some time after then and before he moved to Tulsa, Emily was born."

"Sweet Jesus," Ben muttered quietly. "And I thought *I* had father problems."

"We're talking to former neighbors and tracking down relatives who might have known Tidwell when he lived in Flagstaff," Mike continued. "He only moved to Tulsa two years ago. Seems he had to leave Flagstaff in a hurry. I think he kept Emily's existence a secret after he moved to Tulsa. He couldn't explain her parentage, and he didn't want to stir up trouble. We've interviewed his current neighbors, and they don't know anything about Emily *or* Catherine. Tidwell had evidently discovered it was safer to keep Catherine and Emily at a separate residence under lock and key. I expect that was easy enough to do. Emily was a little girl, and Catherine's mind was disintegrating. I suppose he told poor Catherine she'd be killed if she left the apartment. Or that he would hurt Emily."

Christina was confused. "What I still don't understand

is, how did Emily end up with Bertha and Jonathan Adams?''

Mike stood and faced the outer window. "Some of this is just conjecture, but I think Catherine was losing her mind as far back as the time of the Tulsa move. Years of confusion, guilt, isolation, depravation, and sexual abuse were taking their toll. I think she became progressively unstable. That made her not only unpleasant to be with, but dangerous as well. Tidwell was an important businessman now in a fairly high profile position. What if she got loose? Who knows what she might say or do? At the same time, there was this new little girl, unknown to the world, that, for whatever reason, he was very interested in. He needed a way to bring Emily into his home without creating suspicion.''

Christina was beginning to follow. "So Tidwell *arranged* for Jonathan Adams to find Emily.''

"That's right,'' Mike continued. "Tidwell instructed Adams to investigate the franchise location in Jenks, after arranging for Emily to be abandoned there. He set up the whole coincidental discovery. His idea was that Adams would of course be too old to adopt, but that *he*, the younger, respected, philanthropic businessman and father, would step in and adopt the foundling.''

"That's crazy!'' Christina exclaimed. "A million different things could go wrong.''

"Evidently Tidwell didn't see it that way,'' Mike said. "But you're right. The master plan didn't work out. Something happened he didn't count on. Adams never turned Emily in to the authorities as he was supposed to do, and he never mentioned her at work. They just kept her.

"Time passed. Tidwell was stymied. He didn't want to raise suspicion, but he couldn't let the old couple keep

Emily forever. I'd bet anything it wasn't a neighbor that sent the police officer over to investigate Emily—it was Tidwell. And then, when Adams confided in Tidwell about the problem—because Adams hated Sanguine, but *everyone* loved Tidwell—Tidwell had Sanguine's legal counsel arrange what was bound to be a futile attempt at adoption, while he waited in the wings to snatch Emily up as soon as Adams failed."

Mike leaned back in his chair and thrust his fists in his coat pockets. "I've talked to Derek. He tells me that Tidwell specified that he wanted a young lawyer on the adoption case. Allegedly to reduce the legal fees."

"But really because he didn't want any lawyer assigned who had a prayer of winning," Ben said. He shifted uncomfortably in his seat.

"I'm not sure how Tidwell found out about Brancusci," Mike continued. "Maybe he overheard something at the office, maybe he noticed documents were missing, or maybe he saw Brancusci talking to Ben at Derek's party. However it happened, he knew Brancusci knew about the diversion of funds, possibly knew about Emily and Catherine, and could blow this thing wide open. So he killed him." He glanced at Ben. "Personally, Ben, I'm glad you weren't home the night he came visiting your apartment."

Christina cast a suspicious eye in Ben's direction.

Mike chuckled grimly. "What Tidwell must've thought when the two of us came barging into the office—and accused his *boss* of being the killer."

"And I was stupid enough to tell him that I thought I could get Catherine to talk," Ben said quietly. "Tidwell had probably written her off as hopelessly confused and insane. He didn't realize just how strong she was—or was trying to be. He didn't know that her desire to see her daughter again was maintaining her last vestige of sanity. But I told him.'' Ben withdrew a red handkerchief from his pocket, pressed it against his lips, then put it away.

''In retrospect, it's a miracle he hadn't killed Catherine long ago,'' Mike said. ''Maybe he wasn't a killer yet. Maybe, deep down, he really did love her. Way deep down.''

''She might've been better off if he had killed her,'' Ben said quietly.

Christina reached behind Ben and gently laid her hand on his shoulder. ''I understand Tidwell and his lawyers are planning an insanity defense,'' she said.

''Too true,'' Mike murmured.

''Think it'll play?''

Mike shrugged. ''Hard to imagine anyone crazier.''

''Tidwell knew what he was doing,'' Ben said. ''He's not crazy. Sick, yes. Insane, no.''

Mike nodded. ''And yet, when I arrived at that apartment and he was looking down at Catherine's body, he seemed genuinely affected. Like a father. Only minutes after he killed her.''

''So what did all the business about financial records and crooked accountants have to do with the murders?'' Christina asked.

''Nothing really,'' Mike answered. ''Just another nasty pie Tidwell had his finger in. And, of course, he was using some of the diverted funds to finance the apartment at Malador. That little act of greed proved to be his undoing.''

Mike turned toward Ben. ''And you're gonna love this. Guess what Sanguine was doing with his cut of the slush fund? He was donating almost all of it to the reservation he grew up in. They're creating an educational trust fund in his name, to help underprivileged Native Americans go to college. Well, they were, anyway."

"Great," Ben said. "Now the entire Sioux tribe will probably be gunning for me."

"I suppose those bureaucrats at the Department of Human Resources will snatch Emily away from Mrs. Adams now," Christina said.

Ben and Mike glanced at one another.

"No," Ben said simply.

"No? Why not?"

Ben lifted his head and stared out the window. "Funny thing about Catherine. Just before she died, she drew up a holographic will. Mike and I found it in the apartment. Among other things, she named Bertha Adams as the woman she wanted to raise her little girl."

Christina stared at him in disbelief. "That's not poss—" She reconsidered. "Will it stand up?"

"Who's to fight it? Tidwell's busy at the moment, and no one else has any interest. Even Sokolosky and the DHS crowd won't contest a will executed by Emily's mother."

"But Catherine was insane. Of *unsound* mind."

"Says who?" Ben argued. "Nurse Harriet has disappeared without a trace. I personally spent several hours with Catherine, and I will testify that she was perfectly cogent and lucid. Who's going to testify against me?"

Christina smiled. She leaned across the desk and kissed Ben on the cheek. "You're a pretty good guy, Kincaid."

"Second the motion," Mike said. "But no kiss."

There was a loud knock on the door. Mike opened it.

It was Maggie. "The Executive Committee is ready to meet with you now."

Mike pointed his finger at Ben. "What about . . ."

Ben nodded. "I haven't forgotten." He looked at Maggie. "I'll be along in a minute. I have a couple of stops to make first."

"They're ready for you *now*," Maggie insisted.

"They'll have to wait," Ben said calmly. "It's not going to matter much anyway."

He glanced back at his friends. "Wish me luck."

Ben poked his head through the half-closed door to Alvin's office.

"Mind if I come in?"

Alvin looked up from between two tall stacks of casebooks and briefs. "Please do. I've been wanting to talk with you, but I wasn't sure if you were . . . available."

Ben sat down in one of the leather chairs facing Alvin's desk. "This will only take a second. I just wanted to say that I know I acted kind of negatively when you first told me about you and . . ."

"Candy."

"Candy. Right." He took a deep breath. "Alvin, I was wrong. If she really makes you happy, and you're sure it's what you want, then you should do it, and to hell with what other people say." Ben fell back in his chair, glad he had gotten that off his chest.

Alvin frowned. "Funny you should bring this up, Ben. It sort of relates to what I wanted to tell you. Candy and I have decided to call it quits."

"What?"

"Yeah. It just wasn't working out. It's not as if we really had a lot in common. I mean, you saw her at that party at Derek's. She didn't exactly fit in."

Ben stared at him blank-faced.

"To be honest, she may have been using me."

"No!" Ben exclaimed with exaggerated horror.

"Yes. I think she saw me as her ticket out of the strip joints and into undergraduate school."

"That's awful! I guess you put that idea to rest."

"Well, no. I agreed to go ahead and pay her first year's tuition at TU."

"At TU! That must cost a fortune!"

"Well, it seemed like the right thing to do. There was the little girl to think of."

"A noble gesture, Alvin."

"Also, she had these photographs—"

"I don't want to hear about it, Alvin."

Alvin nodded. "Just as well. To tell you the truth, I don't know what happened to me. I totally lost control. People were laughing at me."

"Say it ain't so."

"Yup. I was lucky to get out when I did. I could've blown my whole career in a single stupid move." He shook his head. "I guess I forgot what's important."

Ben sighed. No comment.

"Good luck with the EC," Alvin said.

"You heard about that?"

"Didn't everybody?" He glanced at his watch. "Derek came in a couple of hours ago asking what I knew about this business with Sanguine and what you've been doing. I played dumb." He looked down at his papers.

"Thanks, Al." Ben walked out of the office.

Greg was talking animatedly to someone on the other end of the phone. Ben caught his eye. Greg flashed his familiar smile, waved Ben into the office, and pointed at one of his visitor chairs.

Ben reached across the desk and brushed a stray hair

off Greg's shoulder. "You'll lose your dapper reputation if you keep this up," Ben said.

Greg whispered thanks and returned to his conversation. Ben sat down and waited.

Eventually, Greg completed his phone call. "Man!" he bellowed. "Clients will talk your *ear* off if you let them." He leaned across his desk "I didn't expect to see you today. Have you already met with the EC?"

"Not yet. I'm on my way."

Greg fidgeted with a pencil. "Well, I hope it all works out for you. We're all behind you, you know. Spiritually, I mean."

"Yeah. That isn't really why I stopped by."

"Oh?" Greg shifted in his chair. "What was it, then?"

"I thought you might want to tell me about it."

Greg's eyebrows moved almost imperceptibly closer together. "Tell you about what?"

"About you and Jonathan Adams."

Greg leaned back slowly. "I don't know what you're talking about."

Very smooth, Ben thought. But not convincing. Not anymore. "You knew him, didn't you? I mean, before you came to work here. And you recognized him, that first day, when you bumbled into my office while we were talking."

Greg did not respond.

"After Tidwell flunked the hair and fiber matchup for Adams, I started trying to think of everyone who had been in contact with Adams shortly before he died. It took me awhile, but eventually I remembered *you*. You did react strangely when you saw him in my office that day. So did he, for that matter." He paused. "I already know part of it. I've done some checking up on you. But I was hoping you could fill in the blanks."

Greg ran his fingers through his hair. "I don't believe I care to continue this conversation."

"Whatever." Ben started to get up. "The police lieutenant is just outside."

"It was just an insignificant incident," Greg said abruptly.

Ben sat back down.

"Totally stupid. Trivial. Back at the Beta house, when I was an undergrad."

"That was in California?"

Greg looked up at him. "Right. It was just a panty raid, you know? I mean, we were a fraternity house, for Christ's sake. It was *required*, practically." He pressed his fingers against his temples. "It was harmless. A minor invasion of privacy, a few dirty jokes, a little mooning, a few photographs. But some uptight bitch in the sorority house called the police—and we got brought up on charges."

"Indecent exposure?"

"Yeah. And breaking and entering—and sexual indecency, too. And just because I was a frat officer, I was named as one of the three instigators. It was awful. We had lawyers, parents, newspeople—everybody screaming their heads off about *nothing*! We plea-bargained down to a misdemeanor indecent-exposure charge. No jail time. But I had a record. And you know what that meant."

Ben reflected for a moment. "It meant the state bar examiners wouldn't let you sit for the bar exam. Not with a police record for sexual immorality, however minor. Probably couldn't get into law school. And even if you did find some sleazebag school that would accept you, you'd never get hired. Especially not at the kind of firms you were interested in.''

"Precisely," Greg said bitterly. "All I ever wanted in my entire life was to be a lawyer. That was all! And after years of planning and preparation, it all went up in smoke. Over nothing.''

"But how does Adams fit into this? I remember that he mentioned he was assigned to the California office for several years.''

Greg nodded. "Adams sat on an appellate academic review panel, part of an effort to involve members of the business community in campus affairs, no doubt with the ulterior hope of securing generous corporate grants. His panel approved the Panhellenic Committee's decision to sanction the Beta house and suspend me and the other two officers for a semester.''

Ben looked amazed. "You mean, all this was just to get revenge for being suspended?''

"Don't be an idiot," Greg said. "I got over that a long time ago. I moved to another state. Changed the spelling of my last name. Started going by Greg instead of John. Finished undergrad school in New Mexico, got into law school in Texas. After law school, I moved again, to Oklahoma, and started working here. In October, I'm taking the bar exam. I paid some bum twenty bucks to put his fingerprints on my application. No questions, no problems. Nobody here knew who I was.''

"Until you bumped into Adams.''

"Until Adams. All those years of moving, lying, and law school flushed down the toilet because one stupid old man turned up in the wrong place at the wrong time.''

"And so you killed him.''

Greg leaned back in his chair. "Sorry, Ben. End of conversation."

"You tried to get Adams to stay quiet, didn't you?" Ben continued. "That's why you arranged the meeting at the Red Parrot. And he was just the kind of old-fashioned, noble sort who might refuse to be bought off. So you killed him."

Greg held his tongue.

"I think you wore your white camel's hair coat. The same one you wore earlier that day to the office. That's why Crazy Jane, the street lady, in her religious, alcoholic stupor, thought she saw a huge white dove. And after you killed him, you continued to mutilate the body, to make it look like the work of some drug-crazed north-sider. That's why you wore a different coat to Derek's party. After you stabbed Adams several dozen times, I bet that white coat was thoroughly disgusting." He paused. "And when Tidwell killed Brancusci, he copied your M.O. to confuse the police."

Greg stroked the side of his chin. "You have no proof of any of that."

"Yes I do. Right here in the palm of my hand." Ben held up the hair he had taken from Greg's shoulder. "This hair is going to match the dark hairs found on Adams's body."

"That's not conclusive," Greg said unevenly.

"We'll see."

Greg picked up the phone. "I'm calling a lawyer."

"Excellent idea. Let me give you some advice, though. Don't hire anyone at this firm." He paused at the door. "Just answer one more question. When you set up the meeting with Adams, did you use my name? Or pretend to be me?" He took a step toward Greg. "When Adams went out to be slaughtered, did he believe he was meeting me?''

"Do you really want to know?"

"No," Ben said. "I guess not."

There were eight men sitting in the conference room. At the head of the long table sat Derek, obviously positioned to preside. A short stack of typed papers lay on the table in front of him. At Derek's right hand sat Arthur Raven, sound asleep as far as Ben could tell. The other six members of the Executive Committee sat next to Derek and Raven, three on each side of the table. They did not look at Ben when he entered the room.

Derek pointed toward the chair at the opposite end of the conference table. Ben sat down.

Derek cleared his throat. "Doubtless you know why you're here, Kincaid, so I won't drag this out. The Executive Committee met yesterday afternoon and decided to terminate your employment."

Ben's eyes focused on a point someplace in the middle of the table. "May I ask why?"

"Don't make this more difficult than it already is. I think you know the reasons."

"I'd like to hear them from you."

Derek rested his palms on the table. "Fine. Have it your way. One: you have repeatedly disregarded the directives of your supervising attorney—namely, me."

"Always with a reason."

"Not relevant. Two: although I have assigned several cases to you in the past few weeks, some with pressing deadlines, you have ignored most of them and focused on one case—and even there your efforts could hardly be termed legal work. Certainly nothing that can be billed.

You are guilty of neglect in the worst way, and that is one of the most grievous violations of the Rules of Professional Conduct.

"Because of your relative youth and inexperience, we have decided not to file a complaint with the bar committee. Nonetheless, Raven, Tucker & Tubb has a global reputation, and we can't allow someone like that to work for us."

Ben tried to contain himself. "Is there anything else?"

"Yes. Three: you violated your duty of loyalty to your clients, Joseph Sanguine and Sanguine Enterprises. Rather than acting as a zealous advocate, you actually worked *against* their interests. That is *also* a grievous violation of the Rules of Professional Conduct."

Ben locked eyes with Derek. "You lost the client, didn't you?"

"Damn right we did," Derek said, departing from his prepared text. "A long-standing working relationship. Sanguine Enterprises represented approximately twenty-three percent of total Raven billings in the last fiscal year. And you lost it. Care to guess how many *millions* in lost revenues that amounts to? Do you have any idea how you've crippled this firm? In addition to attorneys, we have over three hundred staff persons who depend on the revenues of this firm for their livelihood. I don't know what we'll do to compensate for this shortfall. No raises, that's clear. I just hope we don't have to fire anyone." He glared at Ben. "How do you plan to explain this to the staff, Mr. Kincaid?"

"I'll say I did what I thought was right in the best way I knew."

Derek slammed his opened palm against the table. Raven's eyes fluttered a bit at the sound of the impact, then returned to their position of rest.

"Joseph Sanguine tells me he saw you running away from the scene of the break-in at his office with an unidentified female."

"Joseph Sanguine knew I was wise to his embezzling scheme," Ben countered. "That's why he tried to buy me off."

Derek became even more agitated. "Joseph Sanguine contends that you forced your way into his office with your cop friend and accused him of murder."

Ben didn't say anything.

"And you were wrong, Mr. Kincaid. Tragically wrong."

Ben stiffened a bit. "That's true," he said quietly. "I was wrong."

"And what is most incredible is that you did this the very day after that man offered to make you in-house counsel! The day after we thought we had solidified our relationship with Sanguine Enterprises for life."

"How dense are you?" Ben flared. "The only reason he offered me the in-house counsel position was to shut me up. It was hush money."

"If you had found it in your heart to accept his job offer, the relationship between Raven and Sanguine would be as solid as concrete. Instead, it's ashes. Dust in the wind."

Ben drummed his fingers against the table. "That's what it all comes down to, isn't it? The rest of this crap about ethics violations is just smoke." He surveyed the stony expressions of the other shareholders in the room. "I didn't do anything wrong. But you lost a client. A powerhouse client. And now you have to find a scapegoat. Someone to take the fall when you explain to the rest of the firm why revenues are down. And I'm elected."

Derek ignored the remark. "Of course we'll give you the traditional two weeks' notice. We don't want to be unfair."

"Thanks, but no thanks. I'll leave today." Ben rose. "Oh, and Dick?"

"Yes?"

"Your toupée is slipping again."

Without thinking, Derek reached up—then stopped short.

Ben wagged his finger. "Sucker."

* **44** *

By five o'clock, most of Ben's belongings were in boxes. He hadn't really had time to accumulate much in his office, so there wasn't much to pack. Mostly textbooks and other paraphernalia from law school. Once boxed, his possessions were supposed to be delivered to his apartment by the firm clerks.

Ben heard a tiny throat-clearing noise. Bertha and Emily were standing outside the door to his office.

"Have you read and signed all the papers?" Ben asked.

"Yes, sir," Bertha replied.

"Just leave them with Maggie. After the judge signs

them, someone in the office will send you a certified copy. I would do it myself, but I'm afraid I won't be working here anymore.''

There was an awkward pause. Bertha obviously wanted to say something, but she wasn't sure how to begin. "I . . . I have some idea what you've been doing. For me, I mean." She looked down at Emily. "For us. I just wanted to say . . . thank you." She nudged Emily's shoulder.

"Me, too," Emily said, smiling. "Thank you, Mr. Kincaid.''

Bertha put her hand in Emily's, and they walked away.

Ben packed the last book and sealed the box with heavy brown masking tape. He chuckled. *Thank you, Mr. Kincaid.*

He stopped suddenly. Thank you, *Mr. Kincaid*? She remembered my name, Ben thought. We've been separated for over an hour—and Emily remembered my name.

Ben walked out into the hallway. He felt a smile spread through his entire body. The hell with Derek and his crowd, anyway. She remembered my name.

He met Christina at the elevator. They rode down to the ground level together, then walked across the catwalk and into the parking garage.

"I got canned," he said.

"I know," she replied.

"Of course. I should have realized. You probably knew yesterday.''

"Well . . ." She let the sentence trail off. "Let's say I suspected." They strolled a little further. "I for one don't think they treated you properly, Ben. So I quit. In protest.''

"You quit!''

"You heard me."

"My God, Christina, you can't do that!"

"I can—and did."

"Do you think you'll be able to find another job?"

"I already have."

Ben was incredulous. "Already?"

"Of course. I didn't quit job one till I'd located job two. What do you take me for, a fool?"

"Anything but," Ben muttered. They walked down the first row of automobiles. "I don't know how *I* can find work without leaving Tulsa," he said. "The Raven fatcats are bound to smear my name. I may never work in this town again."

"Oh, I don't know," Christina said. "They don't exactly come out of this sewage leak smelling like a rose. I lay odds they'll keep their mouths shut. Even Derek. You'll find work."

Ben shrugged. "I hope you're right."

"But it may take you awhile to find something. And I don't suppose you've had time to build up an enormous nest egg."

"Hardly. Good thing my rent's paid up till the end of the month. After that . . ."

Christina turned to face him. "I've got bad news for you, Ben. Today is the last day of the month."

Ben blinked. "Is that right? I guess it is. I've completely lost track of time."

"I've got a decent apartment, Ben. Not plush, but highly adequate. You can stay with me for a while, if you like."

"Christina . . ."

"Don't worry. No strings are attached. You can sleep on the couch; you can leave on a night-light. And you

don't have to worry about your reputation. We won't tell
Mother. Word will never get back to Nichols Hills."

Ben frowned. "Christina—"

"It's just an idea. You don't have to."

"Christina, *stop!*" He held her in place and looked into
her eyes. "I don't know if it would be fair to you."

"So be unfair. Please. Life is short."

They both grinned.

"Hey, guess what?" Ben said. His eyebrows bounced
up and down. "She remembered my name."

Christina's brow wrinkled until she realized what he was
talking about. "Congratulations," she said.

Ben looped her arm around his, and they walked toward
his Honda. Maybe congratulations *were* in order. He knew
he should feel miserable about losing his job, but instead,
for some reason, he was elated. The gnawing sensation in
the pit of his stomach seemed to have vanished. Perhaps,
he thought, somewhere in the midst of this fiasco, he *had*
done something right. Perhaps it was all right to feel happy
now. It would only last a moment. And what is life but
moments?

Acknowledgments

I have been fortunate to draw on the kindness and expertise of those who have assisted me in the preparation of this book. I want to thank Kathy Humphries and Belinda Cuevas for their assistance in the preparation of the manuscript; Dave Johnson for his help with police procedure; Mark and Dixie Banner for the same, as well as their assistance on matters medical and psychological. I also want to acknowledge the writings of Oliver Sacks and A. R. Luria and their inspirational efforts to explain and treat profound neurological disorders. Most of all, I want to acknowledge the inexhaustible assistance of my wife Kirsten, the source of all good things.

William Bernhardt

**Read on for a sneak preview of
William Bernhardt's new courtroom thriller,
NAKED JUSTICE...**

Apprentice Police Officer Kevin Calley still held illusions
that he might get home early when the squawk of the police
radio shattered his dream.

He snapped the handset. "Yes?"

"Ten-four, Kevin. This is the Box." The Box was the name
given to the daytime switchboard officer for reasons long lost
to antiquity. "Gotta 986 at 1260 South Terwilliger, which I
believe is on your way home. And since you are technically
still on duty..."

Calley pulled his black-and-white up into the driveway of
1260 South Terwilliger. Nice house. Nice neighborhood, in
fact.

Barrett, the name on the mailbox read. Barrett. Good God,
this wasn't the mayor's place, was it? He'd heard rumors
about him down at the police station. Some of the boys had
been called out to his house before, but so far, it had been all
hushed up.

Calley rang the bell and waited. He rang it again.

No answer.

He rang the bell again. "Police," he barked.

No answer.

He pressed his ear against the door. He didn't hear anything,
but the pressure of his head nudged the door open. It hadn't
been shut, at least not all the way. Like someone had thrown it
closed in a hurry.

The door creaked open about a foot wide. Well, hell, Calley
thought. You can't have any reasonable expectation of privacy
when your front door is gaping open, can you?

He pushed the door the rest of the way open and stepped
inside. "Police," he repeated, but there was still no answer.

There was a smell, though, a pungent, putrid smell. Well, he thought, I'll just make a quick tour of the house and make sure there hasn't been any—

He turned a corner and drew in his breath.

There she was. The lady of the house. The first lady of the city.

Formerly, anyway.

She was sprawled backwards over a dining room chair, her feet on the floor, her hands over her head. Her face was bruised in several places; her lips were cracked and caked with dried blood. Her blouse was torn, exposing her left shoulder and brassiere. Blood was smeared all over her body and formed dried puddles on the floor. Her lips were parted and her eyes were wide open, staring at him.

Calley pressed his hand against his mouth, suppressing his gag reflex. What the hell had he stumbled into?

His brain raced. His respiration quickened; panic began to overwhelm him. What should I do? He tried to think; he knew he should do something. He should get to a phone and call headquarters. No, that would leave prints. He'd use his car radio. No, he couldn't leave the house. What if the killer was still here?

Calley fell to his knees and started retching huge dry heaves. It was more than a minute before he could stop himself. What was he doing here? He didn't know anything about homicides. He'd never even seen one before, except in pictures. Why did it have to be him? On his first goddamn week on the job!

Calley took deep, cleansing breaths and tried to steady himself. Pull yourself together, Calley, he told himself. Think of it as a test. A test to see how good a cop you're going to be. When the going gets tough, the tough get going.

He would like to get going, he thought, way far away from this place. But he knew he couldn't. He had to check the rest of the house. He had to make sure...*God!* He couldn't even think about it.

Slowly he covered the rest of the downstairs, making a wide berth around the dining room. Nothing else seemed unusual. With his heart pounding in his chest, he started upstairs.

The first room on the left clearly belonged to a little girl. It was covered with stuffed animals and pink chiffon and Barbie doll accessories. But where was the girl?

There she was. She was lying on top of her bed in the middle of a sea of teddy bears and lions and giraffes. She was barely bigger than they were.

Calley knew even before he touched her that she was gone. Unlike the woman downstairs, there was no sign of blood, no obvious indication of violence. But she was motionless and still—much too still for a little girl. Her skin was pale, as if she'd been drained of blood. Here eyes were closed.

Her wrist was ice old. Calley searched for a pulse, but there was nothing. He held his hand over her mouth and nose. Nothing.

She was dead. Just like Mom.

Calley pushed himself out of the room. His gorge was rising and he honestly, sincerely didn't know if he was going to make it. His eyes were clouding and the walls were beginning to spin. He was losing what little equilibrium he still had. But he had to press on. A test, he told himself. And you don't want to fail.

He continued taking deep, steady breaths, but he still knew he was going to be sick. He pushed his way toward the bathroom he had passed in the hall. His foot made a crackling noise when he lifted it. There was something sticky on the floor. Dark and red and sticky. He followed the sticky trail into the bathroom.

And found the other one. Sprawled inside the tub, her blood splattered across the porcelain. Everywhere.

Calley turned and ran. All notions of logic and duty and honor had been erased by the hideous sight in the bathtub. All he knew now was that he had to get out of there. He had to run and run and run until he couldn't run anymore, until he couldn't remember, until he had purged this grotesque madness from his brain.

NAKED JUSTICE
by William Bernhardt

Published by The Ballantine Publishing Group.
Available in bookstores everywhere.

Printed in the United States
by Baker & Taylor Publisher Services